RHINE MAIDENS

Also by Carolyn See

The Rest Is Done with Mirrors
Blue Money
Mothers, Daughters

RHINE MAIDENS

CAROLYN SEE

COWARD, McCANN & GEOGHEGAN
NEW YORK

 Published on the same day in Canada by Academic Press Canada Limited, Toronto.

The author gratefully acknowledges permission to quote from the following material:

"Begin the Beguine" by Cole Porter. © 1935 Warner Bros. Inc. Copyright renewed. All rights reserved. Used by permission.

"Stardust" by Carmichael and Parish. Copyright © 1929 by Mills Music, Inc. Copyright renewed. Used with permission. All rights reserved.

"All the Things You Are" by Jerome Kern and Oscar Hammerstein. Copyright © 1939 T. B. Harms Co. Copyright renewed c/o Welks Music Group, Santa Monica, California 90401. All rights reserved. International copyright secured. Used by permission.

Library of Congress Cataloging in Publication Data

See, Carolyn.
Rhine maidens.

I. Title.
PS3569.E33R5 1981 813'.54 81-3149
ISBN 0-698-11105-2 AACR2

Printed in the United States of America

Although Bert LaBrucherie, Matt Weinstock, Gene Coughlin, Virginia Wright, and the *Daily News* were all part of the bright Los Angeles of the forties, this work should not be taken as nonfiction or biography.

For: Kate Daly
Dorothy Anderson
Monica McCall

With Love

RHINE MAIDENS

1

I never said I was easy to get along with. I never said I was easy to get along with. I never, never said I was easy to get along with.

You *know* that, Pearl.

Do you know what they have around here? *Snakes*. And I'm not kidding. I am not even kidding. The first day we opened the annex, a colored kid got bit, I had to call the ambulance for him. Do you know what it's *like* out here? At three o'clock the school kids go home, at four the teachers leave. The Unemployment Office shuts up at four-thirty. The Civic Center closes at five, but the Judge likes me to stay until six. To keep things shipshape, he says. Because I'm in charge.

He says.

Do you know what it's like out here, four-thirty, quarter of five, five o'clock? I have to stay here until six, there's nobody here but the custodian. If anything happens to me, I hate to think about it. He's always over in the other buildings, I go weeks without even seeing him, he doesn't have a number I can call. I don't have a number where I can reach him, and we had vandals all the time the first year we were here.

And they hate me. Well, somebody has to do the things that need to be done around here! The typing, the making of

Xerox copies, the answering the phone, the taking messages. Keeping track of the Judge. Arranging his calendar. Covering for him. Running a *whole lousy town* from one set of crummy buildings. The school. The Unemployment. The Civic Center. The Judge.

And out of all the people, Pearl, guess which one has to say no?

They had a snake in the cafeteria, they had two out in the parking lot before they put in the asphalt. I found a scorpion in my own tub last week, dead. How did it get there? I take a bath every day at five in the morning.

What I do after work is this: I get home every night by six-thirty, I get out of my clothes, have a couple of drinks. To tell you the truth, I'm exhausted. There's only one door into my place—if there were a fire, if there was some man in the night—I tell you the truth, I wouldn't know, I *couldn't* know what to do. So what I do is this. I put on my robe over my slip and then I have a couple of drinks. And I'm exhausted, so I go to sleep. Wouldn't *you?*

Wouldn't you? To work like that, every day, I don't care how cold it is, how hot it is, how sick I am.

Sometimes during Johnny Carson I wake up. I watch him and turn up the heat. I don't drink any more after twelve. After one. I get into bed and read. I listen to the sand against the window, the shade push out and fall back against the kitchen door. When the moon is out a certain way, the oil wells along the tops of the hills cast shadows for a quarter of a mile, almost up to my window. I can hear the goddamn things all night.

They say this housing is secure for senior citizens. All I know is, in the three years since I've been here, there've been two rapes and two burglaries. Ida and Bernice don't worry, but they're in the center of the complex. I've got a *corner apartment!*

One night the doorbell rang. I went crazy! It was four in the morning, I was reading. The bell rang. One long ring. Then nothing. My light was on, there was nothing I could do. They knew I was home. There's only one door into my place; if anyone were to come in . . . if there were a fire . . .

I looked up, I looked around my room. The walk-in closet, with six pantsuits in it. Extra blouses. Sandals. The sliding door open. A folded blanket on the shelf. An old suitcase, from when Fran and I were married. The bureau. A lamp from Sagor's, with a nice flowered shade. A picture of Garnet and her kids, on the lawn of their new house. My will, propped up for Garnet to read when I die, cutting out Sandy with only a dollar. I looked around the room, to the door, and the maple knobs at the foot of my bed. This bed used to be Garnet's, didn't it? Thirty years ago? The bell rang again.

Night after night, day after day. I try to tell people what it's like. I tell them at dinner, if I have them to dinner. They laugh at me, or tell me to pull myself together. "Pull yourself together, Grace!"

My door opens into the hall, the light is always on. And all over the room, even with just the one reading light, you can see the sand, a papery layer of sand, like when you file your nails with an emery board, coming in, fading, wearing on everything.

The bell rang *again*.

After years, it has come to pass. What I've been waiting for, for twenty, forty years.

The nights, years ago, in Highland Park, when marriage to Fran had stopped being golf and long walks and going to the beach and playing poker all weekend! The nights when he'd started *working late*. The lights are out, all over Highland Park, all over LA, for all I know, and the kid is asleep. I sit by Fran's big desk in that little bedrooom and look out at the backyard and there is the clothesline—look! Isn't there somebody out by the clothesline! Or behind the garage? And the pigeons next door shuffle around and cough. The dog sleeps in the little hollow that marks out the cesspool at the center of the yard, crushing down the grass. And the moon is chattering along, alive, alive, and Fran isn't working, I know it. Garnet is asleep in the big bed—just until Fran gets home—and the moon, well, I don't mean to be dramatic, but it's trying to tell me something. I'm waiting for something more than Fran with his loose smile and his tweed coat and his bright yellow sweater.

Or later, in the Hollywood Hills, in the seventh year of our marriage, which I read later is the *criticial year*, but why didn't somebody tell me then? Even in the afternoon I'd think, if someone came in through the basement, I could run out through the kitchen. Or, if he had someone *with* him, and they came in through the back, I could *still* get out the front door. Or, *I know* I could always sneak out through the garage (because the garage was attached to the house). Until, once, standing in line in that stinking grocery store on Sunset just off Gower, I read a story in *Family Circle* about a guy who broke in and *cut the phone wires and the power wires and then hid in the double garage so he could catch the woman when she was trying to get out!* And it came to me then, after Fran had left, that there wasn't any point in trying to get away.

That all there was to do was wait.

I used to be a beautiful woman. I *was* a beautiful woman, Pearl. Sometimes I try to tell them—the juvenile delinquents who come in here for the Judge, and say they can't find a job for the work-study program, because of the recession. Those welfare mothers who say, oh, what's going to happen in a real depression? I tell them, "We weren't depressed in the Great Depression!"

But what I want to say to them is this. Look! At a girl, nineteen or twenty, with a twenty-inch waist. (That would be half of what you see today.) Think of that girl in sheerest stockings—half a week's salary—and perfect little black sandals, my foot arching and bouncing, tacking, swerving—think of trim little legs, and hips I didn't even know I had, but I did know about my chest, and what you see today, well, think of all that as a kind of clean, wide, tan football field, with flags and goalposts, and first downs, and ten-yard lines and touchdowns, and people cheering at the sidelines. A whole country, a *nation*, was going on below my organza collar and above my dotted-swiss self-belt. Think of me on payday in downtown Los Angeles. I wore my hair long then, it was a great-looking auburn, the color of a real soft leather purse, and thick, down past my shoulders. I'd just picked up my paycheck for $27.50, and I go down the elevator, tapping my foot, keeping time to the typing I'd done all morning, and walk north on Spring up to Sixth. It's June, and foggy, and all the beautiful women in suits and gloves and little hats are *downtown*, shopping, and the men from the *Daily News* are looking cool, carrying the right newspaper, and at the corner of Sixth and Spring, catercorner, across the intersection, I look across and see you there, Pearl, you're tapping your foot and smiling. I cross over, and without saying a word we go straight into Bullock's, where they're having a sale (they've been having it ten days, and we've been in terror the whole time), we go right in, past the notions, and the old ladies, down to the *Empress Eugenie Hats!* Without a word—only *you're* giggling—we walk right over to two mannequins, just the heads, and take the hats right off them. Yours, the most beautiful sea green with a fluff of pale peach veil, mine in navy blue, with dark blue net and pale blue dots. We walk to the mirror, clamp those hats on our heads. We pay the salesgirl. (Our own checkbooks! Our own names!) We walk west on Sixth to Mike Lyman's and stand there—so beautiful! so terrific!—along with the newspapermen and the businessmen meeting their wives or sneaking their secretaries. The windows of Lyman's are banked with ice, lit up from inside, full of pink shellfish, and bright green limes, and parsley in fresh green borders. Think of us, shown to a table; up front, usually, where the door opened and closed, and people in blue suits swirled in and out, and we gave our once-every-two-weeks payday order. One pieces-of-eight salad. (And two iced teas.)

Even at night, Pearl, I wouldn't be tired. We always had dates then, *think* of the dates we had! The movies at the Million Dollar. Tea dancing on Saturdays at the Ambassador Hotel. Or I'd take the streetcar with you to your place. Or we'd take the bus to mine. Great days. I'd *had* my unhappy childhood and I was done with it. And I hadn't met Fran yet, but I knew it—something wonderful—was going to happen.

I remember a night. I got off work and I wasn't going anywhere particular—one of those heavy, heavy summer fogs had rolled in from the coast. More and more people—in navy blue, in wool and georgette—keep coming out of the swinging doors of the old office buildings and waiting in clumps for this bus or that one. But I feel *so great*, I just can't wait! So I start out to walk, in my new hat, and good sandals, just a couple of blocks to where it won't be so crowded, stepping west on the sidewalk that is almost wet. The buses have their lights on, lighting up the fog, but I keep on walking even when they swerve over toward me. Pretty soon I notice, I *could* walk all the way home.

No hurry, no hurry! I walked all the way out of downtown, past Westlake Park, and the sun was sinking, but it lit up the whole street—was it Wilshire? Was it Sixth? Lines of gray two-story apartments, half in fog, half out of it, and trailing out of window boxes, all that ivy with the tiny little leaves. Farther west—the Ambassador—maybe we'd go dancing that same night. The sun slid down, underneath the fog, and lit the street and then went down, but the light was still there and I was almost home! I'd walked that far. I was out of breath and on my own. I passed the fancy apartment just west of the park. I was walking under that awning they have, when the doorman opened the door for an old couple. They came out, to go to the theater, or just get a cab, but I saw myself in the glass door of that place. I didn't *need* to be rich. Everything was waiting for me—love, and glamour. A handsome man. And we'd change our ways, Pearl! There'd be *four* of us at each other's houses—you, Duane, and Fran and me! Anything could happen, *God!*

What I'm telling you is, the city was beautiful then, and I, I, was beautiful too.

Can I . . . can I get up now? Will they come back? You can hear the sand shifting outside. You can hear the click and hum of the fluorescent light. You can *see* the hum in the lights up there, isn't that amazing? As it clicks, the light changes. As the light changes, it clicks. Two buildings away, across the mall, the janitor, the custodian, is cleaning up. The jerk! The fool! Have you seen how he . . . takes his rag, and dips it in the bucket, and doesn't even wring it *out* before he slaps it, slaps it across the sill, and then the marks, the dirt marks, and the grooves of sand, *stay* on the sill for months, until he gets around to swabbing them again? I've told him about it, and I've told the Judge about it. I've told the people at the school and the Unemployment Office that they ought to complain. The custodian hates my guts.

You can hear the sound, the light feathery sound, of scorpions. *On this floor.*

I've always had trim ankles. And great legs. Even when the waist went and the chest, still, it's true. I have great legs. Unpretentious. No nail polish, no gold anklets, just perfect shoes and perfect feet, perfect stockings, perfect legs. They stay forever, your legs.

When I was waiting after Fran, before Dick, I'd walk the hall at the Hollywood Hills house at night. I used to love the sound of high-heeled shoes. Delicate, sharp, hard, immaculate, *clean.* The sound of high heels on tiles. Even when I was crying and my face and arms were all swollen, and my wrists all swollen and my wristwatch cutting into my flesh, and my period gushing out . . .

Underneath all that *slop,* like waiting for Fran to send a child-support check, what a joke! Or even entertaining the possibility that he might call up to *say hello,* to see how I *was,* and knowing he wouldn't, the fucking, chintzy, cheap, stupid *creep!* Even coming home from those awful dates after the divorce. (Jonah Pimper! Can you imagine going out with a man named Jonah *Pimper?* A name like that. And he had the guts to laugh about it!) Even after two hundred nights with Allan *Bam*ford, I still had great legs.

Allan Bamford. They gripe about television now. But don't they remember what it was like to be *bored* to death? To sit on the couch and you've had dinner and the kid's in bed, and you can hear the kid breathing, and you say . . .

"Fig's got a lot of fruit on it, don't you think?"

Or they say—Allan says,

"Mother's flu is getting a lot better."

And when I wouldn't answer,

"That's *good*, you know? Because I was getting worried about her."

Then he'd say,

"Did I tell you about my classes today?"

I'd nod my head, *Yes.*

Then he'd think a minute. And give me twenty minutes on his classes anyway. Or his *poetry*. Or the papers he had to correct. Or his mother. Dumb bastard. When he found out I'd been married to a newspaperman he went right out and bought himself a tweed jacket *with elbow patches.*

After twenty minutes he'd laugh. And look over at me, shamefaced. Because it's nine-fifteen and he's going to stay until at least midnight because he has nowhere to go except his boring furnished apartment or the Help Me Bar at the bottom of this Hollywood Hill and he *knows* he's never getting to first base with me because *that's my child in there! Do you think I'd do that with my own* . . . She's depressing, and damp, and not above crying in a loud voice to get my attention. But I'm damned if I'll . . .

"And so I gave every football player in the class a blanket five demerits. That's going to keep them all from playing this weekend. They were mad as hell, but it was worth it."

He says it again. And laughs, in his tweed jacket. And leans forward, in a kind of a grunt, to get his glass again, and drinks.

"How about a refill, Grace?" He gets up and takes my glass with him. When he leans forward, the smell of pipe tobacco, and leather, and Scotch, and composition soles, and sweat, and deodorant gets between me and the picture window.

Because the living room in the Hollywood Hills was perfectly laid out. The dusty-rose couch with flowers. The green carpet with the roses worked in. The Spanish-tile coffee table. The bumpy plaster on the walls and ceiling. The *beams* in the ceiling. The four steps up from the living room to the long hall where I'd walk in the night after Fran was gone.

The bullet hole in those same wooden steps. I used to sit at night and wonder how it got there. The antique square piano with the carved, flowery legs that Fran bought and then left when he left. The picture window. The view from the picture window. All of Hollywood spread out in front of us. Downtown to the left. On the right, far out, the oil wells of Baldwin Hills, and on some great days, the rim of the Pacific. Even, sometimes, Catalina.

But this would be at night. I'd be on the left side of the couch, the end table on one side of me, Allan Bamford on the other. *I'd be so tired!* I could only see a few lights from where I was sitting, but I knew all of Los Angeles was out there! Ciro's, the Palladium, the track, the Help Me Bar, Fran—wearing the expensive clothes he could afford, now that he didn't have a wife and kid to support. . . .

And so there were two worlds. The outside world where the fun was: the books, the pictures (because Fran took all that crap with him when he left), the dancing, the parties, the poker, the jokes. Los Angeles with lights; Fran's world.

And closer in, another world. Two feet away, a saggy little stomach, a beige shirt, a clean T-shirt under it, that his mother put in the laundry for him, a leather belt, cheap gabardine slacks, pale fingers holding a pipe, a neck that smelled of tobacco. A balding head, freckled arms, another set of fingers reaching for his glass, and then *my* glass, and where they sat makes twin rings on the coffee table.

The world where I am now, and it's shit. There's something rank and wrinkled in the folds of those slacks, but nothing I'll ever see, and *he knows it*, and you can see it in the set of those damp fingers, and the way he sets his lips against his teeth. You know it and you *know* that he knows it, and it's in that slant of his middle-aged body as he bumps up the other set of steps into the kitchen. That man, this room, and it's only nine-twenty! And we've never even heard of television yet, and the *Daily News* is out of business. Allan's idea of a good time is reading student mistakes to me off the papers he's correcting.

It's only nine-twenty. The kid is asleep, sobbing, or eating cookies in bed and getting crumbs and marshmallow all over the sheets.

He brings back the drinks and sits back in the right-hand corner of the couch. He grunts as he sits. Sweat begins to form on his lip. I'm almost mean enough to ask him to take his jacket off, but I'm not that mean. I sit and watch him. He's never even been *married.* He waits for me to say something. I wait for him to say something. He keeps his hands to himself because he knows better. Is Garnet asleep yet? Maybe she'll wake up, or be sick. There isn't even a clock in the fucking room, and Fran took the record player and all the records. "Perdido." "Adios." "Frenesi." I light another cigarette. Tap tap tap tap tap. Flick a little piece of tobacco from my lower lip with the fingernail on the little finger of my left hand. Move my feet in their terrific pumps. He looks at me in that begging way. He's trying to tell me he wants my body. *In a pig's eye, buddy! You'd have to be kidding!*

"I took a drive out by the airport yesterday," he says. "They're putting up about fifty new houses a week out there. They're a good buy, Grace. If you're a veteran, you don't even need a down payment . . ."

Just Allan and me and his mother and his anthologies of tiresome poets. Doesn't he know that it's always foggy out on those bluffs by the airport, and all the kids who ever live out there are always going to have colds? Every house will have a husband and wife. Every couple will have kids, and a hedge, and bronchitis, and the fog, and rust stains from nails leaking down stucco from sills. Those *couples* (each one of them a light in my picture window), they were what sent me out at night with Jonah Pimper, and Rusty What's-his-name, and Robert E. "Bob" McAllister—fags and married men, anything to avoid the couples, and sick kids, and poor old Allan.

Because what I *wanted* was glamour. Allan never could understand that. Just one of the things that Fran took away when he left. Do you know what used to be the greatest for me? When Fran and I were married, and once a year, on New Year's Eve, the drama editor of the *Daily News* would throw her party. Black patent pumps, or open-toed sandals, and that one year, the terrific black dress with shoulder pads! (It was called a "Nantucket Natural. . . .") Dancing at Virginia Wright's. Every other weekend of the year, poker and smoke, but New Year's Eve, blue suits and a live band! And once Bert La Brucherie chased me around the dining-room table. I'd go one way, he'd go the other way, I'd change directions, he'd change directions . . . And everyone would dance.

"Frenesi." "Stardust." "Adios."

Though I dream in vain, in my heart it will remain. So, on Tuesday nights, when, after three years of "going together," Allan and I took Garnet down to the Presbyterian church at the corner of Prospect and Rodney, to while away a couple of hours while the poor kid drummed up some semblance of a social life—well, there, on Vermont Avenue, just above Sunset, south of Los Feliz, *in Hollywood,* you could still see those graystone apartment buildings. You could see what the city used to be. Hell, they had a *Brown Derby* at the corner of Los Feliz and Vermont, didn't they? Couldn't Allen see that having a drink at the Windsor on North Vermont was a whole different ballgame from killing time at the Help Me? The long dark bar at the Windsor, lit up from behind, and all the bottles shining. The dressed-up women (kind of far gone), the salesmen, the lawyers, professional men, lined up, looking sideways at who came in. The silence, and the jukebox. "Smoke Gets in Your Eyes," "There's a Small Hotel." "Moonglow."

Tuesday nights, seven until ten at night, I'd sit with Allan at the Windsor and drink, even though he couldn't afford it on a high-school teacher's salary. I lived for those nights, and Dick would be there, in something like *moonglow,* looking sideways at me with his puckered rosebud mouth, and his tiny white hands, and his soft white cheeks. I sent him a valentine, care of the bar, he must have known who I was. And poor old Allan telling about how his class of honor students are putting out a *literary* magazine, in his tweed jacket and the smell of Palmolive soap, while fifteen seats down, there's a soft white statue with chubby lips, and once, when I went to the girl's room, he said, not looking at me, not moving his lips, *if I were a gopher I'd go for you.*

Another time he mouthed something at me. "I'm in oil. Remember that." I didn't even know what he was talking about. When I found out, well, you can imagine. Pearl, I was in heaven.

I'm with you once more, under the stars. And down by the shore, an orchestra's playing. And after all the lies and the giggles and maybe four good times in bed, I'm *married* again, to a hopeless drunk. The company has transferred him to the Hellhole of Coalinga and I don't have a friend in the world. The dust gets in the house and the wells make a horrible noise, *night and day. Day and night.* The chubby-faced statue is lying back on his chair, dead blue from vodka or Bromo Seltzer, or throwing up, on me, on my birthday. What for. What for? Running as fast as you can to get to what you're running from. I'm pregnant. Again! In the night, in the company housing I'm going to live in, one way or another, for the rest of my life, there's three eight-ounce bottles lined up, full of soapy water, and three four-ounce bottles, with that puke smell of orange juice and milk. Eight nipples, and eight of those black round disks, those black round disks that shut out all the light—all good times. No dancing! Just heart attacks and varicose veins, and screaming fights in the night and crying out on the back porch while he's in the front room drinking his daily quart of vodka and saying, "I just want to *sit here and fuck,*" and it takes me close to five years of crying on the back porch to figure it out. The reason I found him in a bar, the reason I met him in a *bar,* the reason he picked up on me is pure and simple. *He's always in a bar!*

So my life is ended. Thirty-nine years old with a brand-new baby, and my life is ended. And I don't even have you anymore, Pearl. With Fran, and even with Allan, I had the week in the summer and the week in the winter with you. For fourteen days out of the three hundred and sixty-five I could tell you what I really thought. And you nodding your head and saying, "Yes, hon, I know, hon, it's rough, hon. Yes, it's awful, yes, well, you *know*, I *told* you." And once or twice, "Well, it could be worse, you know. At least Fran's a pretty funny guy." Or, "I know Allan's dull, but he certainly does love you." Or, "I don't think Garnet's so bad. Don't all the kids do that kind of thing?"

More than once, Pearl, I wanted to set you straight. *A lot you know, with one (pretty boring, if you want to know the truth) husband, and no kids and enough money to live here at the beach, and a nice job in a nice office, and your legs are still good, and you keep your tan all year long, and Duane even takes you dancing, doesn't he? Doesn't he?* When, in our late twenties, it comes to me that the Pearl I know is gone. The Pearl of a girl who used to steal the shrimps away from me in every Pieces of Eight salad we ever ordered, the girl who knew as well as I did the difference between the soft, fat beat of Glenn Miller and the wonderful light *trot* of Artie Shaw that goes through every one of his instrumentals, the kid I went to the movies with when we worked downtown, the girl I wanted to name my own baby girl after (but you said no. "Why not make it *another* semiprecious stone?"), the kid who stood by me when Fran ran out and Allan floated out, my Pearl was a middle-aged woman, tired of me, tired of my talk. She'd never had kids; she'd even stopped saying to me, "I'm going to *put* it to Duane, either we have kids, or . . ." She'd stopped telling me how Duane loved catsup on everything. Oh, Pearl, we were only twenty-eight. A sad woman looks at me in the silence in her kitchen, and out in the living room Duane is in his chair like a zombie listening to that jerk who came on at eight o'clock for Chesterfield—why, *why*, Pearl, did we get mixed up with such *jerks?* And you say, "Actually, *I've* been a little worried about my period. It doesn't come for six weeks and then when it does it's such a mess I can't even wear shorts. . . ." And I say dumbly, "It's the change," impatient to get back to the real thing: Allan's stupidity, or Fran's new girlfriends, or whatever it is that makes me the glamorous one. Thinking, no matter what else, I've got a kid and she doesn't.

Except that in a year you're dead.

That same night, down at Balboa, Garnet came in from where she'd been playing in the front yard in the sand. It was summer, and still light. Pearl told Duane we were going for a walk, and we did. Pearl and Garnet and me, walking down the island. We rode on the merry-go-round. (Pearl and Garnet rode, I can't stand that thing that makes Pearl be nice to kids. It's sickening to be nice to kids if you don't have them.) I watch them go around and around. It's summer, mid-July. Pearl is fat now; her thighs clot on the wooden horse. Garnet is sallow in her T-shirt and shorts, hopeless, alone, ugly; nobody loves her. Pearl makes her laugh. Around nine o'clock we get going again for a walk along the whole length of the island. Midsummer. Some sailors left over from the war, dumb sailors and their skinny girlfriends. Pearl buys Garnet a big wad of cotton candy. Garnet stuffs it in her mouth. There at the Aragon Ballroom, where Tommy Dorsey and Jimmy Dorsey and Harry James and Artie and Glenn play, we stop. Pearl says to Garnet, "Honey, look! You can look in the windows if you want to. In just a few years you'll be coming here yourself. Your mother and I used to come here all the time." Garnet stands up against the ballroom wall, her head comes to just underneath the windows. She sticks out her arms so Pearl can catch her under the armpits and lift her up. Pearl keeps smiling, leans forward and *lifts*, regardless of what's wrong in her stomach. *Oh, Pearl! How many times did we really come here; all the way out to Balboa Island? Four times, maybe?* Garnet looks amazed. Her cheeks go slack. Pearl's face is red in the light. "See, hon? Isn't that fun?" Then she goes "*ugh*" and shifts Garnet's weight, bracing the kid between herself and the wall, so Garnet just hangs there like a sack, her ankles dangling about six inches off the ground. The music is nothing I remember right off, and I want to see, anyway, what Pearl sees, what Garnet sees. The fun I almost had. I ease in beside Pearl, and take a look. A thousand, two thousand, three thousand sailors dancing, with their boring girlfriends in short skirts. I recognize the music now, "Peanut Vendor," and it's Stan

Kenton. Nobody can dance to that shit! But they are, and the trumpets are screeching, the place is thick with smoke.

I hear someone laugh behind us. Some cheap bitch with freckles and red hair and cheap flat sandals pokes her sailor boyfriend in the ribs. "Look at that! Two women and that kid, looking in the window like that," and I want to say to her, "*Listen, puke face, where do you think you're going to end up?*" My legs start to blush, I feel the wrinkles, the stretch marks under my butt, why am I wearing these shorts! I want to walk away, just tiptoe away from the dancers and the watchers, but I stand there. (Oh, Pearl, with your tan, waxed legs, *the dearest things I know, are what you are. . . .*)

It started as early as December, late December. Before Christmas, certainly before the new year. They started bringing water pistols in. You can imagine how it went, Pearl, how it *always* goes. The Judge takes it easy, he says at least that isn't a crime. *He* doesn't care, he thinks it's funny, but then he's not the one who has to clean it *up*, is he? He says the blacks are the victims of unemployment and the recession, and it's not their fault they ended up in Coalinga. He says that since Proposition 13, we can't afford the luxury of juvenile delinquents. He says his work-study program, where they muster in once a day after four hours of school, is doing just great. All I know is the black kids, *and* the white ones from the high school across the mall, started playing with water pistols, and pretty soon they're getting confiscated all over the building—and that includes Unemployment and the DMV.

Naturally, everyone brings them to me. Mr. Lambrozini smoothes his bald spot with his left hand and holds the pistols like they're worms and *drops them on my desk just like that.* "Here, Grace, maybe you can figure out what to do with this!" Not just these, these pistols, you know, but this, this, all this, fix the whole thing, all over town; the dust, the heat, the oil, the kids, the water pistols, the vandalism, well, what the hell *am I supposed to do about it?* So I give him the dirtiest look I can, and say, "I'll certainly mention it to the Judge," and Lambrozini stands there for a minute rocking back and forth on his toes and heels and tries to look important, but I just give him my dirty look and he says, "Well, try and think of something to do about it, will you, Grace? Because this *whole pistol question* is getting out of hand!"

By the time the kids come back from Easter vacation we can see out our windows that the whole high school is going down the drain. Even Edna Harris, and she's a real easygoing old girl, has made a complaint. John Poleet, in the journalism department, says they can't get the paper out. Mr. Pfaffanger, in the wood shop, has been up before the board for administering physical punishment, the girls' vice-president has had two tantrums. The first one at her principal, the second one over here at City Hall. *I tell you I've had about enough of this! You tell Rex he can't go on fiddling while Rome burns!* I have to admit the bitch is right.

The very next day Miss Arbogast goes out of her gourd in B10 English. She wrings her hands and cries and cries in front of the room after some colored creep gets her right in the chest. Then some other black bastard gets her, and *then*, from what some of the girls said later, she's wailing away, the tears are cutting down through that awful makeup she wears, and they're going crazy in the class. Poor Elaine is crying and wringing her hands and wiping the water off her chest and out of her eyes, and pretty soon she says, "*All right! If you don't stop, I'm jumping right out of this window!*" And they say, "Go ahead, stupid bitch!" And so she does, and that room is Room 221 and so she falls two stories, and breaks both her ankles. The Judge goes with her in the ambulance to the emergency room, but even with all that, it doesn't look like he's going to take any measures.

That afternoon we're all in the employees' lounge taking a break. The colored kids' families have all been in to take their kids home, a man from the paper has been there to write a story about it, and, I mean, we're all *worn out*. Even Edna's had some trouble in her class and had to wrestle a pistol away from one of her kids. Of course, I don't worry about Edna, she's got the guts of a burglar, I don't worry about her. But we're all in this together now, the high school, the Unemployment Office, the DMV, the Municipal Court. And something is going to have to be done, if it takes federal funds to do it!

Lambrozini says, "Carco is responsible for bringing this element *in* here, let Carco be responsible for getting them out!" Edna Harris looks at me and says, "Grace, the Judge really does have to do something about this now, don't you think?" Well, I am sick of defending him, because she's absolutely right!

She's holding a pistol when she talks. It's a big red one that sells for over a dollar. It's still about half-loaded and I'm about to ask her where she got it when the door to the lounge opens. It's Judge Kirkpatrick. He's just gotten back from taking poor Elaine to the hospital and he's got that look on his face he always gets when he's *going to say a few words.* I wish he wouldn't. I wish he'd cool it! I look over at Edna. You can see where she used to be a real good-looking gal. She's about fifty now, maybe fifty-five, but she always takes good care of her hair and nails. She wears wool a lot, and good silk blouses, I don't know how she can afford them. She says she's allergic to polyester, but I don't believe that, I just don't think she wants to wear the same crap that everybody else does.

The Judge opens the door to the lounge, and stands there with that look on his face. Then Edna raises her arm with the pistol in it, and fires!

I was so proud of the Judge, because in a second, I mean a *second*, he's down on his knees under one of those long vinyl tables next to Pfaffanger and he's hissing, "*Quick, Carl! Gimme a break!*" And Pfaffanger has a pistol on him, naturally, so he hands it to him. Mr. Poleet has always hated Mrs. Bollinger in Unemployment, so he takes out a pistol with only a few drops and squishes them straight into Bollinger's neck. I remember all the pistols I have in my desk, so I get up as dignified as I can (because I'm an *old lady* now, right?) and I walk real slow to the door, the way I used to do when Dick would get his heart pains and I'd walk out to the kitchen for his pills, *slow*. Then as soon as I get out of the door, I run like hell to my office and unlock the bottom drawer where I keep the pistols we take off the little bastards. There must be fifty of them. I scoop them up and run to the drinking fountain and stop up the holes at the bottom and fill the pistols and run back to the lounge.

Pearl, you wouldn't believe it, I mean, it was an unbelievable scene. Poleet has a pistol. Lambrozini has a pistol. Bollinger's ratty old hair has fallen down to her waist, *she* has a pistol! They're all more or less after the Judge. He's down on his hands and knees, Edna Harris is standing over him, one hand on her hip, the other hand shooting away. He's saying, "I'll get you for this, Edna! Don't think I'll forget it." (She's a real nice-looking woman, no more than fifty, I'm sure she doesn't weigh more than a hundred and ten.) I stand a little ways back and say, "Your Honor!" He looks back and I lob him a pistol, one of the big ones. I haven't thrown anything in years! He says, "Thanks, Grace!" Well, God *knows* he should thank me. Then I get one, smash, right in my face. It's that fag bastard Lambrozini. But he doesn't know what I've got in my purse. I reach in and squirt *him!* He thinks he's *God*, you know? God-on-a-Rock. Then I get Bollinger, for all the times she's given jobs to the *wrong kids*, just to make the work-study program look bad. I squirt Pfaffanger for all the times he's come by my desk and said, "Hello, Grace!" Just like that, you know? *Hello* Grace! Who does he think he is, *Hello* Grace! And then Edna squirts me, and laughs, and I squirt her, and the assistant commissioner squirts me, I know he hates me because I won't do his Xerox copies after three in the afternoon, well, why *should* I? What he doesn't know is I still have six or seven loaded pistols in my purse, and pretty soon I'm standing right in the middle of the employees' lounge—did you know that for *years* they wouldn't even let people, *secretaries*, into that lounge? So, *so*. I stand there and shoot. Everyone else has run out of water. The Judge is on his hands and knees wiping the back of his neck with his hand. "I *win*," I say, but nobody is listening.

The Judge, God, he kills me sometimes! He doesn't even

get up, but he wipes off his face with the palm of his hand, and he *says something to the group.*

"Well, I took poor Elaine over, as you all know, and she's pretty shook-up, and she's going to have casts on both feet, but she's going to be all right." I never heard so many people laugh so hard in my whole life.

Was it that night? Or was it a couple of weeks later? That the doorbell rang in the night? I always, I always come home and have a drink, a couple of drinks, and turn on the six-o'clock news. I take off my school clothes and put on a robe over my slip and turn on Walter Cronkite, I hate the son of a bitch, he thinks *he's* God-on-a-Rock! Sometimes I can barely get my clothes off; people don't realize how tired you can get. I sit on the couch and have a couple of drinks and I'm asleep before *Hollywood Squares.* I don't wake up until Johnny Carson. I watch Johnny, I don't drink any more after that. I get undressed and go into the bedroom and go to bed.

There's no back door to my apartment. I read and read and read, and listen to the oil wells, and the tumbleweeds when they blow up against the house, or against the wrought-iron fence around this set of apartments. (But the fence doesn't do any *good!* It doesn't even lock!) Some nights at two, three in the morning you hear someone take a stick and *run it down the wrought-iron fence!* And I lie there, soaked with sweat, waiting for the shade on the window over the kitchen sink to tear, or the window *in this room* to open. Or the little frosted window in the bathroom to ease out, and someone to slide in there, and wait, behind the shower curtains. Around five in the morning, I can't stand it anymore. I get out of bed and go out to the refrigerator for a Coke. I turn on educational television or the last of some late show, and go on in and take my bath. By the time I'm out of the bath, and set my hair in steam curlers, the sun is coming up over those big raggedy hills with their shitty oil wells. I can't see the sun from my place, but the concrete of the American Legion Building is turning pink. I sit in the living room and read until it's time to go to work.

Except this time, in the middle of the night, at exactly

three in the morning, the doorbell rang. I didn't know what to do. My light was on—well, it's *always on at night!* So they knew I was there. Unless they thought maybe I wasn't there. If they thought I wasn't there, then they might come in. I listened. Were there two of them? I have a chain lock on my door, but that doesn't mean *shit!*

The doorbell rang again. I got up and put on my bathrobe without even stopping to shake the scorpions out. I put on my robe, I put on my slippers. It could be something wrong with Garnet, it could be something wrong with Sandy. The doorbell rang again. I walked across the living-room rug, I could hear my slippers sliding on the nylon rug. "*Just a minute!*" I whispered; I could barely talk. I opened the door a crack. It was the police!

"What is it?"

They just looked at me. I had to say it again.

"What *is* it?"

They looked at each other. I hung on to the door, I tell you, I was about to faint. Then the big one said, "*Any trouble, ma'am?*"

"*Any trouble, ma'am?*"

"What's *wrong?*" I said.

"That's what we want to know!" That was the other one, a stinking little pipsqueak punk.

"What are you talking about?"

"We got a report there was trouble. Here in the complex."

I felt like I was going to faint. I faint a lot. I fainted the day I graduated from high school. I fainted the day my mother died. I fainted the day Fran took me to a TB sanatorium to see his sister. (What my mother died of, TB.) I took one look at that poor girl sitting up in bed smiling at me, I took one step into that awful room, and that was *it,* I went right out. I fainted one morning when Sandy was a baby and I'd been up all night with Dick. He was drunk. He'd take one shoe off and *fling* it on the floor. Then he'd take the other shoe and *fling* it! *Oh, I tell you!* After a few hours of that, Sandy started to cry in his crib and I got up and got him a bottle and gave it to him, standing by the bed looking down at him, while he looked up at me, mad as hell because I wouldn't pick him up. He finished the bottle and started to cry again, so I turned him on his stomach and started to pat his back to make him go to sleep. He cried and cried and I thought, Christ! If he wakes up Dick! So I patted and patted and pounded and pounded, and he kept jerking his head up and jerking his feet up and I patted his back, and pretty soon he more or less gave up and put that kind of crusty head of his down on the sheet and closed his eyes, but I could tell he wasn't asleep, so I kept on patting until *all of a sudden* I felt this awful pain in my behind and I opened my eyes and heard an awful scream and there, in front of my eyes was Sandy screaming at me. So I guess *I'd fainted* then, standing up. And fell down on my butt. I had to start pounding all over, and do you think it woke Dick up? *Of course not!*

And that's not half the times I fainted.

So as I held on to the doorknob with one hand and the doorjamb with the other, those awful men began to disappear in blue light.

My God! I thought. What if I *faint?* Then, with just one good shove on the door, especially with the two of them . . .

"There . . . there isn't any trouble here."

"I don't know, we got this call . . ."

"Listen! *What do you know about me?* What do you want?"

(Because, listen. Eight years ago, while I'd still been living in the house out on Z Street with Sandy, before he ran away, I got an obscene phone call! But do you know what I did? The second time the man called up, I made a date with him. I said I'd meet him in that Holiday Inn, up on the second floor, if he'd take me to dinner! He was waiting in the Holiday Inn dining room, he'd made a reservation in my name. So the police came and took him away. But some people got the wrong impression. So these policemen might have got the wrong impression.)

Or, they might not even be policemen.

"Are you sure you're policemen?"

They looked at each other.

"Come on, Hap. There's nothing going on here."

"But, *man!* Where'd the call come from, then?"

They looked at each other. (Where *did* it come from, then?)

It wasn't until they left that I thought: It could be. Bollinger. Lambrozini. The assistant commissioner. Because they don't like me at work. Or *any of the kids* who have to check in at the office.

I saw what was happening.

My God, I thought, I've *got to call somebody right away*. I thought I'd call Ida, she lives just a few doors away. She could come over (because isn't that what a friend is for?). Except when she goes to bed she's usually had a few drinks.

So I couldn't call Ida.

I thought I could call Estelle. Except I don't feel right about calling her up this late at night.

So I couldn't call Estelle.

I could call up Bernice. But she lives down at the other end of the complex, and what could she do anyway?

I thought of calling Edna Harris. She's a lot of fun to be with. She'll laugh at anything! She likes to drink, but she doesn't pass out. She's the only woman I know who actually plays a musical instrument.

I started to dial the number. I really don't know Edna very well, but this was an emergency.

But I'm not sure she likes me.

Then I thought.

I could call up Garnet, but I wouldn't give her the satisfaction.

I could call up Sandy, except I don't know where he is.

I could call Dick, but he's dead.

I could call Allan, but he floated right out there. Dead, dead.

I could call Garnet, but she's *asleep*.

I could call Fran, but he's married again, and has children of his own.

I couldn't call Fran, *are you kidding?*

I could call Mother.

I could call Pearl.

I grabbed my purse and ran out of the house as fast as I

could for the car. Ordinarily I can't see to drive in the dark, but tonight the moon was dead full. I drove out of the lot and down Imperial to where town started. I drove on in, past the motel, past the restaurants, the Penney's, the Buffum's, and right on out of town. I drove east, just those few miles, on that winding road with nothing but weeds and oil wells. I got to Highway 5. South to LA and Garnet. North to San Francisco and Sandy.

I knew Edna gets up as early as I do. I turned around and drove back into town, turning left this time at the Vons and up the street to Edna's place.

Forget it. I drove on home.

I stopped the car. Am I going to cry? Am I going to faint? The dashboard. The moon. The sand. Three oil wells, that I can see from here. One billboard. Advertising where I live. My bathrobe, the *moon*. Sitting there, I could see across the lot to the development. Senior citizens' housing, financed by Carco. And right across the town in the same basic set of buildings, the Municipal Court, the high school, the DMV, the Unemployment. Give me a break.

I was afraid to get out of the car. Safe! No back doors, and aluminum siding to keep in the fire when it starts, so that you *bake* in there, before you burn. Old people living together for company. Strokes. Silly old men wandering out in the bushes so that their wives have to go out and find them. Cancer. You can breathe it out here.

The sun was coming up by the time I sneaked out of the car. I went in the bathroom and started the bathwater and went out to the kitchen for a Coke.

In the next couple of weeks I could see from my window that the high-school kids were going crazy over those water pistols. Usually at school it's always the same. The bad kids out by the bus stop, smoking. The ugly girls working in the cafeteria. The popular girls out on that little bit of lawn in front of the building. The popular guys in back by the football field, looking cute and talking to the coach. And because everybody knows everybody, and the faculty eats with the municipal staff, sometimes, when we're together in the employees' lounge, old Pfaffanger will look out of the window and say, "Jees, can you believe it? Andy Echevarria's found himself a girl, who is she, anyway?" And Edna will put down her cup of coffee. (She doesn't eat any food on Mondays, Wednesdays, and Fridays, to keep her weight down.) "That's one of the McAllister sisters, either Eileen or Kathleen, isn't it? I had them for B10 English. . . ." Arbogast—before she broke her ankles—used to look out, and press those awful handkerchiefs up against her flabby tits and say, "Oh, it's Tracie Reid, that little snit! Doesn't *she* think she's smart enough!" And Edna will look up and say, "Honestly, Elaine, she's not so bad, she's a pretty funny little kid." Or, "A nice little kid." Or, if Edna gets really griped, "Come on, Elaine! She's a *beautiful* little girl." And Arbogast looks pissed off, and blots her upper lip with that handkerchief, because she's always sweating, even inside with the air conditioning. And *outside*, on hot mornings, when she gets out of the car to come into class, there's this giant sopping place from her butt to her knees, like she's wet her pants. And some terrible thing in her makes her pick the side entrance by the bus stop to come in by, right past the bad boys, with that enormous wet butt swaying in the breeze. You see their faces after she's walked by, and some of them look mean as snakes, but most of them look sick. I told the Judge that I bet they were thinking what if the McAllister sisters, or that great-looking Donna McAleer, turned into something like Arbogast.

He said, "You *got* it, Grace," which made me think: Where did he used to be in his playground? Out talking to the coach? Or out by the bus stop, smoking cigarettes? And that made me remember Sandy and those awful boys, over by the bus stop, where I could see them from my desk every morning, looking like they were hiding something, notes or drugs or cigarettes, so that *time and time again*, whoever was working as yard attendant would take a trip over there, and, no, he wouldn't find anything. But Edna, when she took a turn at it, would stay over there for a few minutes and talk, her hip bones stuck out as much as theirs were, her shoulders hunched over as much as theirs were, but even she couldn't help me with him, *nobody could help me* with him!

But now the whole school was a water fight. Popular girls forgot they were popular. They'd come to school with pistols and stand behind the wire fence *at the bus stop*, and squirt the bad kids, even the big black guys! Which gave the black kids reason to come inside to the regular yard, even out on to the *front yard* to get revenge. The quiet little science kids got together and built a water cannon and a bunch of bombs. One day while I was watching, they sent the smallest kid out on top of the pergola and he sent down a couple of huge bombs which drenched those cheap girls, and you could see they didn't have any underwear. Usually it was just the work-study boys and the teenage welfare mothers who made the trouble (in the daytime anyway); now it was everybody.

When I told the Judge he'd have to do something, he said, "Now, Grace."

I was the only one who knew how things were going. "It is mandatory," I'd say, "that when you see someone with those pistols, you take them away."

"Ah, *hell*," Edna would say.

Or Pfaffanger would say, "Would you just make the phone call, so that I can get my equipment fixed? Like I asked you to yesterday? Because those guys out in the *shop*, they've got to have something to *do*. I can't handle them with broken equipment, that's the truth."

That snippy bitch from Unemployment would just say, "Run off these on the Xerox, please!" And then whisper, "I *curse* the day Proposition 13 *ever* went through!" (Because that's why everything goes through my office.)

Then one day, looking at some of the work-study kids eating their lunches in my office, I asked one of them straight out, "*Are you even in this program?*"

He just looked at me and mumbled something.

"What?"

"Old bitch!"

"*What?*"

"Honky bitch!"

I want to tell you, I thought *fast!* I knew that the main reason everyone thought the Judge was so nice was because they thought I was so awful. (Well, why *not?* Isn't that what you're supposed to do? Going to those *Daily News* parties with Fran, even the Virginia Wright parties, everyone saying Hi, Frank! Hi, Frank! Here's Frank! And then, making a *severe* effort to remember my name, Oh, hello, Grace. . . .) Everyone saying the Judge has really worked a miracle with those kids! But *he* knows and *I* know he only thought up Work-Study because the jail was full.

Hell, he doesn't even *see* these kids. I'm the . . .

It's not as if I don't have guts, you know. I've taken enough shit in this world. (I've told Garnet often enough, "You've got to take shit in this world! Don't you know enough to even know *that?*")

"You'd better get out of here, *right now!*"

"Why, *sweetheart*," he said. "Don't get your milk in a boil."

I felt the blood rush up into my head. I was going . . . I was . . . I was going to say something, but three of them looked at each other and got up and left. They'd even brought lunches with them, brown-bag lunches.

"*All right*," I said to the three who were left. "You just sit there and finish your lunches. I don't want to hear a word out of any of you!" Not that any of them had said anything.

Then I put in a call for Mr. Kirkpatrick at the high school. They said he was at the country club, and I didn't have the nerve to call him there.

And the Judge was God knows where.

Then noon was over and the kids left. I called up Ida and told her what happened. She was worried sick, but what could she do?

Sixth period. One of those terrible hot days. You couldn't tell in my office, with the air conditioning. But when anybody came in to ask for something, they were hot and sweaty.

"*No!* You can*not* go home early! I don't care what the nurse said, if you feel that sick you can just lie down somewhere until the bus comes. And that's *it*. That's *final!*"

"No! You can*not* use this phone and you can*not* borrow a dime! How old are you now, Donna, *fourteen?* Haven't I told you a thousand times in the past two and a half years. . . ?"

"No, Mr. Lambrozini, His Honor has told me that I absolutely do *not* have to run off Xerox copies after two P.M. No, I'm sorry, I don't know what an emergency *is*. No, I'm sorry, the Judge has said that *no one* here in the building has permission to use the copier but me. That is a very expensive piece of equipment, and if it were to break, *I* would be held responsible, no matter who was using it."

At three o'clock the last bells ring and the kids leave. At three-thirty the faculty leave. At four the DMV, the Welfare, Unemployment, all close up and go home. (Proposition 13 has been good for some people. The Judge only holds court until noon!)

Four o'clock, and I have to stay here *at least* until five. Four o'clock, and if anything were to happen to me here, the janitor starts with the other buildings. I've asked him time and time again, why don't you start over at this end of the school *Fran*, *Dick?* But he's dumb and he doesn't like me very much, I guess.

And so at four-fifteen they come in. Three black guys. I know them, but I don't know their names. "*What do you want?*" I say with hate, boy, as much hate as I can get in my voice. *You didn't shave on the left side of your jaw! You need a haircut! You smell funny! You're ignorant, stupid! Short! Your jokes aren't funny! I don't know, I just don't seem to feel anything anymore when you do it to me! I just don't seem to feel happy with you anymore!*

One of them walks over behind me. He grabs my chair. Oh, my God! All of a sudden I'm looking at the ceiling. Oh, Pearl! This is what I've been trying to tell you. It, It, It. I wasn't wearing a pantsuit, I was wearing a skirt. It was finally going to happen.

"Oh, don't," I said.

"Stupid old bitch," he said. Then, "Corky, you got any twine?"

"Twine?" I said. "You've got to be kidding! You're going to be sorry for this!" But my voice came out quavery and old. "The custodian's going to be here soon!"

"No, he ain't."

So then they've been watching. I open my mouth to say, *So you've been watching.* But that guy is looking at my mouth. I put my hand over it. I press my legs together.

Another guy, a fat one, says, "Can I sit on her face?"

Corky says, "Oh, *man!*"

The fat one says, in a white boy's voice, "Well! If you want booty, you can't be particular!"

Corky takes a piece of twine. He ties it to the back of the chair and tries to run it under me, but he can't.

"You fucking bastard! Do you think I *care?* Do you think I even *care!*"

My voice so mean it frightens me.

"You stupid, fucking idiots! So *what?* So *what?*" I can't even see them. I can only see red.

All the time the twine is going across me, back and forth, from one chair leg to the other, from one arm to the other. I can't hear them, I can't see them. Then I hear a noise; I look at them again. Corky is finished with the twine. He stands by the door, looking cool. (Like Dick's rich nephew after Dick died: "*Well, here I am, folks! Don't all start screaming at once!*")

"*You make me sick,*" I scream at him. "You make me want to puke! Don't you know that about yourself?"

The fat one has the middle drawer of my desk open. "Here they are," he says, and pulls out the green plastic bag of pistols.

The three of them stand along the wall. Looking at me. Oh, God. Like people look at old women in the street. In restaurants. At parties.

"*Well?*"

The one with the pistols leaves. The others go out right after him.

Six-forty-five the custodian comes in. He thinks I'm dead

because I'm not screaming. There's blood on my face and neck because I've bitten my lips and tongue. "Oh, my God," he finally says when he sees I'm alive. "Oh, my God, Mrs. Jackson, thank God you're alive!"

I think for a minute of Fran in the old days. Fran with a few beers in him, telling little Garnet, if she started reading *Captain Horatio Hornblower* maybe she'd end up reading *Moby Dick*, or telling her about how much fun he'd had when he was a boy and so poor, and that was why it didn't matter how much money we had, holding little Garnet on his lap—before he left, of course—and looking at her dead in the eye and saying, "The thing to remember, *always*, kid, is nothing bad can happen to you."

The custodian unwound the twine.

They can call you guys a lot of things, I moved my lips at him, *but all you really are is liars*.

2

Friday, April 10

I am very sorry to have to start this course—and this journal—with an apology. Your first class seemed very interesting indeed, and I was—I actually am—looking forward to this quarter very much. But I was called away by a family emergency for the better part of the weekend. Missed two out of the first three days of my classes. Not a very good start, is it? (And it's funny that my mother, who never has been very hesitant about pointing out my shortcomings, is at least indirectly responsible for this one.)

She got sick over the weekend, and my children and I drove up to the little town where she lives now, to see if there was anything we could do. It was the general consensus—I should say it *became* the general consensus—that we should bring her back now for a short visit.

I'm not too sure what you want us to put in these journal entries. So I want to ask you to bear with me. Even though I have been taking extension courses for several semesters, this is the first time I have actually enrolled in daytime university classes in, well, I think, over fifteen years. There is some doubt at home about whether I will be able to do it, and of course I should say that if it looks like (looks as if?) I won't be able to fill my obligations at home, then of course I'll have to drop. But I very much want to be able to finish. Because I see so many women are doing just that.

Well! I can't think of too much more to say in this entry. You said you would read these things and not mark much in them, is that right? I'd like to ask you to be *very critical.* I'm very conscious of not being able to express myself, and it's something I want to improve—as much as I can in eleven weeks. (Only, now it's ten.)

You asked us to say what other classes we are taking. In addition to this class in composition, I am taking a History of Los Angeles, to celebrate the city's bicentennial, a brush-up conversational French class called "Verborama," because my husband and I have tentatively planned a trip to Europe this summer—if we can only get our children to consent to go to camp—and Psychology I. (I took it twenty years ago, but forgot it.)

I'll close with one last thing. I remember learning in an English class somewhere, that it isn't "right" to start a sentence with the word, the letter, I. But it isn't right to use the "passive voice," either, is it? So if you're writing a journal—I mean, if you're supposed to be writing about yourself—how do you do that? (I expect you can see from this entry, that I've been out of school for fifteen years. Sometimes it seems like fifteen centuries.)

Saturday, April 11

You say that I should "make up" those two meetings I missed by writing about where I was when I "should" have been at school. Actually, I think I'd rather write about something else! But, here goes. I didn't think I'd have time to do homework on the weekends, but I took my children to their lessons, my husband went in to work for the morning, and my mother, who has trouble sleeping nights, is sleeping late.

Well. Last Monday morning, while I was still doing my laps in the pool, I got a phone call. I always hate when there's a stranger on the phone, who, as soon as you pick up the phone, calls you by your last name. I always remember when David, my little boy, fell out of a tree and got his concussion. Or when Debbie, my daughter, got in trouble with the girls' vice-president for not wearing panty hose under her overalls. Can you imagine that? It was right after that episode that we decided to put them both in private school.

So even though it was going to be my first day at school, I was doing my laps, because I watch my weight. My husband has told me several times that I have a lot of "natural" beauty, and I may not be terribly smart, but I'm smart enough to know what that means. I was doing my laps, and, my God, why can't I *get* to it! A woman who lives in my mother's apartment complex called up and said my mother was "sick."

Only, she wouldn't say how sick, or what happened. So I got to be the one who was worried sick.

I really don't know how to tell you about this. Anyway, I called the school, got in the car, went over to school where Debbie and Davie were waiting. We started the drive up to Mother's. Actually, I don't know how specific you want this to be. I drove through Beverly Hills, over Laurel Canyon to Oakwood School (ordinarily I'm part of a very good and conscientious car pool), and then out the San Diego Freeway, over to where the valley (how horrible it is out there!) turns into those scrubby hills, then over the hills, onto the Grapevine, and then onto Highway 5, which, I guess you know, cuts up through the middle of California, and some of the worst-looking country in the world. Once we were on 5, it was a mere 250 miles up to the town of Coalinga, which, for several ungodly reasons about twenty years ago, is where my mother decided to live.

I guess I should say that while I was driving (it was about ten o'clock in the morning, and we had the air conditioning on) I got a strange idea that we were the only spot of color in about a hundred square miles. I'm not just talking about the Volvo I drive, but, looking in the rearview mirror, I saw my two beautiful children. They were both sulking, naturally. Davie had been playing baseball, and when he does that, or any other physical exercise, he turns bright pink. (Our Mexican gardener calls him Camarón.) Debbie was wearing one of those bright new green T-shirts that say "OZ", from that new store they have now in Century City, Bijou, and a bright orange sun visor on her head with the word "HEAVEN" on it. The visor came from the other new store they have in Century City named—why can't I be clever about this?—Heaven.

Neither of them was speaking, either to each other or to me. They're at a difficult age, and besides, I guess I can go ahead and say it, they hate the drive up to see my mother, and they're not too crazy about my mother either. They blame it on me, and I don't blame them. When they were little, you could always keep them going by saying *Wait for the Cows!* Because just before you take the turnoff to Coalinga, there is this terrible pen of cattle, halfway up the middle of the very worst part of California. It's not a farm at all, it's just stuck in the middle of the desert, thousands of cows and steers being fattened by hormones, waiting to be sold and die. Once, when I was driving my mother home after a visit, we had a flat tire by there, and we went into a Spanish-style house right in the exact middle of those cows. It was built around a fabulous courtyard. The handles on the faucets in the basin were gold, and on the back of the toilets they had a ticker tape which fed out nothing but information about cows! It was really quite amazing. We got this once-in-a-lifetime look into another whole world which was doing very well without the world of television. But try and tell my *children* that. Now, if I were to say something to the kids, like, "Wait for the cows! Can't you hardly wait to see the cows?" I know the kind of answer I'd get.

You see, I'm very proud of my children and I've raised them a certain way. I've been around enough to know (no, I haven't "been around" at *all*, but I've seen enough growing up here to know that in "Hollywood," Brentwood, just like anywhere else, there are two ways to live, two ways to grow up). I don't want to be—I can't be—one of those Hollywood mothers who spends her afternoons getting daisies hand-painted on her toenails for forty dollars a toe. And both my children have to live on an allowance. They have to buy a lot of their clothes in Heaven instead of Saks. But still, they take tennis lessons—well, so do *I*, take tennis lessons, but they're *good* at it. But they're thirteen and fourteen, and it's gotten to the point where everything I say

Something has just occurred to me. I must say here that I'm not at all sure I should be taking this class. I don't need to graduate because I don't need a job because I don't need the money. I thought I wanted to express myself because I see women everywhere who say they want to express themselves and then they go ahead and express themselves. But couldn't that be harmful in some ways? I'm not even talking about people reading this "journal." My husband has a shredder at home, and every week, when I shred his things, I can certainly shred this. But aren't there things that can be harmful to know?

I was going to say that everything I say to them now, they look at me like I was their mother. I mean *my* mother! And that's after, I don't mean to tell you this, I don't know how many tennis lessons, and trips to the psychiatrist for me and them, and thousands of sandwiches I made with my own hands, not out of white bread, because it's bad for you, or lunch meat, because it can give you cancer (and I grew up on it), but sandwiches made out of pita bread and alfalfa sprouts and breast of chicken, and I might as well say I'm really taking "Verborama" so I can help them with their French homework. Whenever we travel, it's certainly Ian who does the talking; I'm not going to go opening my mouth in a foreign country. But they look at me as though I were my mother. Am I still as far away from them as that? And isn't that harmful to know? If I didn't know it, or write it down, couldn't it slip away into the past without me noticing? (Or them either?)

You ask me to be "specific and visual." Don't misunderstand! I know you said it to all the rest of the class, and I know I shouldn't take it personally. My husband, who actually *is* almost always right about everything—in his profession he has to be—says I take everything personally. It's just that I don't think there's anything to be specific about, on Highway 5, for instance, or Coalinga. We have an artist friend who had a picture hanging in the living room of the Bob Newhart show for years. She's very interested artistically in the highway to Gorman. She made us a present of one of her "Gorman Series," but even though her work gets more popular every year, I can only hang that picture in the den. Because it's only a highway, and sand, and the same truck over and over. I have trouble seeing it as "art." I guess that's because I've made the ride too many times.

You say that if we keep looking at something over and over, we'll be able to figure out what it means. All right! My children and I made the ride up to Coalinga to see if she was okay, because my mother's neighbor said she'd been sick. After six or seven hours of driving, we made it to Coalinga, and drove through town, on out to my mother's place. My mother lives in an apartment complex, financed in part by Carco, the major business in town. So, because the rents are greatly reduced, it's an ideal place for senior citizens. (If any place for senior citizens can be ideal.) We got there around four-thirty in the afternoon. It was still over a hundred degrees outside, and the sun didn't look like it was ever going down. That's the kind of place it is.

How do I do this? I feel silly writing down what actually *did happen*. You say that this is true for everyone in class, that we don't "respect our lives." Well, here goes. We spent almost the whole first afternoon in someone else's apartment, because that's where my mother was, and Ida, her neighbor, who seemed to be taking care of her, had asked us all to dinner. That was very nice of her.

How do I expect to get college credit for this? The apartment had paneled walls. There was an enormous cuckoo clock which every fifteen minutes made a terrible noise. But even worse was the ticking the clock made in between. The couch and chairs were very old-fashioned, and every place that could have a doily on it did have a doily on it. There were Hummel figures on knickknack shelves. (Nobody we know now owns a knickknack shelf, there aren't any anymore, except there are still quite a few in Coalinga.) Ida, a very nice friend of my mother's, whom I don't know very well at all, had made us an enormous dinner and put on a hostess gown, even though it was the middle of the day. The whole house smelled of roast turkey, and she was making brown gravy, even though, as I say, it was *hot*. She had made up a lot of broccoli. I saw, when I went out to the kitchen, that she'd opened up three Birdseye packages. (Still, it was very nice of her.) She even had wine for us, which I had mixed feelings about, since—as my husband points out, and certainly I can't contradict him on it—I like to drink a little too much. (I can see that sentence works two ways, but it's true, I *like* it too much and I *drink* it too much!)

Red wine in the middle of the day when it's over a hundred degrees outside and ninety degrees inside doesn't go down too well. I had a couple of glasses. I noticed my children started giving me looks and then they went outside. There's never anything for them to do up in Coalinga. They never understand why we go up there, and I suppose that's something really good that I've been able to give them in their lives. (Although I grew up for a good part of my life in Los Angeles, and came back to go to college here, I spent my high-school years in Coalinga.)

We sat down to a very heavy lunch, or dinner. There were

Ida and Estelle and Bernice. I think they are all Carco widows, all friends of my mother. I don't see them as being like my mother at all, but what do I know? They are soft and plump with white skin and white hair and, usually, skirts. They look like they buy their clothes at Sears, and they make it a point to compliment each other on their clothes. I'd taken considerable trouble, considering the short notice, to dress for this trip. I had a Gucci bag and some very good pants, and a top from I. Magnin, but I could see I'd dressed wrong, pretty much as always. These are women I've known since my mother moved up there, and I must say I don't like them very much and they don't like me.

It's not that I don't like them. They're very kind and good. But they do things like hang their skirts from a bureau drawer and then explain how it keeps out the wrinkles, and they don't have to walk over to the closet to put their skirt on in the morning, so they're one step closer to getting dressed. Do you see? They wash out their stockings, and they pull them out when they hang them up, so they'll be in their perfect stocking shape. And where did all that get them? They had their husbands and their children (I *know!* That's all I've got!) and sometimes they even traveled in foreign countries. They are so sweet, and eager to please. One of them had a tapeworm once. Am I getting specific enough?

And now, of course, at night, they drink together, and get angry about life, and cry.

I'm getting off the subject, so maybe I should say exactly what the dinner—served at five in the afternoon—was. Turkey and broccoli. A dish of lima beans. "Manzanita" jelly, bright pink, homemade, and holding its shape from a jar. Mashed potatoes and butter (margarine). A fruit salad, at least it *was* fresh fruit, cut up on separate beds of lettuce, and the dressing was boysenberry yogurt. Those rolls that are half-cooked, and then you brown the rest in the oven. Red wine. When I saw it I knew I was going to have to eat it all, and I did. (Luckily I've enrolled in a dance class as well this semester!)

No, what I meant to say was, I looked at all the food so carefully prepared, and so carefully set out, and the white linen tablecloth used for special occasions. You could see that the creases came from someone who used a hand iron, it wasn't ever sent out to the cleaners. I looked through those fluffy curtains that the woman had on those windows, and I saw those oil wells they have all over the outskirts of Coalinga on those bare hills they've got up there, and I looked at the round thing of red jelly moving around on the saucer, and I felt the most incredible feeling of pain and sadness. I'll be honest and say it wasn't for them. It was for me. That I'd tried *so hard* to go *so far*, and there it all still was, worse than ever.

Also, I should say, because you say to use direct quotes, that one lady, when she found out Ian stood a good chance of having the second feature picture ever produced in mainland China, started saying things like, "Oh, Garnet, dear, I hear your husband just came back from China!" And then I'd start to say, oh, something like, "Yes, I." But then Ida would say, "*Bernice* was in China once!" And so then I'd say, "Really?" And then Bernice patted her lap and kept saying, "Oh, just in World War II." And Ida would say, "She was a nurse, you know." The last thing on this earth they wanted to hear about was my life. I guess it's flattering, at my age, to be thought of as a juvenile delinquent. In fact, my mother did have terrible times with my brother, and I think his bad reputation, through the years, has spilled over on me. Also, I think it's fashionable (?) for all their children to have turned out bad. I've heard only good things about one of them. He works on a nuclear submarine.

I don't want to say that this was a bad trip. Actually, they are very nice ladies. And Mother's particular friend, Ida, has several things in her house that I wouldn't mind having. A hand-carved coffee table from India, for instance. A cut-glass bowl, a very beautiful pink color. A nice wall hanging . . .

My reason for going up there, for missing these first two classes, was (specifically!) trying to find out what had happened to my mother. We had gotten that phone call, but nobody would say what was happening. Even Ian, my husband, offered to drive up with me (he's very good about those things), but naturally I said no. But I was in this room, all the food was on the table, those women were looking at me as though they really knew me, as though they knew who I was. The kids were already playing outside, and I could have guessed up front, as Ian might say, that Davie would begin practicing his karate chops and end up beheading a neighbor's concrete birdbath.

I'm only trying to say that it was time to sit down. All the food was on the table, you know how turkey with dressing is (maybe you don't, you're a man), it gets congealed, and it was beginning to congeal, and my mother wouldn't come to the table. Ida has an old chesterfield, is that what they call it? A big, square chair with big arms, very brown and down to the ground, and there was my mother (I know just this morning you advised against using "there was" because it is not "strong"), but all I can think to say is, there was my mother, sitting in a chair. Like that bomb, the Big Ben they loaded in the airplane, before they bombed Hiroshima. Like a big black bull in a box. Like, you know, like those old Billy Wilder jokes where he says we'll have a, you know, just one of those average big-bulls-in-a-box shots? I know I don't tell jokes very well, but the point of that is supposed to be, you don't *get* big black bulls in a box every day.

This is not a complaint about my mother. I wish I could say that in a way that someone would believe me. Or that I could believe it.

Let me try to do it "visually," the way you said in class. I was in a very sad place, on a very hot day, with a big turkey dinner and four old ladies. I *hate* to call them that, but that's what they are!

My children were outside, I could see the shiny blond tops of their heads, they were doing something in the yard which goes around the apartments. They hadn't broken the birdbath yet, but Davie was picking on Debbie and I felt, I knew, that in an hour or two she was going to be crying and he was going to be hitting, and these poor old ladies were going to have some damaged property, and I just felt sick about it. I'd had two glasses of wine in the middle of the day and I *knew* I was going to have more. I was already worrying about getting back down the highway and home before midnight. You don't know how I dread spending the night up there.

So the essential thing would be, to get on with it! To eat the "dinner" these nice ladies have fixed and find out what's happening to Mother—I mean, did she have cancer, I suppose is what I thought. I was all set to give her a talk on not being hopeless, or how there was the laetrile clinic in Tijuana, or the Simonton method of self-hypnosis (I guess that's another Billy Wilder joke, the whole idea of telling my mother about the Simonton method of curing cancer).

But there we were, and my mother wouldn't come to the table.

That's really all I can say about that moment! She wears those boxy pantsuits like a lot of secretaries now, but she isn't very big. In fact, she's quite small. And she was sitting in that boxy chair, well, I guess I've said it. The top of her head barely came to the top of the chair.

The thing is, I haven't said yet, those women are all extremely fond of her. They really love her! They started talking to her almost like she was a cranky dog that they were crazy about. "Come on, Grace! Come to the table, now!"

And if I hadn't known better, I'd have thought she was having a nervous breakdown instead of cancer. You could see, that's what *they* thought she was having, but she wasn't having any *nervous breakdown*. I mean, that's just *her!* I would really like to *see the day* when someone fixed a dinner for me and I had the nerve to just sit there and not go over and eat it. It is just a day that would never happen.

And I got this terrible feeling of fatigue. I started to sweat, really sweat. I went over for another glass of wine because, really, I've seen it all before!

The women were standing around her, looking concerned.

My mother said, to *them:*

"Why'd you bring *her* up here?"
She was talking about me!
My mother said, so meanly, "Jesus Christ! As if I haven't been through enough!"
It crossed my mind that my mother had been raped, but I'm sorry, I just couldn't believe it.
(And I want to say here that those women, whom I've always tried to like, were all of them nodding their heads, like, yes, it really is terrible that *she* has to come up here, after everything *else* you've been through.)
Outside, Davie took his first whap (is that a word?) at Debbie. Debbie started to make this horrible, ongoing noise. I don't blame her. It was about a hundred and ten degrees out there, but I didn't want them to have to come in here, either. . . .
One of those women, I think it was Ida, looked over at me. "Garnet, you have no idea what your mother has gone through." They all looked over at me as if whatever it was, was my fault!
I went over and had my fourth glass of wine. All I wanted to do was to lie down. And not because of the wine. But because my mother had been *going through* things for so long, and after a while I really get to believe it,· that my mother, even at her age, is really *going through* things, and all the rest of us are just *dogging* it, you know? All the rest of us are only living.
I said something like, "Would it be, wouldn't it be, a good thing, if we sat down and, actually, discussed what happened? We could have something to eat."
All I can say is, my mother looked at me like I was a piece of shrimp, and she hates shrimp. But listen! In restaurants she always orders a seafood salad *with no shrimp*. Never a tuna salad, but a seafood salad! Then she asks if they put any shrimp in it. They usually say no, God knows why. Then she looks through her salad with a *fine-tooth comb*, until she finds a piece of shrimp. Usually it's not even a whole shrimp. It's usually a quarter of a shrimp. When she finds it she puts a fork in it and *rams* it around on her plate. Then she says she's

going to faint. Or she starts to cry. Or sits there with her arms folded and watches us eat. Or she looks out the restaurant window with the tears streaming down her face, while *someone*, a husband or a boyfriend, but usually one of her lady friends says, with all this reverence, "Come on, Grace, you've *got* to eat something!" Although my mother is far from thin. But her eating is totally over for the night, and she stays up all night throwing up, and crying and scratching her arms until the blood comes, and everyone has to come home early, and for thirty years at least I've wanted to ask somebody, even *her*, why not order a *hamburger!* Which is like saying to her: Don't worry Mother, if you've got cancer, they've got this wonderful new method on these *cassettes!* All you have to do is listen to these tapes.

What I'm saying is, that's how my mother *goes through* dinner, don't you see? While everyone else is just, you know, eating?

I knew, already, she'd done it to me again. She made me miss two classes, two days of classes, because I ended up staying that day and night and part of another day up there. I've taken est. I know I'm "responsible for my own condition." But how is it, when I finally get to a semester, a point in my life, when I can finally "take hold," that events, *my mother*, start to happen? And when I take a class where I'm supposed to keep a journal, my life, which most of the time I would describe as happy, and myself as a happy person, turns into something else, so that when I simply have to describe my life this week, it's something that shames me and makes me—no, I know, nothing makes me do anything. But I know, there's something, someone in this world who knows every awful thing about me. Seeing that person is like tripping a lever. Everything kicks back to another place and time, and I forget who I am and that I'm a happy person, as happy as anyone I imagine has a right to be, and there I am again, watching my mother *go through it.*

We never did eat that dinner. It just got worse- and worse-looking, while my mother made a little bit of a *scene* there, and

Davie broke the birdbath. The neighbor came over to complain, but when she realized what my mother was going through, she stayed and tried to make her feel better. I began to realize that we'd be spending the night up there, so I phoned the motel for reservations.

I'm still not sure what happened to my mother. I guess there's nothing medically wrong with her. And I don't think she's crazy. If she is, she's crazy like a fox! And while her friends and neighbors seemed to think she was wiggier (?) than usual, as I say, I've seen all that stuff for, well, *over* thirty years.

I might say as well that she got a leave of absence from where she works. She wasn't fired, I know that. I called up her boss, a judge who's also the justice of the peace and town manager up there. He said some kids from the high school had "given her a hard time" and that he and the rest of the staff had decided Grace deserved a few months off. Then he told me how wonderful she was.

Always with that sense of reproach! Like, how could you have let those kids do such awful things to your wonderful mother? Or, how could you let her suffer the way you do? The thing that gets me is, he's known the family for years, he *knows* better. But the main thing is, my mother is on a medical leave for a few months. She's not fired. He told me that so many times it really made me worry. She has a pension. (So that even if she has terrible children like my brother and me, she's going to be *all right*, don't you see?) And not a financial burden.

I'd be lying if I said I wasn't relieved.

But she won't be going back to work for months, and here it is just the second week of April.

If she doesn't get better, the implication was, she won't be going back at all.

I'm going to end this entry in a minute. I want to ask you, do the extra pages count ahead? Because I want a good grade in this class. I plan to write again tomorrow, if I can, so that, for this week, at least, I'll be even with the rest. My family thinks I can't do this, go back to school, and this time I don't just mean my mother. My children are embarrassed by it, and although my husband is a very kind man, I think he's embarrassed too. But I want to try. And I think even *I* can manage twelve units. I would love to get good grades and show them.

My mother is only sixty-three. She's never been sick a day in her life. She throws up a lot, but never during the racing season.

I don't think I have to say here what I fear the most. Ida (Mother's friend), told me, just plain told me she wasn't going to be responsible for Mother living alone up there. Evidently she's been crying a lot and banging the walls. (How could I say to Ida: That's just what she does.) Ida knows it anyway. She's known her for . . . not as long as I have, but a long time. And I could tell by the way she wouldn't really look at me that she

I think they've just *had* it with her up there. Like my father *had* it. Or my

Forget it. The main thing I see is, they just *took* her like a big volleyball, or something smaller, and harder, that you can hit with a racket, and batted her over to me.

My brother isn't within hailing distance, so I'm *it*.

That's what my mother used to say. I'm *it*.

My mother is only sixty-three. She's as strong as a bear. And for now, anyway, she's coming to live with me.

Sunday, April 12

I stayed around at Ida's until about five. I couldn't stand to call Ian and tell him about Mother coming until the next day, so I just left a message at the studio that I'd be staying overnight. (Such a harmless message!) Ida, once she got her point across, let me off the hook. She said why didn't I just take the kids over to the motel and get some rest, maybe a swim. I suppose underneath it all, she felt pretty bad about it. Friendship has its obligations too. (Do you think, if I go on with this class, I'll get in the habit of writing that kind of sentence?)

We went over to the motel, the only one in town. In high school, sometimes, for a birthday, three or four girls would check into a room for a slumber party, or, sometimes, for a prom, a couple would check in there for a really magic evening.

The kids had their suits, and they swam all through the afternoon and into the night. I swam too. I'm that much of a Brentwood matron to think about finishing my day's laps. Pretty soon we went in and had a gorgeous (by Coalinga standards) buffet dinner. The kids were pretty good, they didn't ask me any questions.

I knew things were going to get terrible, is what I'm trying to say, but that one night at the motel was pretty nice. I guess you could say it's the good part of my adolescence. The dry grass all around, and the way the lizards come right out by the pool, and the noise of the oil wells, which some people hate, but I think, almost, sounds like the ocean. I didn't spend much time growing up in that godforsaken town, but I did spend some. Parts of it were pretty. I still like periwinkle because for some reason they've got a lot of it up there growing out from concrete-brick walls. It's like little blue stars.

The next morning we wanted to get an early start, but Mother was throwing dishes all around the kitchen so we didn't. Ida and Bernice tried to make it seem like it was unusual, but I just laughed. I was feeling pretty awful about the whole thing by then. I told them, *and* Mother, that I'd take her down to LA *for a short visit*, if and when she calmed down, but not before.

Then I went back to the motel, and Debbie and Davie and I spent the rest of the day by the pool.

The next morning I drove back by. They'd called me by then, and said, "Grace is all packed, and she's so looking forward to visiting you." Again, like all this was my fault for not wanting to visit her. *Well, who'd want to visit her?*

And I'll just say here that one of the things she broke the day before was a dark red Catalina pottery coffeepot, one of the few beautiful things she's ever had, one of the few nice things my father ever left her, and one of the very, *very* few things I was ever going to inherit.

That's a Billy Wilder joke.

There was a, what do you call it? An unspoken agreement, a tacit agreement? That Ida would clean up if I'd take Mother away. She had this heartbreaking little suitcase we put in the back and there was a fight between the kids about who had to sit in the back with her, and we started out of town toward Highway 5.

By eleven o'clock we were on the road south. We passed the cows, on the left now, and none of us said a word about them. My mother was in the backseat. A more logical way of doing it might have been to put the "grown-ups" in the front seat and the kids in the back. Except I was *not* going to have her up front with me, not while I was driving, and I have to add, she'd do anything, even sit in the backseat, so as not to have to sit next to me. She was in the back, catercorner behind Davie, and sitting next to Debbie, who didn't like that one bit.

Things got off to a great start when my mother looked over at Debbie, who was wearing another Oz T-shirt, the one that says, "Toto, I have a feeling we're not in Kansas anymore!" and also her little Heaven sun visor. Mother said to Debbie, who had worked a good forty minutes that morning putting her hair in two little ponytails so that they came straight out of the top of her sun visor, "Take off your hat when you're riding in the car!"

I looked back at Debbie in the rearview mirror, and she was looking straight ahead, right through me, past me, out to the sand and the fences whizzing by, and it was still a good hundred miles until we came to a good truck stop. We hadn't been on the road more than ten minutes.

My mother said, "Take off your hat when you ride in the car! *Didn't you hear what I said?*"

I saw Davie beside me shudder all over like a python at the zoo. I think he'd just remembered it was going to be a six-hour drive.

"When you're *riding with me* in the car, and I say take off your hat, young lady, you take off your hat!"

I was terrified. But that Debbie! She doesn't go to Oakwood School for nothing! She isn't friends with the daughter of a consumer advocate for nothing! She folded her arms and stuck her lip out. Her hair was coming straight up in two blond sticks out of her sun visor. We had miles left to go.

All of a sudden, and you have to say one thing, my mother can certainly surprise me, she lunged across the upholstery and snatched the sun visor off Debbie's head, or tried to, except Debbie had anchored the visor onto her ponytails, so it was as if my mother was doing her best to scalp her own granddaughter. My mother made more trouble in the first fifteen minutes of the trip than both my kids did the whole time on the way up.

My mother got the visor and sat on it. Debbie was crying with rage, and I'm sorry to say, I was crying too. Because I knew this was only the beginning. Then Davie, who can be really a terrific kid, opened up my purse, which was sitting between us on the front seat, found my cigarette case (I hardly ever smoke anymore, but Ian gave me the case for our tenth anniversary). Davie pulled out a cigarette, pushed in the cigarette lighter until it was ready, lit up, blew an enormous cloud of smoke all over the car, and turned around in his seat to look at his grandmother, who looked—I could *feel* it, I didn't even have to look in the rearview mirror—like a shark in a bathtub. Davie held the cigarette pointing straight down like Jean Paul Belmondo in the old French movies—he gave his air-ace look and said, "Let's play a parlour game,

Grandma! Let's play Geography! Because time flies when you're having fun!"

I started to laugh with the tears on my face, and I could see it even struck Debbie funny. My mother actually considered the situation and said, "Yes, well, okay, if I don't have to write anything down, because you know, I get sick in the car."

And Davie said, "Finland!"

I said, "The Dardanelles!"

Debbie said, "Samoa!"

(Do you see how the game works? Does your family ever play this in the car?)

But Mother couldn't think of anything, and she said Debbie was cheating to give her an A to work with. Debbie gave her a truly ferocious grin and said "Abyssinia? Albania? Atlanta? Afghanistan?"

My mother said, "I don't like little girls who sass!"

Davie said, "Let's go the other way around the car. What about Newfoundland, Grandma?"

But no. Mother had to take her letters off Debbie, and Debbie was mad enough and a good enough student that she gave her an A or an E every time.

I see this journal entry is long enough, but I don't want it to go by without at least saying that maybe a half-hour later Debbie gave her one "Argentina" too many and I heard my mother say, "You disgusting little girl!"

Which was bad enough, but then I got to hear my own daughter rap right back, "You disgusting old lady!" Davie took a deep breath. I got a very clear and sudden idea of why kids take drugs.

It went on that way for a lot more hours. But I want to emphasize there was nothing very much out of the ordinary about this. Or, rather, the unordinary part was what Debbie said back, with her little visor locked under my mother's behind. The unusual part was my mother's look of surprise when she heard those words, and I thought of how much more her husbands and her children took without ever thinking to answer back. I thought that my mother has always been very good at dishing it out, and never very good at taking it.

It was ten o'clock that night by the time we drove up our driveway. The kids were asleep. Mother was awake but not talking. Our home in Brentwood, South of Sunset, North of San Vicente, is two-story fake Tudor, with an expensive mansard roof. There is a beautiful jacaranda tree in front, and several night-blooming jasmines in back. And a side yard, which is my favorite. We have "room for a tennis court," which in some ways is even better than having one. We only have a part-time maid. We don't have a burglar alarm—I guess we should—and we certainly don't have a circular driveway. Our gardener is good, very good, but he doesn't sweep or rake much. You're always stepping on something crunchy out on the lawn.

I really love my home, much more than I could ever say. I drove up in the dark, and I could see, by a certain light in the den, that Ian was home, reading scripts. He works very hard—for us, and for himself.

I pulled up in the driveway and turned around in the seat to look at Mother. There was a big yellow moon, and it lit up the inside of the car. I saw my mother looking at the house, with contempt. It was as though she already saw the twigs on the lawn, the thousand holes in this little "fabric," I guess I could say, that I've been working on the last fifteen years.

I guess you could say that that was when I got depressed. And I mean more than depressed. I saw her looking at my house and I felt a really terrible despair. My brother and I fought my mother. My brother lost and I got away. I didn't win. I just got away. And it's like those vampire movies. You don't win against vampires. You just persuade them to fly off somewhere, and then you hope to God they don't come back. They do, of course. I felt a black despair. I just felt like I couldn't go in there with her and let it start again.

She said, "Well, are we just going to sit here all night?" Then she said, "Isn't *he* going to come out here and help us with the luggage?" But there was an awful lot, a *lot* of time between each sentence. And she didn't make a move. I almost have the feeling she didn't want it to start again either. She's older now, she isn't immortal.

Here is the kicker. I really love old Grace. Sometimes, on my "bad" days, I watch *General Hospital.* I know you'd never watch, but there's a woman, my favorite, Tracy Quartermain, on that show. If Tracy Quartermain were forty years older and was two million dollars poorer, she'd be like my mother. Just so *awful!* I love her. Like you love the idea of the end of the world? Or all the ground squirrels in Brentwood and Bel Air and Topanga Canyon rising up and giving themselves one good shake, so all their fleas fall off into thousands of expensive rugs, and every Beverly Hills wife and kid and even husband swells up, turns black, and dies in horrible agony from the plague? That's how I love her.

How my heart breaks for her, you could almost say.

I want to go back, for a minute, to the three days in Coalinga.

I think I mentioned the picture by our friend in the living room of the Bob Newhart show? The other reason I watch Bob Newhart—the reruns, every afternoon before the kids get home—is that I have been told I look, and act, like Suzanne Pleshette.

I am a fairly cheerful person, I think. If you know how hard I've worked for what I have, well, you couldn't know, nobody could know.

Not when I was in the apartments, because nobody could fool those ladies, but when I was with the kids, alone in the motel up in Coalinga, I felt like quite a beautiful woman. The people at *New West* called Suzanne Pleshette an aging starlet once. I was angry, then I thought, there are worse things to be. I'm not terribly pretty, but I keep moving, and I smile.

I stayed two nights up in Coalinga in that motel. The proprietor is an Armenian, God knows why he decided to come and live his life in that dreadful little town. He recognized me, I think. But I was there alone this time, except for the two radiantly beautiful young kids from my new, made-up life. Mr. Albarian was alone in his motel. He gets very few customers—or rather he depends on Rotary meetings, juvenile delinquents, which I was for a very short while, and casualties from the accidents on Highway 5. There were none of those that night. But every night Mr. Albarian has his wife make a big buffet. He opens the doors of his lobby out to the swimming pool so that you can hear the oil wells and the cicadas. He lets his buffet sit there under orange and yellow lights, which he thinks will drive away the bugs, and sometimes they do.

I was able to sit there, with the whole buffet to choose from, and the kids laughing and talking out in the pool, taking turns diving off the edge, gliding in and out of the water, and I—even in Coalinga—could really see that I was lucky, and beautiful, and had style.

Do you know what my mother used to say when a new friend of mine used to come over? I'm speaking now about after my stepfather died, but before my mother moved to where she lives now. She would look at someone, I don't care if it was a girl scout or some poor guy who was dropping by to take me to a football game. She'd say, *"Who's that jerk?"* And the person who had looked so good to me at school or work would shift, after what Mother said, to look like the jerk he or she really was. Once, when my brother was only ten, he made the mistake of coming home, *walking* home, with a little boy about four years older. "What did he want?" my mother started asking, and she asked it so many times and in so many ways that we had to *beg* her, me crying, my brother screaming, not to call the cops on the fourteen-year-old boy. But six years later, that kid got arrested for flashing, right on that street. A neighbor wrote to tell us about it, and my mother wasn't surprised. I wasn't surprised either.

The real break with my mother came, not when I moved out, or left town, but when Ian began to come around. There had been other boys. One who brought me flowers every time we went out, but he had a habit of saying, "We was just sittin' there shootin' the breeze." Even I could see he was a jerk. There was another one who certainly knew how to kiss, but his hair was crimpy and he didn't have too much of a sense of humor.

I guess my mother was right about him too, except he came down to LA and made a fortune in television commercials. Ian and I run into him all the time at parties. She was right about some of my women friends. Two of them turned out to be jerks. There was once a boy I really liked a *lot*, he was a cashier at Ralph's—that was back in Coalinga. She seemed like she liked him, but then she said his shoulders sloped and he had the beginning of a gut, and didn't those freckles make me sick, and, God, he thought he was a big shot with his car! And besides, he was just one step up from a box boy. And once, when he took our groceries out to the car as a favor, she tipped him. That was the end of *that* little romance.

When I brought Ian home she

She's never been terribly considerate of other people's feelings. She called him a Jewish jerk. As in, "Who's that Jewish Jerk?" She was certainly right about the first part. His folks changed their name so that *he* could have a better life. And he was the one who thought up "Ian" because he liked the idea of coming from Scotland. Also, he was thinking of himself as a producer even then. Ian for Ian Fordyce. Evans for Robert Evans, whom he admired even then. "Ian Evans presents . . ."

But how was I supposed to know about the second part? Because the thing is, my mother is often right. I had a friend once who married a homosexual; my mother called it, right on the button.

"Why doesn't that Jewish jerk bring over some wine, if he's going to stay for dinner? Do you think you could get that Jewish jerk to mow the lawn, instead of just sitting there watching television?"

(Of course, in fairness to her, she's been through a lot in her life. She probably doesn't mean half the things she says.)

There are times you have to hope for the best. My mother

was, has been, almost always right, but I married Ian.

So when she sat looking at this house, my house, you know? I heard all her words, so clear, so clear, she didn't have to open her mouth to say them.

3

Tuesday night, April 14

Now that Mother has been here a few days, I think I should say that last time I wrote I exaggerated some of the things that went on. Now that we're all back at the house and the kids and I are back in school again, it's hard to believe some of the things that happened.

So *now,* I don't know what to write! I can say that Angel, the gardener, brought over a dozen pony packs of marguerites this week without being asked, he does such a good job on the yard, it is certainly worth the money we pay him. Or, that I drove Ian's car for the weekly shopping yesterday. I can see, really, what they say about the Mercedes, it smells so nice, and there's no noise at all, you feel like a different person, a better person somehow, and in honor of having that car, I did the shopping at Jurgensen's instead of Alpha Beta.

Yesterday afternoon, after classes, I had in a couple of friends to play cards with my mother and me. Mother's always been a card shark, and she was the big winner yesterday, so that pleased her, I think. They are women I don't see too often, but they were nice. And in fact, I do know that all around me here in Brentwood there are women who spend long afternoons playing cards (or shopping), and with their mothers. So Mother is that much closer in that respect to a "normal life" than I am. I do think she had a good time; at least she didn't say she didn't. She does get impatient with the way I play, and I don't blame her. She says I don't know how to play.

But, really, I never had time to learn! I don't think she realizes that if I hadn't worked hard during that time when most people are managing their bridge techniques, I wouldn't be where I am today. (?)

(When I was shopping at Jurgensen's in Ian's car, I got so carried away with that vision of the good life that I bought huge Guymas shrimp and papaya for dinner last night, and that's after everything I wrote you about Mother and shrimp. I had to fix her a toasted cheese sandwich, and she ate alone out by the television set. I imagine it was my revenge for losing at canasta?)

I'm finding this hard to write. I guess I might as well say that the best thing I did in the last four days was last night when Debbie went outside to feed the dog and came back in and said that Angel's new marguerites had some snails on them. I hate that! Ian was working upstairs in the bedroom, Davie was on the phone, Mother was asleep in the den (I can see that we won't be using the den much anymore), and I couldn't think of those little plants out there, getting eaten up. We have a whole plot toward the back part of the yard, which is only for cut flowers. I got the idea from Candy Spelling's ranunculas, she had forty square feet of ranunculas, and last month her whole house was full of the most beautiful fresh flowers every day.

(I should tell the truth. The two times I was over there last month, there were flowers everywhere. But I sure wasn't there every day.)

However. A dozen pony packs of marguerites can turn into a lot of daisies, if the snails don't eat them. So I thought about it and then I got the table salt and a flashlight and took

Debbie with me. We went way out to the back part of the yard, and the snails were going mad out there, except Debbie and I did away with three hundred and twelve of them! We were out there almost two hours, and she was wonderful. There's nothing more wonderful in the world than a thirteen-year-old with the giggles. And nothing more terrific than Debbie with the table salt going "eeyuu!" each time she got another one. We put all the snails in a bucket for Angel, he'll be very pleased. But we didn't tell anybody else about it when we went back inside, and when we got back inside the house it was a little embarrassing.

Reading this over, I don't know what to think.

I feel very strongly that I'm a very lucky woman. In a world full of trouble, I have no reason to complain. I know that a house, and a husband, and two nice children are not supposed to be the things that make you happy anymore, but they make me happy. (Or at least they don't make me unhappy.)

Thursday night, April 16

Last evening Ian and I left Mother home with the children while we went to a screening. Afterward we saw Richard Burton in the lobby with a nice, quite shy woman, and we all went out to La Masia for something to eat. I can't tell you how funny and strange it was to go in there with a real superstar, and to watch him talk to the waitress in that marvelous voice, and then to hear him order—where everyone has scampi and herbs, or artichokes vinaigrette—a mashed-potato sandwich. He ate it, too! It was just revolting. The girl, who was one of those real on-the-make beauties who

(I imagine) are always after Ian, was very proud when the four of us went in there. It was very crowded, the way it always is, and she was very tall and blond and kept turning her head so that her hair was flying around like a conditioner ad on television. I don't blame her; it's a hard thing to be a young single actress in Hollywood. But when that sandwich came! She was one embarrassed girl. And you could see that Ian was thinking of all the other people we'd seen that night whom it would have made more sense to have dinner with.

I don't want to make Ian sound like a conniver. He's not. He's very hardworking and nice. *Not* the kind of person you read about. He's what they call a line producer, which just means he's the one who gets everything done. He's worked on many series, keeping them on the air for season after season. He's at an interesting point in his career, he's looking for a chance to do a feature film (I think he's dreaming, but of course that's how he got started, and, as I say, he has this possible deal with China), or at least get in a position to do some two-hour movies for television—at this point in his life, after all his hard work, he deserves more power, and more credit. But I suppose every wife in America could say that about her husband.

To tell you the truth, I hate those screenings. I especially hate the part before the film goes on and the lights of the screening room are turned up bright the way they were last night. Did you ever read that Jane Goodall book about the chimps? These people look nicer than chimps, and I'm sure they are nicer, but there's a lot of that swinging around. Mr. Coppola was there last night, and I've always felt so sorry for him since he didn't get the Academy Award and his wife wrote that book about him. What I mean to say is, he comes in, he's all furry, he sits down, he looks straight ahead of him, he waits for people to come up and take hold of his hand, and not as many people do anymore. Do you remember the chimp who had all the happiness because he found the gasoline cans to bang together? Well, Mr. Coppola lost a couple of his cans, is the only way I can think of to put it.

The men, I don't have to tell you, are worried about their hairpieces. It's the only thing they don't come right out and talk about, and under that bright light some of them look pretty awful, and some of them look good, but besides, there's all this other activity. People move up and down the aisles, the beautiful nervous actresses and the "girlfriends," who are safe—for now, anyway—and some of the wives who are so old and have so much of a stake in the community property that their husbands will never leave them.

The girlfriends talk to each other. The wives, especially the old ones, sit down in groups of two or three and look straight ahead, bored to death. I feel sorry for the actresses. Most of them are really very nice. But I'll tell you the people who make my flesh crawl. The assistant producers, the assistant directors, new writers trying to sell something, the agents, the people still in their twenties who really, well, there's a woman I know who uses so much cocaine that she really looks more like an Easter bunny than a girl. She has a really amazing pink twitchy nose! (I don't want to say anything against "dope" itself, because I don't know that much about it.) But I do know this woman went to a school like Smith or Bennington or Vassar, and she has this high, fluty, well-bred voice, and her nose is like Rudolf the Reindeer's, and what she does is this: When she sees someone, like Ian, she doesn't wave or come over and say hello. She kisses her own wrist (I would like to *see the day* when I'd kiss my own wrist in public!) and then blows this kiss over to the person whose attention she's trying to get.

When you get four or five people like that at one table, it can be . . . just sad, I suppose.

So that I guess one reason I came back to school is because when I look in the future I don't want to be those wives, and I'm too old to be the girlfriends, and I can't act. But those go-getting women are, to me, the worst.

Since nothing much else has happened this week, and since you said we might want to do this, maybe this is the night to spend some time writing about my life. I was born and brought up right here in Los Angeles. My grandparents are all dead. I can say I had a happy childhood. My father was a newspaperman. We lived in Highland Park when I was growing up, before the war. (Isn't it funny, that when the other students in your class say "before the war," they mean other wars?) We had a good time, I think. At that time I was an only child. My mother was a housewife and happy to be one. What I mean is—I was watching some Brentwood housewives the other day in the parking lot of that little farmer's market they have—my mother was like they are, when she was young, only we didn't have money, of course. When I was eleven my parents separated, and the next five years were the most unpleasant ones of my life. Then she remarried. My stepfather and I didn't get along, and I went out on my own very early. My mother had a son from this second marriage, and my father, ten years later, got married again, and he has a young son too. I have tried to keep up with both parents.

After high school, I decided to move out. There wasn't any money for college; I moved back down from Coalinga to Los Angeles and I went to business school for one semester. But I couldn't stand it. I got a job selling Orange Juliuses in the May Company basement, and took drama courses at LA City College at night. I don't know what it's like now, but back in the sixties it was a very exciting place. I worked behind the scenes, making costumes. I had a girlfriend—we have since lost touch—and we used to laugh so hard, we got into real trouble. I think it probably even affected our grade. Anyway, at a cast party that same semester for a production of *Candida* I met my husband. His father had a grocery store on the east side, and he had defied him by becoming a drama major. (To tell the truth, he wasn't a very good actor. It's a good thing he decided to learn how to produce.)

We fell in love right away. I think it was a mature decision for both of us. He knew if he was going to make it in the tough world he had chosen he would need a woman to work hard for him (I don't mean to sound righteous, but it's true) and that he probably couldn't afford a "Jewish Princess" at that time. And I'd always heard that "Jews are good family men." It wasn't until I was twenty-five and already married four years that I heard some of my father's stories about "business trips" in Chicago, and the *worst person in them* was his Jewish partner.

I don't want that to sound anti-Semitic, but it's true. *Anyway*, I worked while Ian finished LACC and then UCLA and then sold his first *Bonanza*. By that time his father had more or less forgiven him for everything, including marrying a gentile. And helped him out financially so we could buy a nice house and then this house. When Ian finally got his own series, I had those fantasies that he would leave me, because it's happened to everybody else I know. But he didn't, and although we've had our troubles

Reading this over, I see there's one thing I left out. I suppose it's silly, but I think it belongs here. (Maybe you could tell me what you think, in the margin?) I've always been faithful to my husband. And I didn't go out too much during that one year I was living alone; I think I knew that if I got in trouble I wouldn't have anyone to fall back on. But I did go out with a nice boy named (Stewart?). One night we came awfully close and he kept saying "tomorrow." "Tomorrow I'll take you home and introduce you to my mother." Looking back on it, I know it doesn't sound like he was going to be a "bad customer." But all the time he was saying that he was also kissing me, we were alone in his apartment, and I got very indignant! (You know, in the early sixties it was still very important to be a "nice girl.") So I went home angry.

Thinking back on it, I guess he was very nice. Probably the nicest person I ever met. And I made it an absolute point never to go out with him again.

Do you know something interesting? (And then I really will end this boring entry.) He went on in television, but he never was very successful. (So, you see, I made the right choice!) He became a character actor, and not very successful.

I meant to write this because my mother is staying here

with us, but there's almost nothing about my mother here. It's very late and this is the most I've written. You often say in class we should write about our family, so I hope I'm not too bold when I say I really think I should get extra credit for this. I love my mother very much. She had to raise first me and then my brother. It was a bad set of "accidents," I guess you could call it. First my father left and then my brother's father died.

It has always been important for me to keep up as many ties as possible. I have remained friends with my father over the years, and have made it a point to see my mother at least three times a year.

My brother is a sixties dropout. I have his phone number, but I haven't seen him in some time.

When I was growing up, all our neighbors, even the poor ones, went on vacations in the summertime. Before I met Ian, I had never been beyond the city limits of Los Angeles except up to Coalinga. They say that anything is possible here in Los Angeles (Southern California), but I'm not sure that's true. It *is* true that I have a beautiful home and a handsome husband and two wonderful kids, and even the opportunity to go back to school to find out what "life is all about," but when I look around me, I see all of West Los Angeles filled with women who have just that much and no more. I am certainly not complaining. But I do wonder sometimes if they feel as strange when they go out to screenings (or whatever) as I do.

Saturday afternoon, April 18

Mother is lying down, after what, I imagine, has been a fairly awful excursion.

I think the card game got my hopes up. I thought we could go out to shop. Well, my mother hates it.

But I did think we could, we should, go and visit my brother. Where I get these ideas, I don't know. Ian says I'm a fool. I suppose he's right. I do know I'm crying now, and I'm not the type to cry.

For reasons I'll go into later, I thought it would be best not to meet at home here, but to go out someplace. Mother hates elevators and basement parking lots—I'm not too crazy about them either. Any place too fancy wouldn't be right. I finally decided on Nate'N Al's, the deli across from Jurgensen's in Beverly Hills. It's crowded all the time and all the comedy writers have breakfast there and I guess I thought the "vibrations" would be so cheerful there that no one, my mother, me, Sandy, would make a scene.

I think I already said, Sandy is a "dropout." I suppose every family has one now, and what I dread above everything in the world is that one day Davie is going to take off his karate jacket and stop kicking people and announce that he wants to play "lead guitar," like the sons of half of all the women I know.

I really have mixed feelings about it. I left home just about the time my brother was born, but I know what it can be like to grow up in a house where they're not exactly crazy about you, and I think music can be a defensive as well as an offensive weapon. What I mean is, my mother used to complain about Sandy watching Dick Clark. What she meant was, every afternoon Sandy came home by himself and watched Dick Clark to learn the newest dances. He danced so long and so hard that he wore a hole in the rug. That can't be right, you know?

The truth is, Ian and I are responsible for taking Sandy to a few clubs in the old days. He'd come down for a week or so in the summer from Coalinga, and we were just young kids in the movies, so we'd take him to the Troubadour to hear—was it the Mothers of Invention? Captain Beefheart? The way you'd take another kind of kid to see a ball game. (I also think it's quite possible he found his first marijuana at a party of people from City College, where we were all so happy then, just to be making it. It all seems very strange now, but I think we thought then that we had found some kind of heaven on earth.)

My mother didn't want to do it. She hates Sandy, or says she does. She says he's just like his father. (She says that about me, too. Never that we're in any way like her, which is just as well.) She didn't want me to call Sandy up. Well, she had her share of phone calls in the night about him, and neighbors complaining, and once she found a hypodermic in his room. (Once she asked me, "Is he on top?" She meant pot.)

But I thought: He is her son. He is my brother.

So ten o'clock this morning we drove over to Beverly Hills. I thought the whole scene might interest my mother, all the men who thought up *I Love Lucy* and *My Favorite Martian*, and *Mork and Mindy*, all scrubbed up in their medallions and shaving lotion, all eating the good food their mothers probably used to make for them, because comedy writers are very fearful people, as I'm sure you know, and I think they use the food to cheer themselves up.

And, it's different from Coalinga.

And I usually see someone in there from when Ian and I were first married. They're almost always doing well. God knows why I thought Mother might like that.

So. We walked down Rodeo Drive. Everyone was out shopping, everyone was having fun but us. We got to the deli and I had one of those unpleasant little shocks. I saw our reflection in the glass doors, only for a minute I didn't recognize us. A tired middle-aged lady with an exhausted look on her face, with a tiny little lady who didn't look all *that* much older than the other one. It didn't make me feel too marvelous, I can tell you.

Then we got inside and—maybe you know—it's a great place, always crowded, the restaurant on one side, the counter, where everybody holds a number and yells, on the other. My mother raised her voice as only she can and said to me, "You didn't say this was a Jewish place!" So that I got to be humiliated in front of a hundred people, some of whom were my acquaintances and even my friends.

Because I couldn't think of anything else to do with her, and because the hostess was giving us this truly terrible look, I took Mother to the rest room.

Every deli I know, no matter how clean and pretty it is out front, has these stuffy, crowded, not very clean rest rooms. Naturally Mother began to say, "What's that terrible smell? You don't expect me to go *in there*, do you? I think I'm going to faint! I don't know why you dragged me in here anyway, you know sure as hell he's not coming. When did he ever go anywhere he said he was going to!"

And so on. Except we weren't alone in that little crowded place. There was a person who was taking off eye shadow and mascara and wetting a paper towel to scrub off lipstick the way, sometimes, somebody does when they want to start all over again. This person, who was crowded right in there with us, gave a huge grin. My knees started to shake, but Mother didn't notice. She did really, because she started in on me in another whole way.

"You wouldn't look so *tired* all the time if you'd stop being so pure and start using some makeup. You don't teach in an *elementary* school, for God's sake! You don't have to be a *good example* to anybody."

I thought about saying that I know from actresses that makeup only helps people who already look good. Or about telling Mother that *she* never used anything in her life but lipstick, or—even something she might understand—that the way you tell a gentile in this town is if they stay away from the hair dye and the eye shadow, but I simply wouldn't open my mouth. The other person caught my eye in the mirror and said, grinning, in this very high voice, "Doesn't it frost you when you start getting lines around your mouth?" And then, right to my mother, "*Nothing* can help *that*, you know!"

Mother looked right at this person, and it looked like she

was so put out by being spoken to by a stranger that she went into a booth and shut the door.

I opened my mouth to say something, but the person put a hand on my arm, gave me a squeeze, and left.

And when we went back out into the restaurant, Sandy was waiting for us in a booth for four. Mother and I sat down across from him, and looked.

He is a rock musician now. I have no way of knowing how successful he is, although I did see once he was booked into the Starwood. He is not "punk," at least I don't think so.

What he looked like was: he has a very pale, clear face, with a lot of black curly hair, very carefully styled. There was some glitter on the flesh above his eyes. His "top" was almost exactly between a shirt and a blouse. It was pure silk and very expensive. I knew the one it was, from Theodore's. He looked drowsy but nervous. His fingers were very thin and gray. His eyebrows were plucked pencil-thin. He had four golden chains around his neck. He was as far away from Coalinga as it is physically, mentally, morally, possible to be. His voice, when it came out of him, was strained and low. Would it be correct to say he looked like a double exposure?

I don't approve of women going on about their suffering. I do believe that with luck and persistence and three hundred dollars to est a lot of that can be avoided. But in that booth there was such a wall of pain that I'm surprised the waitresses didn't feel it. And I'm going to try to remember what we said (because, as you say, some of this may be valuable, later, to our children or grandchildren), but I can't remember exactly. I think because there *was* that certain amount of pain, and the past, that we

We novocained ourselves, is what I was going to say.

I know I said, "You're looking great, Sandy," although I had real trouble looking at his face.

And then when we ordered, I guess that showed something. I had scrambled eggs with tomatoes, no toast; Mother said she was too sick to eat, and then ordered ham and one egg over easy; but Sandy just ordered melon. Mother hated that, but Sandy gave us a big smile and said he's been on a liquid fast this week, and lost four pounds on the first day. He did look hungry. He said altogether he'd lost seventeen and a half pounds and with any luck, by the end of the month he'd be able to wear a size three. Then he smiled and said to both of us, "I do have a lot of discipline. It takes discipline to do what I do."

For the last several years, I always try to meet Sandy in a public place. I realize, by now, that I come from a somewhat peculiar family and that it isn't fair to foist it off on my husband *or* my kids. So I met Sandy the last time in the Swiss Café, which, I imagine you know, has either that pretty patio out back or the darkest inside restaurant in the world. Well, he brought a friend with him, and by the time lunch was over, the maître d' called me over and said even though he knew I was a good customer, or *because* I was a good customer, it might be better for everybody if I didn't come in with those people again.

So that's why I thought breakfast might be better this time.

You say to try to use our "senses" in these, to be visual, et cetera. I can say that although Sandy is my brother, he doesn't look like our side of the family at all. He has a little round mouth like a drawstring purse and little round cheeks like the hamster I once got for Debbie (and she lost it in the central-heating system). In fact, Sandy, through no fault of his own, looks almost exactly like my stepfather, and I have real trouble looking at him. It used to be a refrain of my mother's that I was exactly "like" my father, and it used to drive me wild. But this morning I could almost see what she meant. Because Sandy is like his father.

I might as well say that breakfast this morning was one of the worst ideas I ever had in my life. It was like this. Mother looked at Sandy—her own son!—as though she couldn't see him very well, as though he were several blocks away instead of just across the table. I could feel her tense up beside me, and then she began to ask him questions.

"Sandy! Where do you live?"

"Hollywood."

"*Where* in Hollywood?"

"Like, right in the center. . . ." He looked over at me.

"I said, *Where in Hollywood?*"

Then Sandy said, "Over near Vermont. Near Western."

If you could have seen my mother's face when she said, "Vermont and Western don't even *cross!*"

So then Sandy said, "Vermont. West of Vermont. East of Western. *Near City College.* I thought I might take some classes there." Then he looked over at me, to bail him out. "Didn't you take some classes there, Garnet?"

But before I could answer, Mother was at him again.

"Are you *working?* What do you do for a *living?*"

"I can't work now. I had an accident."

By that time I could feel my mother's own mean look of disbelief all over my own face.

"What *kind* of an accident?"

"I was driving a delivery truck and someone ran into me. The truck wrecked itself, and I got fired. So I got a lawyer to file a disability claim."

We just looked at him. The waitress brought our food. He began to eat his melon. He's such a little guy!

"I really hurt my neck," he said to us. "It's only right I should get some money." Then he looked over at me. "My music is doing pretty well," he said. "I was booked into the Palomino last month, but it fell through. Someone stole all my equipment."

Mother began to rap her nails on the table. Oh, that noise!

Then Mother asked him, if you only knew, the most ludicrous question.

"So when are you going to get married?"

But all he did was laugh. "I don't know! When are *you* going to get married?"

She just looked at him.

He teased her for a little bit. "You could, you know. You still have a very young complexion."

It was something to see my mother. She answered him in

such a loud voice that some of the comedy writers looked over at us with very nervous faces.

She said, "I wouldn't get married again if you paid me! Not under *any* circumstances! Not for *any* reason. Not to *anybody*. Why would I want to do *that?*"

I surprised myself. "It's safe."

They both looked at me like I was crazy. So then I had to turn into Mrs. Middle Class America again, just for their benefit. I told them you had to work at marriage. (All I can say is, it was a fairly bizarre morning.)

Then Sandy thought he could tell me he'd never liked Ian very much. I didn't say: That's all right, he never liked you very much either.

What happened then was something that happens sometimes in our family. So many bad things have happened to us and we have had so many bad quarrels that we reach a certain *level*, and it's as though the whole thing speeds up. We sit, or stand, or whatever, and it's like that joke about the prisoners who tell jokes by number. There's a moment of very thick silence, like that moment when you remember the war dead on Veterans Day, when we remember all the bad things we've gone through together. I know that the air in Nate'N Al's got thick and blurry, and my ears began to buzz. If we'd been at home, this would be when the "fur would fly," and that's why I try to arrange these meetings in public places.

They were both smiling. I suppose I was too. Then Sandy looked over at me and started to talk in a different way.

"I *was* married you know, can you believe it? But what I've really done lately is travel a lot. I've been a lot of places since I've seen you last. I spent a year in Alaska. Did you know that? I went with a guy and we spent a whole winter in a lean-to he built himself. Not even a cabin. A lean-to. We went through a whole winter there. And then I spent almost a whole year in Bolivia and Peru. We went through some hard times. . . ."

"How did you live?" (I asked him that. Because it's so hard to live, just in Brentwood.)

"We went up into Belize—that's down in Central America—for a while. We lived in a house on stilts. They have crabs there, they come out of the ocean and walk into the streets and try to walk right up the stilts. And I went to Europe twice, I don't know if I told you that. I stayed in Belgium, most people say that's a real dumb country, but it isn't. I lived with a seamstress, my friend's mother."

"How did you get the *money* for all that?"

The answer is drugs, of course, and I have no real idea whether my mother knows the extent of the problem.

Sandy was still talking along.

"You want to know when I was really happiest? I was really happiest when I lived with Harley in the Hawaiian Islands. Have you ever been to Hawaii? Kauai? On the leeward side?"

I kept thinking that Joanne Woodward had one, Carol Burnett has one. Almost every family in America has a son or a brother or sister with a bit of a drug problem. But he looked so sad and thin. And it made me feel so terrible that he would spend his time trying to tell either my mother *or* me anything.

"If you want, after you get to Hanalei Bay, you can pack in, you can go beyond, over the hill, and live on the other side. You can live in a tree house. A lot of freaks do that. You stay back from the beach and live in the regular jungle."

My brother never gets out in the sun, and so his fingers are almost blue. It took me all this time, just looking at him, to figure out that maybe he wasn't on a liquid fast at all. Maybe he just wasn't getting enough to eat.

He was talking right to me. "You know how—when I was in high school—I couldn't do *anything?* No, you weren't there. I keep forgetting. Anyway, I was like everyone else in that dumb school, I couldn't learn how to do anything. . . ."

"There were plenty of things for you to do! You just hung out with the troublemakers! Do you know what happened to *me* a couple of weeks ago?" my mother asked him.

"Out there in Hawaii I finally learned to swim. I had all day every day for a year on the most beautiful beach in the world, so I finally learned to swim. Every day I took a swim, for miles. All by myself. I got so I'd swim all the way out, by myself, past that point. You know that point? I'd swim out to it and past it, and the currents would meet there and keep me just at that place. You could look way far! Past where the road goes. Where no one lives. And those green *hills*, you know? If you'd taken a little something, they were something."

My mother jumped up and stood in the aisle. The waitress saw her and leaned in around her to take the check. Sandy was still talking.

"So that's what I've done, you know?" He was looking right at me. "But, don't laugh. I still think I'd like to have children."

Mother put her two fists on the table and yelled right at Sandy. "Where do you *live?* What's your *phone number?* Why do you say you don't have a *job?*"

Sandy almost gave it away. "I have a hair appointment, and they're real strict." Then he got up and left.

I've been writing this off and on all day since we got back. I'm in bed now, Ian's asleep beside me, he's been out in the sun so much that his back matches the brown in the bamboo pattern of the sheets.

They're new sheets. I made Mother go shopping after breakfast. I think the linen section at Bullock's Westwood has a good chance of being the safest place on earth.

Looking at Ian—who fell asleep very early this evening—I have to say again he's the most handsome, considerate man I know.

I also have to say that, just to round out a perfect morning, my mother stood outside Nate 'N Al's on a perfectly beautiful sunny day, said she was going to faint, and said it was because she'd seen Ian, my husband, in there with another woman.

After we bought the sheets, she went into her room and shut the door, and didn't come out, even for dinner. I wonder about a woman who sees infidelity everywhere.

Before she said she was going to faint, Mother made sure to

tell me she'd never even been to Europe, that nobody ever took her *anywhere*, that she'd worked like a dog all her life, with no thanks.

And I, always the straight man, was actually standing there, talking to her. "Well, Mother, you could always get a charter flight . . . ."

4

April 20

I don't know whether I've said it or not in this journal, but I'm an est graduate, and while I realize I have a long way to go, I have come far enough to know I'm beginning to lose my patience. This is the beginning of the second week, and I've decided—and I've told Ian, I told him last night as we were driving home from a party—that this visit is going on for three weeks and no more. (I even kidded him and asked him why *he* doesn't make a fuss like other men do about their mothers-in-law. Of course, he isn't that kind of person.)

But I mean it. I've worked too hard to have everything go down the drain because of one mean lady. On the other hand, I want her to go home having had a "good time." Don't ask me why! I know you can't go around trying to please people, especially you-know-who, but I imagine there are some things that a couple of weekends of consciousness raising, no matter how intense, aren't going to change overnight.

And now I guess there can be a shift in tone. But I'm still going to be talking about Mother! When she's around, that's *it*, you know? There isn't anything else.

Today we had another magic day. In the morning, because she said she wanted to go shopping, we went shopping. I will *only say* that after three hours we neither one of us had anything except two very bad tempers. (I do have to say that after three stores, when she complained that everything in those stores was for thin people, and why was I trying to make her feel so bad, I then took her to Lane Bryant and she said everything in that store was for fat people, and why was I trying to make her feel so *bad?)*

Anyway, I'd made reservations for lunch at the Ambassador Hotel. There's a group of women who meet there once a month to have lunch and discuss books, at least that's what it says in the brochure. One of my friends has a mother who goes, and since I'm getting to the point where if I look at another deck of cards or drink another whiskey in the daytime, I might begin to faint myself, and since I know Mother would loathe any of the groups *I* belong to, like the World Hunger Project, or Women For, and since I'm falling behind in all my homework anyway, I thought, well, this is it! I'll take her to this lunch, and nobody, *nobody*, will be able to say I didn't do my best.

When we were driving down Wilshire Boulevard, she started peering out of the car in that nearsighted way of hers. She's so little, she's like a kind of bad Pekingese in a pantsuit. I was, in fact, so angry at her by eleven o'clock this morning that I was entertaining myself with the fantasy of bringing my fist down on the back of her neck as hard as I could. She didn't seem to feel much better about it all than I did. When we drove up to the hotel she said, "I used to come here and dance with your father."

I was mean enough to say, "I can hardly believe that."

"What do you mean! I used to be a great dancer! *You're* the one who can't dance a step!"

"I didn't know Daddy danced."

"You'd get him drunk enough, he'd do anything. See the Brown Derby?"

We were driving right *by* the Brown Derby! How could I *not* see the Brown Derby?

"Do you remember when you were . . . let's see, you couldn't have been more than six or seven years old, when some of Fran's relatives were out here visiting and we took one old battleax to the Brown Derby and your father ordered a beer, and then another, and she said, 'Why, Frank! You've already had your beer.'"

I gritted my teeth and said, yes, I remembered. But why is it, when my father tells that stupid story, that I think it's just a sweet, harmless family story?

Mother was really "taken out" by the sight of the hotel. "God, we used to dance at the Coconut Grove. God, can you believe it?"

I can't tell you how hot it was in that parking lot and how depressed I felt. And all around us, expensive cars were pulling up and more older women and middle-aged daughters were getting out of the cars. All around me, you could *feel* those poor women beginning to sweat. I guess both my mother and I were in a pretty bad mood by then.

So when she said, "Who *are* those jerks?"

I shot right back, "They're *ladies*. Just like you."

And she said, "*Well*, why don't they *do* something? Don't they have children to take care of? Or houses to clean up? Or a job?"

I was very snippy by then. "Obviously not."

So she started in on me. Again. "Why can't you learn to play cards or have some laughs, or have some fun? What do you think you're trying to prove? Why can't you play a decent game of poker?"

I didn't say that women of my social class don't play poker, but I don't think I had to. I mean, I'm not my mother's daughter for nothing.

We went in the basement side door and up a big staircase. Mother started to breathe heavily, but she didn't say she was going to faint. She did say, very audibly, "Jesus Christ! Don't tell me you go to things like this when I'm not around. Because *I* don't believe it."

She just went right on with her basic theme for the day.

"What *do* you do all the time, *anyway?* I mean, I don't see you and Ian ever having anything like *fun!* Don't you get nervous? Don't you get tired of just SITTING AROUND?"

Several women turned and looked our way.

"I've . . . been staying home especially so that we can spend time with you during your visit."

"Don't worry! I'm going home soon! You're going to bore me right out of the house!"

"We have social obligations because of Ian's work."

"Yes, but . . ." Then she started twisting all around with her purse under her arm, peering into corners. "The Ambassador, my God. I came here, my God, before I even met your father. Do you remember, Pearl? We'd come here after work, we'd get the afternoon off sometimes for a tea dance . . . you don't even *dance!*"

"Well, I know it!"

"Two weeks ago I had a dozen women over to have lunch and play bridge. They spent the whole day!"

"That's very *nice*, Mother!"

"Well, answer me this! Do you call this a good time?"

"*No!*"

"*Well*, then?"

Then I got her over to the registration table and shelled out forty dollars. Then I got to try to pin a name tag on my mother.

"Are you going to wear one of these or not?"

"God in heaven! They make me want to puke." But she finally let me. "Can we at least go into the bar and get a drink beforehand?"

I think every other woman there had the same idea. There must have been a hundred women there at the bar, each one with a double martini in front of her. We saw Joyce Haber, who used to be a gossip columnist for the *Times*. She was going to be a guest. My mother recognized her.

"How old do you think she is?"

"Exactly my age."

"*She* looks pretty good."

I ordered another.

"I didn't know you were so crazy about drinking!"

I began to look around that bar. Outside was all that beautiful sunshine and life, and where was I, you know? I began to think: Why me? Why me?

A lady came to the door of the bar and shouted, "Girls, girls, come on, now! They're ready to begin."

I am not what you'd call a feminist, but I am thirty-nine years old, and I'm not a girl.

My mother had to finish her drink, which for once in her life she decided to drink very slowly, so that by the time we got inside the main room, all the tables near the back were filled up. They marched Mother and me up near the front, the way I seem to remember they do when you're late for church. They sat us down at a big table in front of the dais where seven or eight ladies had already begun to eat.

I sat down with my mother on one side of me and a woman with a kelly-green pantsuit and orange hair on the other. She looked over at me, and this is what she said: "Hello! My name is Andrea, and I don't do anything!"

I couldn't think of anything to say.

"I never *have* done anything, and I'm proud of it." She had a double martini in front of her. "This is my third one of these, I think that's all right, at something like this, don't you?"

"It's all right with *me*," I said. I'd already asked the waiter to bring another one, and asked him to bring some wine with lunch.

They all wore hats, they all were dressed expensively. They all were over sixty. They had little crazy eyes.

And I don't like to write about what they said, except some of it was pretty funny, if you were in a mood to laugh. A lady was the center of attention at the table.

"Gay! My dear, *you* can't *use* a word like 'gay' anymore! Those nauseating perverts have taken it away from us. It's like when that Italian—what's the name of that awful Italian?—"

"Sinatra," one of them said. "She's talking about Sinatra."

"When *Sinatra* took '*mother*,' a wonderful word like

'mother,' and made it into a dirty word! Of course, he wasn't a fag!"

"That's right," Andrea said.

"But our *governor!*"

"Of course, he came from the seminary, that's *fag land!*"

"Do you know what I saw the other day?" A woman right across from us. "A man with his penis *painted white*, do you believe it? Well, what are you going to do about something like that? He waved it, just like that! And then he said hi!"

At least I had the pleasure of seeing my mother silent.

Somebody else asked, "Whose fault is that?"

The lady across from us took a shot. "It has . . . to be . . . the fault of the American woman, that's who! Do you think fairies would be sleeping with fairies if they'd been given half a chance?"

Andrea, beside me, had lost interest. "Do you know what my husband bought me for Mother's Day? A golf cart, wasn't that something? Of course he didn't fool me. It was really for him. But there it was—of course we live right on the golf course—when I went outside on Sunday morning."

"I play golf," my mother said. "I play golf two or three times a week after work. They have some good courses up where I live."

So then, besides everything else, I got to feel left out. Because I don't play golf anywhere. (She's actually right, you know; when you look right at my life, I haven't made many arrangements for having fun.)

Andrea took hold of my arm. "He did up the whole thing with yellow cellophane, you know, with a big bow. I was surprised."

The woman who'd hauled us out of the bar went up to the dais to speak. (And I don't expect you to believe this, but I took notes.) "For years now, haven't you all wondered why we don't *do* things with our lives? Why we sit night after night watching *television?* Do any of us remember what it was like for us before we had television? Yes! I'm *sure* you do! Do you think—and I'm sure you'll agree with me—that any of us will *ever* equal the pleasure that all of us have felt, when, after a day of work, we used to sit down with a good book?"

All the women clapped like maniacs. If you could have seen my mother's face!

"Some of us have asked, I know many of you have asked *me!* What *is* it about Los Angeles! Why can't we have *salons* out here, just like they do in New York! So now some of us have gotten up the nerve to approach that wonderful woman whose books we've all read with such attention for so many years."

To tell you the truth, I've forgotten her name. But—what can I tell you? She was the spitting image of Mother. She grabbed the microphone and began to roar into it.

"I don't want any introduction! *Can* the introduction!"

"This woman doesn't *need* an introduction!" the moderator said hastily.

"Before I do anything else," that crazy woman said, "before I do a damn thing more for *anybody!* I want to take this opportunity to salute, the most handsome, the bravest, the greatest man in the world! CLARK GABLE!"

It went on like that for two solid hours.

There was a second speaker. An actual college professor, if you can believe it. Talking about the role of women in modern America, but nobody listened to her, so after ten minutes she gave the microphone back to the other one, who led cheers for Tyrone Power and a few others. They brought the professor a double martini and she drank it and another one.

Afterward I went up to talk to her. (Partly because nobody else did.) She asked how I liked it, and I thought the best thing was to say my mother was a little disappointed.

But she said, "Well, at least you got out of the house."

The college professor had had too much to drink.

When my mother came back from the ladies' room, the professor asked her how she liked it.

Mother said, "It made me want to puke."

The professor gave her a big smile. Then she said, "Far-out. I really mean it."

April 23

In the two days that remain to me of this subject matter, I'd like to clarify my position about all this. What I'm saying is, by next Monday my life will be back to normal. I can catch up on my other homework, but, just because I won't have so much to write about, this journal will fall off. (I can't build many pages on ordering a new king-size bed, at least I don't think so, and if I began talking about ideas, I have the terrible suspicion I'd begin to sound like Andrea and her golf cart.) So, since I guess I'm an optimist, I have to believe that I received this visit from my mother so that I could have a chance to review what some people might call my primary relationships.

Like: I took my mother to the beach. She hated the beach. Sand got in her bathing suit, and she managed to sunburn the soles of her feet.

She sneers at the way Debbie makes her bed. Debbie can't/won't make square corners.

She's told Davie to clean his glasses so many times that he's stopped wearing his glasses.

We like to serve wine with dinner? She hates wine with dinner, she says it makes her sleepy.

We never drink hard liquor. That's all she does drink. And she doesn't hold back.

We took her to the movies in Westwood last weekend. We thought she'd get a kick out of the whole spectacle. She hated Westwood, she said she could remember when it was beanfields, so, *so what?* She said standing in line made her feel faint. And she hated the movie, of course.

So she shouldn't have to stand in line, we took her to a screening. What an awful night. There were journalists there, she hated them, she said she could spot them a mile away. ("I can tell those bastards from a mile away! They're just as phony as they always were!") She hated the TV critics. ("What do they have to wear those hairpieces for! Don't they know they look like fruits?") And especially the movie. ("It made me want to puke.")

She hates our friends:

"Who's *that* jerk?"

"Who's that fat jerk?"

"Who's that slob?"

"Who's that slob?"

"Who's that drunken slob?"

"Who's that phony?"

"Isn't that phony a fag?"

The irritating things about all this are: (a) she usually is at least partly right, and (b) she only tells me or the kids about it, so that Ian ends up thinking she's kind of cute.

I forgot to say. She hates my clothes. She asked me the other day if I was trying to look like Myrna Loy. And naturally she hates my cooking because it has wine in it. And she hates my housekeeping—I don't want to get into that.

She won't learn how to play backgammon. She says only "rich bitches play that slop." She won't play tennis. "I used to play. But my health won't allow me to play now." We took the kids to play miniature golf: "It wouldn't be fair for me to compete. I'm a decent golfer." But she won't play real golf! "I don't know anybody down here, and I absolutely will not play with strangers."

And culture isn't the answer. I drove her out to the Getty. I thought we might have a picnic, or that—I don't know—we could look at the sculpture for a while and then I'd reward her with a whiskey and soda at the Charthouse. I may as well come out and say it, I thought we might even walk for a while on the beach! Even as I write this, I have to laugh. She's right, I *am* dumb. How long, how long, how *long* will it take me to learn? We didn't even get into the first gallery of the Getty, of course. We didn't even see the gardens, we didn't even *blink* at the Pacific! She got sick in the elevator and that was that. We turned around and came home.

And you should see her face when I turn on the cassette tapes for Verborama.

On the other hand, if you notice such things, you might have noticed—if you even know who I am—that I had a person in class with me on Monday. My mother. Do you know what she did? She spent the entire hour passing notes to me. She'd point first at one person, then another. (Not you, of course!) "Who's that jerk? Who's that slob? Who's that fag? That looks like a real N.F.!" (N.F. means "No Future." That's what she used to call boys who called me on the phone. She still calls Ian that sometimes.) But then after class, a couple of people came up, and she gave this sweet smile and shook hands with everyone. And, you may have noticed, she has a wonderful tan and a healthy complexion, she's a very, God, she's a very pretty woman. So today a person in this class came up to me and said, "You have such a nice mother." And the person in class misunderstood my answer. "A friend?" she said. And I had to say, "No! A fiend."

Which doesn't make me look so great.

I'll just say two more things. I told Mother she should think about going home next week. I don't even know if she heard me. She started up, another refrain I've heard for many years.

"Just remember one thing. There's an envelope on my desk at home. With your name on it. My will. Everything goes to you! Not one penny to Sandy!"

"Yes, but—"

"And if I have a stroke! You're to tell them immediately to *pull the plug!* Got that?!"

"But I'm talking about *now!*"

"Got that? *Have you got that?*"

"Yes, Mother."

"And don't forget my retirement money. That goes to you too! Because I don't want him to have one penny!"

But then, when I think about the money she's being such a fiend about, and remember that, for all her work, it represents a week's pay in Ian's working life, after deductions, I could weep.

And why don't I help her?

I'm writing this in bed. I told my husband some of the things I've written here. I told him my worst fear, that I'm afraid she wants to stay here forever. And that there was no way I could stand it.

Then he said, "Would that really be such a bad idea? This is a big house."

I couldn't believe what I was hearing.

"No, I mean it. It would be like a regular baby-sitter. When we wanted to go away for a weekend."

"She hates the kids!" (Although, I have to say, I know that's not true.)

"This is a big house, we certainly have room for her."

"Ian, what are you trying to do?"

He wouldn't look at me. "Nothing. What would I be trying to do?"

I couldn't answer him.

"No matter how you two might not get along, she's still your mother. And even out here, even in this city, even the way we live, it's good to have some family around. If anything should happen, don't you see?"

"Happen?"

Then he said he was terribly preoccupied with an idea for a new pilot, and he turned over and went to sleep.

And here I am.

Of course, I've known he's busy. Which is one reason why I've made plans for Mother and me to go to a seminar on money management this weekend. The kids are going on a field trip to Catalina—that private school does come up with interesting things—and Ian is working, and even while Mother was trying to leave me all her money, I was thinking I could help her to manage it.

God.

What all this is, of course, is that she makes me think of the past. And I've worked so hard to put together a decent present that I can't stand to think of the past. Would you deliberately go out and sprain your ankle? Would you invite a sprained ankle to come and live with you?

I will not think of the past, I'm not interested in it, I don't want it. I don't have contempt for much, but I do have contempt for those people who shake their unhappy childhoods at you all the time.

But before the past? Before the bad stuff started happening? I remember a person who loved me. Once, in the first grade, I went to spend the night with a little girlfriend. In the night I woke up and remembered this beautiful woman singing "That Old Black Magic" in her kitchen. I cried until that whole family woke up. Because the beautiful woman was my mother, and I wanted to go home.

5 A.M. Saturday morning (Sunday morning?)

Well! I don't know how to begin. Let me say it's late at night, my overhead light is on, and I can *see* the aura, the energy coming up off this paper! I am going to try to write in perfect harmony with my own thoughts, trying to be a perfect part of the material world while, at the same time, "hooking in" to a greater spiritual or cosmic energy which will move my pen across this paper.

Do you really think it will work? (Do *I* really think it will work?)

I should have known, when they called the seminar Green Energy, that it wasn't just about your ordinary, average, "T Bill" accounts!

I'm feeling wonderful as I write. We went back to the Ambassador Hotel. My mother told me once again that she used to dance there with my dad. And we even ducked by the Coconut Grove, and there were all those potted palms and old people. (Although at the time, I wasn't in love with it, just thinking of it now is *far*-out!)

I bet you can't imagine what my mother said when we went up to the registration table.

First she said, "I hate this!"

Then she said, "Who are those jerks?"

I think in this instance, words really failed her. Because behind the table there were three young guys dressed up like dollar bills. I took one look at them and started to laugh. The first time in months I laughed like that. They were all dolled up in green tights with T-shirts that had the pyramid with the eye on one side and George Washington on the other. And green shavings all over their heads.

Naturally Mother wouldn't go up to the table. I just grabbed her and pulled. You should have seen her when I paid five hundred for the two of us.

"I'm telling you for your own good," she told me. "You're a fool."

"Cloris Leachman took this seminar," I told her. "So did Joanne Woodward." (Actually, Cloris did est, and Joanne likes horseback riding, but what the hell.)

"I'm going home," she said.

But I was up for a good time. Or, just the sight of those people gave me courage.

"Go home if you want," I said. "Ian's working, and the kids aren't home, they're in Catalina."

You know what she said? In a *murderous* tone? "I used to go there with your father."

"Yes, well, all I'm saying is, if you want to go home, you can go home. If you want to stay here, you can stay here."

"Listen!" My mother does not like to be crossed!

But the girl behind the desk had been listening. She was smiling! "Terrific," she said. "I really mean it!" She said to me, "It's great! The ones with the most resistance are the ones who really get it in the end."

Then she said, "You're really beautiful," to my mother. "I want to tell you, you really have a high energy level. You're going to do just great in the training."

They gave us a questionnaire. We sat down with some other people out in the hall to fill it out. Here were some of the questions:

Do you want to Be Rich? Explain.

Do you want to Be Happy? Explain.

What do you think about "Rich, Famous, and Free"? Explain.

Are you willing for your Sex Life to increase?

Is there such a thing as "Enough Love"? Explain. Be specific.

They made me laugh just to look at them. But Mother was getting really upset. She wanted to go over to the bar for a drink before the thing started, but I told her they didn't want you to drink or smoke or take any drugs for the duration of the seminar.

She was very upset, but before she could say anything, the three little dollar bills got up and danced us in. My, it was strange, very interesting.

I have to admit, I really had expected something with interest rates and estate planning. I heard somebody say, "Have you done this before?"

And someone else say, "I've done them all. Successful Living and Feldenkries and TM and est and the est graduate sessions and Leonard Orr's Rebirthing, and I've been Rolfed twice. . . ."

"As long as I get rich, I don't care."

"Is that what they're supposed to do here? I heard it was a real spiritual thing! I'm not sure I'm ready for all that other stuff."

"I've heard it's the most fun of all."

"Oh, well! Okay!"

I guess my feelings right then were just *so happy* to be out of my daily life (and so happy to have something fun to write in this journal), and so happy to be away from responsibility and what I was used to on a weekend that I decided right then to have a good time and worry about being "silly" or "stupid" later.

A young man came out, and God knows he wasn't worried about sounding silly.

"Oh, I'm so happy, I'm so happy, I'm just so happy to be here with you, to allow you the space to get past your considerations about the wonderful message you're going to be receiving, to really get clear on what your life is about! Because life is not about suffering! Because I want to tell you right now, before the Man even comes out here, that your life is not about suffering!"

Everyone cheered, and I don't know, I couldn't stop laughing. I guess it was those little kids dressed up like money.

"Because your life is about happiness!

"Because you are a fun-happy person!

"Because your life is about prosperity and wealth!

"Because you are a prosperous and wealthy person!

"Because you are enlightened, happy, and wealthy!

"Because you are divinely irresistible to happiness!"

That sentence made a real impression on me. What an interesting idea. They don't have Happiness I and II at UCLA. Not even in Extension.

"Because you are in love! Yes!

"Your life is *about* love!

"You're a millionaire in love!"

I heard the people around us begin to sigh.

"Okay, then," the man said. "You're ready for the Man. But remember, no drinking, no smoking, no headaches, no sick stomachs. We're just not going to let you be creative in that direction. And believe me! When you leave here on Sunday night, *you'll see a different world out there!*"

A young guy came out. He was wearing a green business suit and glitter in his hair. He was handsome.

"This is a game about money. Take some money out of your pocket, as much money as you can be accountable for."

"What's that?"

"What does he mean?"

"I didn't bring any money!"

"Doesn't he have enough of our money already?"

Even I began to get suspicious. But for twenty minutes I hadn't thought about my mother, or what was going to happen in the future, or how I could please get rid of the past.

The little green people stood at attention. They were going to play, and some other assistants came out.

I'll just say what happened. First, my mother and I both took out the same exact amount of money. The Man started chanting.

"This is a game about passing, and what you get to do is pass. You'd better stand up to be able to pass. Now, pass! Pass, pass, pass, pass, pass!"

My mother and I just naturally turned away from each other. I changed dollar bills with a nice-looking woman on my right. Then with a tall, well-dressed man in his thirties. I must have been around my mother too much; I instantly thought he must have been a homosexual. (Later I realized it was because he changed money fair and square.) An assistant passed me a five! I put it in my pocket. Then I changed ones with a woman in her sixties. (I thought: Someone nice for Mother to talk to.) Then I changed with a hippie freak who reminded me a lot of Sandy. I held on to both bills for a second, I didn't want him to try anything, but the poor guy didn't have any strength in his fingers. Then I changed with a prosperous-looking older man, and then with a kind of beat-up-looking little teenager in a shawl, who gave me ten dollars for one! (I have to say I was wearing some very expensive-looking white slacks and a navy-blue linen blazer; I guess she thought I should have the money.)

I took out my five, and a little kid about Davie's age came by and showed me his two empty hands. I gave him the five and he stuffed it down into his pocket, which was *bulging* with money.

The Man said, "Now, this is the last pass!"

I was waiting for the game to end, and I still had the ten-dollar bill in my hand. Then this bony little hand, a man's hand with scrabbly little fingers and manicured nails, just lifted it away from me. I looked around and it was a good-looking guy in a perfect cream-colored cashmere and spotless white chinos.

I couldn't believe myself. "You bastard!" I said to him.

"Yeah?" He was laughing, and he held my bill just out of my reach.

"Give me my money! You're not fair!"

When he kept on laughing, a voice came out of me. "I hate your shoes!"

He actually faltered, and I finished him off. "They're so . . . Jewish!"

He kept my money, but I spoiled his fun.

The game stopped.

"Well," the Man asked, "what happened?"

That little kid stood up. "I'm *rich!*" he said, and everybody clapped, but I know I wanted to kill him.

The older man with the lanyard had ended up beside my mother. "A lot of the charming ladies here have relieved me of my money. But isn't that what money's for?" Mother looked at him.

But listen. By this time a girl had started to cry. She really made a fuss. "It's not enough that you charge us an outrageous price to get in here, but you send your assistants out to steal all the rest from us, even down to our small change! You ought to be ashamed of yourself!"

Then another one stood up, in tears. "That was all the money I had in the world," she sobbed. "My last twenty dollars. I even quit my job so I could come here this weekend. That was my food money. My cab fare home. So won't the person with my twenty-dollar bill please give it back to me?"

"Accountable is accountable," the Man said. "I really mean it. Do you see?"

"But I didn't *do* it," the girl moaned. "I was just standing there."

"You took out the twenty."

"I didn't have any change!"

All the assistants started to laugh. Even the Man cracked a smile.

"See? This is just one example. You think you're just standing there, but you're creating things all the time."

The man who stole my money stood up. "Wait a minute! You're saying we're responsible for everything that happens to us?"

The Man smiled. "Well, by now it isn't exactly a new idea."

Even with a pocket full of money, that man hated it. "Consciousness-raising shit!"

"They say it in est too," someone said. "They're saying it everywhere now."

"Well, you're a dirty fucking liar!" The girl went into tears.

"Somebody take care of her!" the man in the lanyard said. "Don't just let her suffer like that."

Right then is when I should have noticed. That poor man wasn't any more than four inches away from my mother.

"I had an awful childhood! I'll tell you the truth." The girl was really crying. "I was a battered child. How can you say I was responsible for that?"

"I say so," the Man said.

Then, I'm afraid, I embarrassed my mother forever. Because I jumped up and talked.

"I *see* it! I see what you mean! I thought I was a winner in this game! For a while I was! But I gave a five to that little boy—who's rolling in money—and then *that man stole* . . . no, wait! I was just standing there, like a—"

"Like a *turkey*," said that guy, who, I guess I don't have to say, was a dead ringer for Ian.

"Yes! You awful man! And I let you do it!"

"You got it, sweetheart!" At least I cheered *him* up.

"So you see?" I was panting with excitement.

"So, what did you find out?"

"I thought I was a winner! But I was a loser! I guess that's all I found out."

I heard my mother, clear as a bell, from across the room, whispering to the man with the lanyard, "She always was a little slow on the uptake."

But to me it was a revelation. The hours just peeled by. People got hungry or tired or left. I paired off with a thirty-year-old exporter (who really *was* a homosexual) to ask and answer the question What do you like about yourself? Do you know what he said to me? He said, "I like my *teeth!*" Of all the ways to answer that question! I'm not saying it was profound, but it seemed so sweet to me.

Then we asked each other what was keeping us from having what we wanted. I did that exercise with the battered child, and I told *her* a thing or two. *She* ended up looking like a queen. Then we were supposed to ask "What in life would make us truly happy and satisfied?" I ended up doing it with some silly dope addict who kept saying, "All the coke I could ever use, that's all, no, that's really all I'd ever want!"

I don't know how to say this, Dr. Newman, and I hope you're not thinking, like the man who took my money, oh, just some more of that . . . consciousness-raising shit. But I was having the time of my life. I knew it was stupid. But I think, I *know*, it's important, when you start having a good time.

Things got pretty weird. I mean, they started to *sing*, all those cute little dollar bills, "I'm a millionaire miracle, a millionaire in love." And I blush to admit it, but they wanted us to get up and dance. I got up, I did it. I almost died, but it was actually fun.

Late that night a woman stood up to say, "Don't you think it's sad that we have to go to *such lengths* to find out what we should know, what we *have* known, I guess, for such a long time?"

The Man said, "It's only sad if you make it that way," but I thought: Oh, God, yes, it is sad, it's more than sad.

It went on until about four in the morning. I don't know if it was simply fifty people in a room having a good time, or if the cosmic energy they kept talking about really does exist, but I do know the *air* seemed to get thicker (I'm so glad this journal is just for your eyes), and the people—who my mother would say were certainly jerkier, even, than the old ladies at the lunch—the *people* began to get shiny! My face got tired from smiling. I mean really tired. But I couldn't stop. Even now, while I think of all of us standing at the Ambassador, where (don't remind me! My mother and father used to go dancing under those paper palm trees) we all stood and planted roots in the carpet and grew leaves on ourselves and went into bloom, I'm sorry, it just seemed so *funny* to me.

Toward the end of the evening, three different people told me I was beautiful. I spend a lot of time on my appearance, but people don't always volunteer that I'm beautiful, so that struck me funny too.

Oh, I forgot to say! I looked around at one point to see my mother becoming a tree, but—did you already guess it?—my mother and the man with the lanyard were gone. I'm sure I'll worry about it tomorrow, but at the time all I could do was laugh.

5

I knew right away I had to get out of there. Those fools! Can they seriously think that when you've been with them since the day they were born, you don't know what's in their *minds?*

I never had a real family. We were poor enough, we were the kind of family that dies of TB. But now! *Now* they don't even *have* TB! It's like you spend your whole life getting ready for trouble, and then they spring something *else* on you! You know my family now. Ex-*husbands*. One in a beach town, one in hell. Deadbeat kids. One a dope fiend, the other a moron. No one you could call on. No one to help you. What I am trying to say to you, Pearl, is that I was alone. My friends that I loved, dead. Dead or old. I could see now I couldn't go back to Coalinga, I'd die from it. I couldn't go back to that job. I'd die from it. Did you ever think about *mandatory retirement?* And how you die right after?

Another set of words to go over in your brain. *Bored to death.* They set you loose in the maze.

She had me in that room. There was no way I was going back to the house, because if *she* was too stupid to know her husband was screwing himself silly with that girl I saw him with, *I* wasn't. How could she be so stupid, how could she be so *dumb* as to leave her own house to stay in a hotel for two days? How could she even be a daughter of mine? Where was she *raised*, for Christ's sweet sake, that she didn't know that your own bed is where husbands love to do it best (and leave the stains there, and arrange for you to do the laundry)? *Never* leave home in the afternoon, *never* leave home at night!

But I couldn't tell *her*.

And who knows? I could be wrong.

By God, it tickled me to come out a winner in that pukey game! And then the next morning, when we were marching around:

"I'm a millionaire!

"I'm a millionaire!

"A millionaire in love!"

I was marching around, but I certainly wasn't singing. I was dying for a drink.

Even in the middle of all this crap I kept thinking how much fun it would be to tell it. To Fran. Except he was on another whole wife. To Dick, just to drive him *nuts*. Except he was dead. To Allan—it might get through that jerky dimness of his. To you, Pearl. But there was no one. *No one!* It was getting to be like a terrible joke. It was getting to be the truth.

If you could know how it *ate out my ass* to see that house of hers! Those Oriental rugs. Those *matching couches!* Those ashtrays you could use for a deadly weapon. Those Chinese *screens*. When I ask her where she got that stuff, she pulls that look on me, boy, that look! I remember from when she was a kid and I'd be telling her off, a look like someone had reached in her head and scooped out all her brains with a spoon.

"The *decorator* did it." The decorator! Jesus Christ! And in my room! She must have known I'd be in a position to call on her for help one day, because you know the color I hate worst? Pink. You know the color the guest room was? Pink. I am not even kidding! Pink walls. Pink ceiling. Pink carpet. Some kind of salmon-colored spread. And a big pink thing on the wall made out of yarn that looked like cirrhosis of the liver. When I said something—I said, "You sure didn't hesitate in your use of *pink* in here"—she got that look on her face and said, "It's the decorator. He likes to experiment with colors in the air, you see? He's turning the air pink in here. Did you notice, it's yellow in the living room, and blue in ours? He's very expensive. From Palm Springs."

But Ian is color blind! She knows it and I know it. That's what I'm up against.

And the garden. Every morning I'd wake up in this sea of pink. Like puke, and I'm not even kidding. And she'd already have the sprinklers going outside, whap whap whap whap! Lawn and hedges and birds of paradise! She's working on another whole sea of green. She's turning the outside into a swamp. Your basic South Sea *isle*.

I get up in the morning, she's out in the kitchen taking labels off cans! "Aren't you even going to write something on the goddamned *cans?*" I ask her. "Otherwise, how're you going to know what's in them?" She gets that look on her face. "I forgot about that." Thirty-nine years old and she *forgot about that!*

One morning last week I woke up and couldn't find a cigarette. It's cloudy, for once the sprinklers aren't drowning that pukey lawn. I get on my robe and go out to find something to smoke. There's Garnet in the den, in what looks like a mountain of yellow paper!

"What's *that?*" I ask her. She looks as smug as a plum. "These are Ian's secret papers, Mother. He won't trust anyone but me to put them through the shredder." Who cares? Who *cares!* He would have to *pay* me to read his papers! She didn't even think to get a grocery bag to put them in. "Someone's going to have to vacuum that *up*, Garnet!" So she gets that look on her face. Like a big pudding. *You pudding!* Sometimes it's all I can do to keep from telling her that.

I tell you, they've got a life, it would make a strong man weep. She goes off to that school, she's got her little card, you know, she's got that little *student identification* card. She puts those pukey kids in a wagon, she drops them for their tennis lessons. Since when do kids have to have tennis lessons? What I did, and what you did, Pearl, we went out on a court with a racket and we *hit the ball!* And that pukey little kid takes karate! Pow. Pow. So *what*, you know what I mean?

And then they swing on their swings in their backyard and they swim in the neighbor's *pool*. The little darlings. It makes me want to puke. The only one with any brains is Ian. Don't they know where all of it *comes* from, all their *rugs*, their . . . *gravy?*

And the food in that house! When I stayed home, with Fran, with Dick, you knew what food was. Baked apples. Spanish rice. Apple brown Betty made with Grape-nuts. A fried egg. A piece of halibut on Friday night, not that I ever believed in that shit, but because it was Friday, you ate fish, that was *it*. In her house it's like that *rug*. Everything is so groused up with sour cream and wine and onions and paprika and Accent and cinnamon, you *can't eat* it!

I told her that; she looked like I pistol-whipped her. "You're right," she says, "I know you're right about that, Mother." So the day after that, everyone in the house is eating lettuce and melon, with strips of *prosciutto*. Carrot slices with little bits of lox! Cottage cheese whipped in a blender with celery! Some days I go out in the kitchen, I look in the refrigerator. I'd finally get so I'd just *ask* her. "Don't you just have some saltines and an *avocado?* Some Triscuits and a piece of *cheese?*" She'd have the cheese, but not the crackers. One time I asked her, "Don't you even have a can of *Campbell's Vegetable Soup?* Don't *tell* me you haven't got that." But she gets that *look* on her face. "You know I took all the labels off, Mother." I didn't even take the trouble to answer her.

I get the feeling there must be a lot of women in my kind of trouble. Because women live longer than men, don't they? And they can't all go live in old folks' homes. Jesus Christ, not for twenty more years. So from sixty to eighty, what the fuck do they *do?*

Sometimes my heart sinks.

My heart sinks in my body. Because the women I know now, Pearl, they're from another world. Of course they like to drink. They can be fun some of the time. They're all right.

But they make desserts out of magazines! They brag about their fucking sons in Harvard Law! They say, "Charles and Eileen asked me to come live with them, naturally I said no, but they told me I have a home with them anytime I want it!" And then they smile and deal out the cards.

I don't want to really get *on* this, but do you know what Elaine Arbogast gave me last Christmas when she drew my name at work? A ceramic pair of praying hands. I stayed up for hours at night looking at them.

Whatever happened to the women who used to be *you and me*, Pearl? Who used to go with Fran and Duane over on the big steamship to go dancing at Avalon? Or when you two finally got married and you had that new muddy lawn outside your apartment and Fran stuck the big firecrackers in the mud and POW! all over your new apartment! *Laugh?* Where are the people who used to laugh like that? Where are the people like Virginia Wright, the drama editor of the *Daily News?* You know what I mean? The *drama* editor?

Sometimes I get an idea—I get an idea of *all over America*, the girls who used to be so great in the twenties and thirties and forties. They're sitting in somebody's kitchen now. Their husbands have died or skipped, and they're sitting out in their married daughters' yards or at one of those new kitchen tables. Their daughters have got them slicing mushrooms, or slicing up those goddamned carrots. And they're *never* going to get out—I don't care if they live in Cleveland or Houston or Pomona, they're never going to get out until they're so old they can't get out. And that's when they're *shipped* out.

Oh, I forgot! When I was standing at her sink, right next to the Mexican maid, cutting up green pepper for that goddamned cold tomato soup they eat. She comes in with some folder or other and says, "Mother! I've been thinking, for *all* of us. Isn't it time we thought about joining a funeral society?" I told her right then. "*If you think* you're going to get out of paying for my funeral when I've left you every penny of what I've worked for all my *life*," but she said the

California undertakers have the legislature sewed up, and this society was a blow to big business.

I said to her, "What about joining the interior decorators' society? You could save some money doing *that*, and strike a *real* blow against big business." She looked like she's about to cry—that *look!* That orphan look. Then she said, "Actually, I do have a decorator's license. And we do save money that way."

I told her, "You join a burial society over my dead body!"

She didn't even laugh. How can she be Fran's daughter?

So within a week of coming down, I knew it wasn't going to work. With the sprinklers and the pink air and maybe twenty-five years of my life to live, it wasn't going to work. *Don't* ask me why. I couldn't stand her, that's why.

There was one woman in that hotel room, she was my age, and she looked pretty good. I must have been desperate, Pearl, she almost reminded me of you.

Or—I used to know the prettiest woman, Jeannie Butler. She was married to somebody, Christ if I remember who. But when we'd play poker with Matt Weinstock and his wife, or Gene Coughlin, or Hugh and Virginia Wright, sometimes they'd be there. *He* was okay, but she was beautiful. Later, when I was married to Dick, I managed to keep in touch with Jeannie. We went to the races once, she wore real pearls and drank a whole bottle of Jack Daniel's she kept wrapped up in a bag. Do you see what I mean? This woman had the *style* of Jeannie Butler.

So I got next to her.

"Listen," I said. "Excuse me for asking, but don't you find this kind of . . ."

"*Yes!*" she said.

We were sitting down now. And I was as far as possible from Garnet, who was sitting there with the sappiest smile pasted on her face.

"My daughter's thirty-nine years old . . ."

"Yes! I saw the two of you together when you came in."

"Do you have children?"

"I'd hardly call them *children.*"

We both looked over at Garnet and laughed. "I have two," I said. "I never see one, and I see too much of the other. How about you?"

"Three," she said. "All married and out of town. And three grandchildren. They cry all the time. Listen, I know it's silly to ask, but did you grow up around here?"

"Los Angeles High School," I said, and held my breath.

"Pasadena High, '32."

"That's amazing." I felt shy.

"Have you been to many of these weekends before?"

"What?"

"Other weekends."

I guess I just looked at her.

"Actualizations," she said. "Prosperity. est. I know! It must be Pierre! Didn't we work together at Pierre's Polarity Massage!"

"How old are you?"

"Sixty-two." She was real bright about it. "You must be right around there. Oh, but you certainly don't look it, any more than I do. Tell me, what do you eat?"

"Huh?" She honestly took me by surprise.

"I'm a vegetarian. You must be too. You don't get a complexion like that for nothing."

It's true I don't eat much meat. It costs too much. But I got a vision of all the Baby Ruths in my desk drawer, and the ocean liner full of Hill and Hill blend which I'd drunk just to get to the age I am.

"I don't eat much meat," I said.

Then that smarmy little jerk was back up at the blackboard. (And how I resented being told to do anything whatsoever, especially by that creep!)

"What were the things in life which have kept you from being, doing, or having exactly what you want?" he said. "Pair off, and ask each other that. Then say thank you. Don't say anything else. Just say thank you."

That woman turned to me with a sappy smile on her face. "What were . . ." she began, but I turned, like butter wouldn't melt in my mouth, to the other side. There was this fairly decent-looking guy, in his middle sixties, like a lot of the rest of us. (I don't know where they dug up this bunch, but they were either old farts or hippie freaks, not much in between.)

He was tall and skinny. He wore a brown sport shirt and good slacks. His face was longer in the bottom half than the top; he wasn't too gorgeous. He wore glasses. Around his neck he wore one of those creepy leather things old guys wear, but this one looked better than a lot of them. Like a shoelace, a long suede shoelace, and holding it together, a brown polished stone as big as an aggie. He looked like he had somebody to take care of him, but he was here alone.

"What were the things in life that have kept you from being, doing, or having what you want?" he asked.

"My husband, whom I loved more than anything else in the world, left me," I said. Well, what else was I supposed to say?

"Thank you," he said. I just sat there and looked at him.

"What were the. . . ?"

"My wife, whom I loved more than anything else in the world, died," he said, "after a long and terrible illness. I have had no joy since then."

Poor bastard. "I'm sorry," I said.

"No," he said, "you're—"

"Thank you."

"What were. . . ?"

"After my first husband left me—*for a secretary!*—my second husband *died!*"

"Poor kid!"

"Well, what were. . . ?"

"My children are gone, grown up, I hardly ever see them. Of course, you know that story. I have a very nice place down in Santa Monica at the Georgian apartments. Do you know where that is? But I'm alone. I . . . don't have much fun. That's why I'm here, of course."

"Thank you."

"What. . . ?"

"I feel the same way. For many years I had to work as a secretary to raise my kids. It finally got to be too much for me. . . ."

"And how are they now?"

How can anyone really know? One of them's supposed to be in trouble. The other one's supposed to be okay. I wouldn't bet on it either way. "They're all right."

"What are. . . ?"

"Oh! Well, I had the usual responsibilities of a family. I always felt that I might have been a decent . . . composer, but I married early and had the boys to look after—"

"Okay, wind it up now! This is your last answer!"

"—and so about the only thing I was qualified to do, well, I had a pretty good education in the sciences *and* the humanities, so I wound up as an engineer and then a businessman, for thirty-seven years! Do you remember when they sent that first machine to the moon, without any men in it? And it had that three-legged wheel base? Well, I suppose I shouldn't say it—"

"Come on now, finish up!"

"But I had a pretty large hand in that."

"THANK YOU!"

Everyone started to clap. (God knows why.) But he kept on whispering in my ear.

"Just as soon as the boys went out on their own, my parents started needing some help. My sister and her husband did what they could, but most of the responsibility fell on me, of course."

Up in front, two kids in their dollar suits were talking about *enthusiasm*, and how the trick was to see *abundance everywhere!* Oh, Pearl, if you'd only been there. Because right next to me was something worth getting enthusiastic about, something as rare as the dodo bird, do I have to tell you?

Without even having to turn my head, I could see an eligible single man, a little older than I was, with money in the bank. I'd lived for twenty-five solid years in Coalinga—tell me about it!—and I can say for sure they don't have those guys in low-income apartments. They don't have them around City Hall.

Without blinking my eyes, I looked over at what I could see of him—just his upper legs, and his right shoe and sock, because he'd crossed his right leg over in my direction. Those slacks—brown gabardines—were clean and pressed. His legs were thin, and as far as I could see, only a little bit stringy. Polished loafers. Not bad. And a sock which looked like it probably went all the way up to his knee. Without looking right at him, I already knew he had most of his hair, cut real short, you know? And he was pretty tan.

He looked like a guy who gets out a lot. Someone who plays golf. He wore one of those baggy short-sleeved sport shirts.

To tell you the truth, he looked like a namby-pamby *jerk*, the kind you wouldn't touch with a ten-foot pole if you were twenty-five and he were thirty. Or if you were thirty-five and he were forty. But those are the kind of guys that *survive*, Pearl! Those are the guys that live to tell the tale.

For the first time in months and years, I looked straight down. *Oh*. Disgusting. I've let myself get disgusting. I'm going on a diet right now.

Over on the other side of the room, Garnet got up to talk. She was all dolled up in a linen blazer with little post earrings and her hair back in a barrette. She looked like a tired anchorwoman.

"Is that your daughter?"

"Yes."

"Excuse me for saying it, but you seem *younger* than she does."

And he might have been right! Because no matter what, I never let my hair get messy, and I take good care of my hands, and my shoes are always in perfect condition.

My legs aren't bad, either. At least he could see that.

I have to tell you the truth, Pearl. Even that first night, he didn't look like Fran. You know that no one, *ever again*, could be like Fran to me again. You could tell by looking at this guy that he might like to drink. You could see that under his eyes and around his nose. But . . . things *didn't strike him funny*. He wasn't . . . a newspaperman.

But up against Dick, he looked like a fucking angel.

The person he really reminded me of was Allan. . . .

When I think of the nights, when I was married to Dick, and he would be sitting dead drunk in his chair! And I didn't know what to do. I just didn't know what to do! I'd finish the dishes and put Sandy to bed and try not to wonder where Garnet was, what cruddy furnished room or strange bed she might be in, and it would come to me. I'm forty-two years old and I have absolutely nowhere to go to get out of this and there's nothing on God's green earth I can do about it! I'd sit on the back porch in Coalinga and look at the clothesline and the oil wells and the tumbleweed. And think of people all up and down the state in the same terrible boat as me. And I'd cry. I'd cry and cry and cry and cry. If only I'd been able to make it with someone like Allan.

What was it that made me *not* be able to make it with someone like Allan? Because Fran and Dick were certainly different, but they had the one thing in common, they were bastards.

So right here next to me was everything I couldn't stand in Allan. Only more so. He must have a bank account. And he said himself he had an education. And it seemed like he said he had only one marriage. (Of course, they'll lie like a rug. But he seemed too *simple* to lie.)

I'm not such a fool that I don't know when my life is going to change, and I had nobody to *nudge!* I had nobody to *poke*, nobody to pull out a cigarette with and have a laugh. Why doesn't anybody around here play poker? But I knew that you'd never find this kind of guy sitting up in that jerk shirt at a poker table.

They wanted us to get up and dance. "I'm a millionaire! Yes, I'm a millionaire! I'm a millionaire. . . ." About half of everybody got up. Well, how the hell do they expect you to dance to a nance playing a *guitar?* Those jerk assistants wouldn't pull you up, they'd *stand* over people who were too embarrassed to get up, waving their jerky hips all over the place and snap their fingers—trying to look *hip!* Trying to look *with* it! Garnet was still sitting down. She finally had the brains to look embarrassed.

"You didn't tell me what your name was."

The poor guy was stuck in his chair, frozen solid. But he mustered up some good manners.

"Ed. Ed Cochran. From Dallas. Originally, that is."

He was terrified I was going to ask him to dance, and he was right.

Because I know that in any group, if it divides up, you've got to be in the one that keeps moving!

"Just stand up, Ed, and I'll dance around you. It's safer that way."

Things had moved too fast for him. He was probably still back with balancing his checkbook.

I pulled him up on his feet. "My God," he said. I bet he was sorry he ever *heard* of the Ambassador.

I grabbed Ed's hand, pulled it over my head, circled under his arm. I saw Garnet looking over at me and blushing.

Some big bearded bozo came skipping over to me and tried to put his arm around my waist. *Nobody* puts his arm around my waist! Not in twenty-two years!

So I snarled at him. "Butt out of here, buster! Can't you see I've got all the man I want?"

He went barging off. He smelled bad.

Ed stood there like a stone while I moved around him. (About a fourth of the people were still too scared to get up. The jerks!) My feet, still neat-looking if I do say so, began to twitch as if that guitar-playing fag were Artie Shaw.

"Did you ever used to do *this?*" I asked Ed.

"Oof!"

I guess he didn't used to do it.

The Man himself sidled his way over to watch. (You didn't see *him* dancing! Hell *no*, you didn't! He just waved his arms, is all, and gave a kind of a smirk.)

"Come on, Ed! Show him you know how to do it!" Memories came back, of poker parties late at night, just breaking up, and me grabbing hold of Matt Weinstock for a few turns, while Helen stood back and said, "Come on, Grace!"

I grabbed Ed's old bones and pushed out from them again. "Do you remember 'Nola'? 'Kitten on the Keys'? 'Frenesi'? Didn't you ever used to go *dancing?*"

"No."

But that part was over, and all over the room, people were sitting down.

"You were sure the belle of that one!"

No thanks to you, buddy, I thought. But I just pulled out the old butter-wouldn't-melt-in-my-mouth smile.

The guy who ran the seminar had something to say. (For a change!) "Don't you see how it's really wonderful? Look at that wonderful old couple over there—don't you see how it's really possible to finally *get off your positions?*"

There were a few claps from the people around us. Not everyone thought we were the hit of the evening. And Garnet kept her back turned to us.

To tell you the truth, Pearl, I'd about had it. Spending a weekend making a goddamned fool of myself is not my idea of a good time.

Now, I was pretty sure I had a *look* left in me. Not the kind of look I used on Sandy or Garnet. Another whole look. I didn't even know for sure if I had it left. I hadn't used it since those nights in the bar, sneering across the purple dark to Dick. *You big gorilla!* You think you're pretty smart, don't you, you big gorilla! I knew I was taking a pretty big chance. Because like I said, this wasn't a joke. This was my actual life. But I reached down for my look. *You big gorilla!*

I took Ed by the arm.

"Don't you think you might buy a girl a drink? Or are you planning to stay around *here* for the whole weekend?"

His face changed colors like a jukebox. I'm not kidding you, he looked like an octopus on a rock. Then he took a deep breath and said good-bye to raising his consciousness and his two hundred and fifty dollars.

"Why . . . sure! There's a nice place, right by my apartment, where we can go."

And so we ducked out of there, past the door of the Coconut Grove, where the *regular* dancers were doing regular *dances*. "I used to come here a lot," I told . . . Ed, and squeezed his arm.

We hustled down the stairs of the main lobby to the side entrance. Walking pretty fast. I had the weird idea that if they could, or if they'd noticed, they'd send some "assistants" after us.

"My daughter goes to college," I said. I couldn't think of anything else to say. "But I should tell you right now, *I* didn't go to school. My mother was sick all the time I was growing up. I had to go to *business* school."

"You poor kid!"

"Oh, it wasn't so bad," I said, calming down. "We had some pretty good times."

We had found his car in the lot, a Ford LTD, spotless.

"Nice car," I said. To tell you the truth, I was beginning to get a little antsy. "I should have told Garnet where I was going."

"You can call her later." And I saw he was just as nervous as I was. I gave him a kind of pale gorilla look and said, "Say, I bet you don't pick up people all that often."

He laughed.

"I didn't know what a good time even *was* until I was forty and the kids were grown."

I didn't know what he meant by a crack like that. But I was in a car on *Wilshire Boulevard*, with a man my own age. Beggars can't be choosers.

He hunched over the wheel and cocked his head to the side

as he talked to me. "This is a good car. I let my son maintain it, he does a good job. I have a Winnebago too, for camping trips. Do you like camping?"

"Oh, *yes*." (I'd never been camping in my life.)

"Good! That, to me, was one of the saddest things about losing Madeleine. We had a wonderful garden, you see. We raised all our own vegetables. Madeleine preserved things, and we dried all our apricots and peaches, without sulfur. And then we took them camping."

"Mmm."

"So when she passed away, you see, I had a garden full of good things, and I couldn't even bear to go out into the backyard."

"That's tough."

He had to stop for a red light. It must have been around midnight. On both sides of the street, first-run movies were letting out. On the right side I saw Dolores' Drive In. You and I used to go there, Pearl, for hot-fudge sundaes, forty years ago.

"I like hot-fudge sundaes," I said. "Did you ever used to go to Dolores'? For those sundaes?"

He looked like I'd peeled back a blanket. "*Did* I! But, you see, Madeleine was a great follower of Adelle Davis. I don't think I could eat refined sugar now."

"Did you say where you were taking me?"

"You know, I've been a widower for almost two years. I won't say it hasn't been lonely. Right after Madeleine passed away, both my boys asked me to come and live with them. They were very nice about it. I really think they meant it. Then, when they could see I wasn't going to do it . . ."

"Why didn't you?"

"For one thing, it would have meant favoritism. That I liked the one boy over the other. But really, Grace—it *is* Grace?—they both live in the valley. I'd been married thirty-three years. I didn't want to be around that kind of life any longer."

"What'd they say to that?"

"They tried to get me to buy a condo in Leisure World. I

had the money for it, and they said the property would only appreciate, that it had to go up."

It's a long way from an apartment in Coalinga to a condo in Leisure World. I kept my mouth shut.

"But the thing about a *condo* is that it's just the same thing! Except that there aren't any kids, and somebody else mows the lawn."

That speech sounded like he'd rehearsed it and told it to his sons maybe more than they wanted to hear.

"So do you know what they wanted me to do then?" He gave me a kind of shit-eating grin.

It was weird sitting in that car with that guy. I'd been away from men for years, but it was all coming back to me. Just sit *still.* Nod your head *yes.* Wag your head *no.* Ask questions, the dumber the better. (And wait until afterward to tell them what you think!)

Ed saw me smiling and went right on. "So you know what they tried to get me to do then? I have to give them credit, they were only trying to do the right thing, they were worried about me living alone in that big house. Well, they tried to get me to sell the house and give all my money to Dr. Westmoreland!"

"*I* know about that guy!"

"Yes. Well, I went down myself to look at his original place, right here on Wilshire." He thumbed over his shoulder and back toward town. "It seemed like a pretty good idea. You give him your money, he takes care of you until you die. . . ."

"I used to walk right by that building when I was a secretary, when I was only eighteen. That was a great-looking building. It had a porte cochere. It's a good-looking apartment house."

"That's what it still is. But . . . Grace, I tell you. I went *in* there, and of course my father knew him, and Madeleine's father knew him, and I saw all those widow ladies in their print dresses and all that . . . well, it *wasn't* that, because they have that where I live now, but just . . . I went into the dining room to have lunch. And it was a *good lunch.* Roast beef, and special diets for the people who had problems. But, you see"—and this sounded like he'd rehearsed it too—"all those people were really from my parents' generation. They'd been missionaries. They'd been ministers. They'd been deacons. They'd been Masons. They'd been Rotarians! If I'd decided to live there, I'd have been perfectly at home. As my own father would have said, I would have been with the right sort of people. But between you and me, I'd *had* it with the right sort of people!"

The poor guy. Did I say, Pearl, he was wearing a short-sleeved shirt?

I thought of Fran for the millionth time in my life. Living in a *beach town*, with a *young wife*, a beautiful life I'd never have. I knew he must be old now, but I couldn't get past what he looked like *then*, before we were married, the first couple of years we were married. He had class and he had style, and it never mattered how much money he had. He wore long-sleeved shirts, and tweed jackets. And sleeveless sweaters. You'd *never* see Fran in a short-sleeved shirt. What makes handsome guys bastards? (A simple question I've been wondering about all my natural life!) So that the nice guys are turkeys you wouldn't touch with a ten-foot pole. . . .

Ed hunched over the wheel, looking at me. What have *you* got to smile about, turkey! His smile drew out at the edges. He was frantic, poor bastard. Because it was my turn to talk.

"So what did you do then?"

"I gave myself two weeks. And I thought to myself, Ed, you've lived around this city since you were twenty-nine years old. But you don't really know it at all. And I got in the Winnebago."

Jesus. When I think of what Fran would have said about the jerks who buy Winnebagos.

"I drove, I drove, to all the places I'd ever heard of, looking for places to live. I drove down to Leisure World. It was nice, but not what I wanted. I went out to Palm Springs. It was nice, but the anti-Semitism really got to me, Grace. I've never been much of a liberal, but do you know a Jew can't even get a cup of coffee at the Thunderbird?"

To pass the time I began to think of all the drinks I'd ever had. Whiskey sours, at the Ambassador, when I was a kid. Cans of beer, cold cans of beer, standing around in white shorts when I was married to Fran. Brandy alexanders, with you, Pearl. . . .

". . . Riverside. I had some idea of settling permanently at the Mission Inn. But you could cut the smog out there with a knife. Then I drove south to Murietta Hot Springs. Of course, that was *all* Jews, and, Grace, believe me, if you've ever seen one of those eighty-year-old women hauling themselves out of a hot spring. . ."

Sometimes stingers are nice. If you're not planning to eat anything. And in the thirties, with Fran, when we could almost afford it, Scotch. Fran and Dutch Van Burkleo, when we were out on a Sunday drive. The guys, out at Mother's Pub, on the Devore cutoff near the Lytle Creek Winery, sitting with glasses of wine in front of them, but drinking Scotch out of a flask. And when the food came, Fran put his veal cutlet into Dutch's wine. . . .

"I went as far as Las Vegas. Do you know I'd lived sixty-six years of my life and never even been to a casino?"

Straight bourbon. When we'd play poker. But I never got drunk!

"I like to think of myself as broad-minded, but after one night of Don Rickles and one night of Redd Foxx, I turned right around and came on home."

Margaritas. When Fran and I went down to Aguas Calientes for the races. Made out of tequila they'd probably put together the morning we drank it. Gee, they were good! Those margaritas, and I had that real good-looking one-piece bathing suit.

"I began to think I might have to spend the rest of my *life in the Winnebago.*"

God knows, I never had much to say to Garnet, but when she was pregnant with Debbie, I came down and spent a week with her. They were still in their old house then. Around eleven at night, after Ian went to bed, she'd go out to the kitchen for a mason jar and pour about a pint of tequila in it. She had fresh lemons, and Damiana from their trips to Ensenada. She'd make us two margaritas, about a pint each, and load them up with kosher salt.

"I went up to Santa Barbara. It was a little too expensive. And I wasn't going to buy a condominium *anywhere.* I actually spent a day down in Venice. But it was poor."

"*Say,*" I said, and I could hear the rasp in my voice, "when do I get my drink?"

"After *two full weeks* in the Winnebago, I found it. I know a little bit about research, after thirty-two years as a technical writer, and I'd started—maybe you could tell from the way I told the story. . . ?"

He gave me a big smile, and I smiled back.

"I'd started in a series of concentric circles. As far east as Palm Springs, as far north as Santa Barbara, as far *out* as Las Vegas, as far south as Del Mar. I even took the boat over to Catalina to check out the western parameter, but they didn't have any concerts or plays, and the library there is terrible. Then I came *in,* little by little. I figured I should end up roughly in Playa del Rey or Santa Monica. After fourteen days, of course. And one afternoon, I did end up in Santa Monica, just about where we are now. And by a strange coincidence, only one quarter of a mile from my own sister."

I'd forgotten what it could mean, to be in a car, on an endless trip with some turkey who loved the sound of his own voice.

"I walked up and down this strip of grass—can you see it? Can you see where we are now?"

I looked where he was pointing. I couldn't see shit. "I'm afraid I don't."

"There's a wonderful strip of grass here, it goes for a couple of miles, the whole length of Santa Monica."

"Mmmm."

"These are all *bluffs,* don't you see? We're at the end of the land. We're hundreds of feet above the blue Pacific!"

Am I really going to be able to do this? Am I really going to be able to tough this out? I began to think of salty dogs, over in Ida's apartment after work. Just the two of us, watching the six-o'clock news, too flaked out even to talk. Half vodka. Half grapefruit juice. Lots of ice. Lots of salt.

"At noon on the second day, I needed something to eat. I asked a man on a bench right here on the bluff, 'Where's a good place?' He pointed right across the street. 'The Bellevue,' he said. I went right over. It was Friday. I had a bouillabaisse all by myself, and I tell you, Grace, that is an experience. I ordered a half-bottle of wine, and then I ordered another one. Because I knew I had found it."

He turned right, and right again, and pulled into a parking lot.

"I asked the waitress, 'Where do all these people *live?*' Because they *looked* just like the people in Westmoreland's dining room, except they all were tan, and they all had double martinis in front of them!"

It's funny, a martini is one of the few drinks I could never get completely enthusiastic about.

"She said they came from the Georgian, right down the street. After lunch I went there. They had a place empty on the sixth floor with the most beautiful view of the ocean. I didn't have to think a minute, I said right then I would take it."

He drove into a parking lot and whipped me out of the car.

"Afterward I walked back here. The restaurant was closed, and that's when I found the bar. I had a champagne cocktail, to celebrate my new life."

He opened the padded-leather door of the Bellevue. It had mirrors and leather, it was a good-looking thirties bar! The lighting made me want to cry, because it reminded me of Fran.

"But this is a nice place!"

He smiled. Poor bastard. All he wanted was a good time. I was trying to think whether this was the kind of place that might have a good margarita, when he ordered a bottle of champagne.

I hate champagne! I hate any kind of wine, it makes me sleepy and sick. I was going to say something, when they brought over the bottle. It was Dom Perignon.

"We should celebrate," he said, "because this could be a new life too."

It tasted *good.* And it went to my stomach and started to work. All my life I've tried not to fool myself. I was trying not to now. But that bar got to me. I thought: Fran, you didn't take it all away from me. I thought: Pearl, there've been places in the world like this all along, and we spent such a little bit of time in them.

We didn't talk any more. We sat. We listened. I could see what he meant. It was a bar full of people our age. But it was another world. (And yet, I'm ashamed to admit it, I was already mad at him. Why couldn't he have stopped on our way out at the *Brown Derby?* Why couldn't we have stayed at the Ambassador and gone to the Coconut *Grove*, for Christ's sake? Why did he have to waste almost an entire hour of a perfectly good night driving his stupid car along Wilshire Boulevard and telling me the story of his boring life? And I began to think that so far he hadn't asked me *one question* about *my life*, not *one damn thing!)*

(But I'd be goddamned if I'd tell him anything anyway.)

So I began to wonder about when he was going to take me home.

Because if that bastard thought he was going to get anything out of me after one stinking bottle of champagne, Pearl, he had another think coming!

The bar was crowded. A couple of real old guys were at the far end by the windows, wearing those white patent-leather shoes they must do a land-office business in somewhere in this city. A couple of stools down, there was an older woman—my age, all alone. She was neat, and clean, not drunk. A couple of good-looking women in the booth next to us. And a couple of fags, maybe as young as fifty, in the next booth over. The place was small enough that we could all keep an eye on each other.

Somebody's night nurse, still in her uniform, came in, and sat up at the bar.

"I'll have a glass of strychnine," she said.

"Ah, *Maud*," one of the guys said from down at the end of the bar, "it's not *that* bad!"

"Just a joke, honey," she called back. And to us, because she saw we'd been listening, "Just a joke."

"Isn't this place wonderful?" Ed asked me.

One of the two old guys was trying to put the make on the good-looking woman alone.

"Haven't I seen you in here before?"

"I come in here every night."

"I knew I'd seen you in here *sometime.*"

"Every night. When I get off work, from five-thirty to about seven-thirty. Then I watch television, and then, at eleven-thirty, just after the news and before I go to bed, I come down here for two more. That way I don't get into the Valium thing."

Half a frozen enchilada in the morning, half at night. That and a One-a-Day vitamin pill and you keep your food bill down to five dollars a week. All the weirdness you can get into, Pearl!

"Well, I was sure I saw you around here," the old guy said.

She just smiled. "I'll have my second, Al," she said to the bartender, and the guy with the patent shoes was weighing in his mind whether to buy it for her.

"He's going to blow it," I whispered to Ed, "if he doesn't get his bid in there."

Ed gave me some *star-struck look.* Like he'd finally met the woman of his dreams.

She bought her own drink, and the jerk closed in. I guess he figured after she'd bought her own second drink he had nothing to lose. She was going to leave sometime soon, and it might as well be with him, right?

"May I tell you something?" he said, leaning over the bar toward her.

"Sure!"

"You have a wonderful complexion."

"Thank you!"

"No, I really mean it. And you're a working woman, too, isn't that right?"

"Sure!" She was beginning to feel the second drink.

"What I mean is"—he leaned right in there and got confidential—"you *should* be looking tired. Here it is almost midnight, and you look bright as a dollar!"

"Thank you."

"But your skin is so *smooth!*" The other guy in white shoes made a quarter turn away and gestured to the bartender for another drink. Ed poured out the last of our bottle.

"Well, I try to keep it that way."

"Most women around here, they've been out in the sun so much, their skin gets like leather. Around their *eyes*, you know? They think a tan looks good, you know? But after—"

"After a certain age, every woman should stay out of the sun."

"Big *deal*," I whispered to Ed.

"I don't know about that. All I know is, you have a lovely complexion!"

"Yeah," his friend said.

She finished her drink and gave them both a big smile. "I *have* to stay out of the sun. I never go outside without a whole lot of sunscreen and a big straw hat."

I knew it before she said it.

"I have skin cancer. You probably saw me in here about six months ago, all black and swollen up. I looked terrible. Every six months, I go in for that treatment. But as long as I stay out of the sun, and am real faithful about doing that, the doctor said I'd be all right. I kept on with work all through it!" She raised her voice a little, since the man in the white patent leather shoes had sunk back about a foot away. "They were real nice about it. I only missed one morning of work. Now I have a real quiet enjoyable time around here. I try to keep myself busy."

"That's swell," the guy said.

The woman with skin cancer finished her drink and picked up her purse. You could see she liked to be home in bed by midnight. The nurse looked over at her and waved her drink. Her strychnine had turned out to be a Rob Roy, double.

"Great stuff," I whispered, and dug Ed in the ribs. It was what Fran used to say. I hadn't had a chance to use that expression in a fair amount of time.

But my elbow went into dead flesh.

"Say! What's the matter?"

I thought maybe he wasn't as used to drinking as he let on.

His face looked like it had been through the tenderizer. "Madeleine died of it. Skin cancer."

"Not that kind. Nobody dies from that kind."

But he couldn't answer.

"Ed! How's your money situation?"

He looked up at me. A face I've seen myself sometimes. At five in the morning. After I've taken my bath.

"Are you as rich as you look?" The voice that made Garnet cringe and cry. The voice that made Sandy run away. But it got results, and that's why I used it.

He had his head in his hands. The nurse, the fags, the bartender, were looking in our direction.

"Because I don't care if it *is* expensive! I want another bottle!"

"It took her eight years. First the face, like that. Then the spots on her ankles. Then her pancreas. It took her eight years."

"Oh, *come off it!* Do I get a drink or don't I?"

"Of course," he said, and signaled the bartender.

"Listen, Ed. Nobody here is going to die!"

And while I said it I remembered one of Garnet's boring Hollywood stories. Jacqueline Susann telling that English actor in the Polo Lounge, "You're not going to die, Larry!" And they were both dead in a month.

"Listen," I said. "You think death is the worst thing that could ever happen to you? Death would be a *pleasure* after some of the things I've been through!" I could have given him an hour (or eight) on my husbands, my children, my childhood, the tea and toast I ate three times a day during the Depression. But we were in a swell bar! And that was French champagne in front of us. (And I could see the punk smiles on those human dollar *bills* we'd just left, if I began my sad story.)

So I kept still while the bartender opened the bottle. And when it was time for a toast, I gave Ed my *big gorilla* look.

"Good times, huh?"

"Oh, Grace!" he said, and gave me a big teary grin.

6

Pearl, I wish you could have seen them the next morning, ruffling their feathers like a lot of owls. Garnet was having a well-bred *fit*, you know? Because she'd had to cut her weekend *short*. This was the kind of thing she'd really wanted to do *all her life*, and it was something she'd thought we'd *have fun doing together*. But there was *no point* in *staying on there* if I was going to run off like that, and really, come to think of it, they were all lucky even to see me again *alive*, the way I'd run off with that person, and right in the middle of a *process*, and Debbie, David, if *either* of you happen to answer the phone and it's the Prosperity People, for God's sake tell them your grandmother got sick. . . .

I heard all this, Pearl, standing in some kind of butler's pantry they've got between their enormous kitchen and their *Formal Dining Room*. I went downstairs, expecting to find them in the kitchen, with poor old Garnet in her ratty robe watching the *Today Show* and trying to palm it off as public service, and the kids already off to school, but I'd forgotten that this was Sunday morning, and the poor fool believes in *Sunday Breakfast*. (Just like she's still got those bumper stickers on her car, "Another Mother for Peace," well, who the fuck *cares* if Garnet Wickendon Evans is *for peace* or not!)

I'm going out from the kitchen, through the butler's pantry, and I hear that harping, whining *voice.* I don't know how Ian can stand her, except he's got those ratty-looking bangs coming down on his head, maybe he's *got* to stand her. They're sitting up to the dining-room table like four fools. There's not even a place set for me. They've got silver dishes *with covers* on the sideboard. Something in them smells like . . . I don't know, dog shit.

They're all out there. They've got big bright blue cloth napkins in their laps, and Ian is wearing a white terry-cloth bathrobe with a monogram. I know enough about this place by now to know he's been *doing his laps.* David and Debbie are sitting up to the table playing Look. Or Davie's playing Look. It's something brown. He opens his mouth, and Debbie looks at him and gags. Then his mother looks at him and he shuts his mouth until she thinks nothing's going on and Debbie calms down, then he opens his mouth again and Debbie gags again. And all on the same mouthful! Doesn't the creep know he looks awful enough without trying? He doesn't have to make any effort *what so ever!* And Debbie's no prize either.

Did I tell you they were eating out of *baskets?* They had their fancy Sunday-morning china, except instead of being on a tablecloth, every one of their stupid plates was sitting in a basket? *Only Garnet* could think that up. And the poor fool was sitting there in a *morning gown.* She'd put on mascara even though it's only ten in the morning, and she'd brushed out her hair all the way and so it looks like Brillo, and they are sitting there, with a big bowl of roses in the middle of the table, and she knows I'm allergic to roses.

"You know I'm allergic to roses," I told them.

Ian stood up. What a jerk. It's his own house! Why should he stand up? His robe fell open, but he had his trunks on. Debbie stopped squirming and looked at me like the spoiled little slug she is. Even David shut his mouth.

"Leticia," Garnet said to the Costa Rican just standing there in a white uniform watching the four of them stuffing their faces. "*Una placa para la mamacita.*"

I don't know Spanish, Pearl, but I knew enough to know *that wasn't* Spanish.

"Would you like . . . . Leticia to serve you, Mother?"

"No, I wouldn't like Leticia to serve me!"

By that time Leticia's brought out another table setting. Under the silver covers there're eggs left, and sausage, and sweet rolls. I turned around to Garnet and gave her a big smile. "I thought *you* were on a *diet!*"

"Well," she said, "I am. Only this is Sunday morning."

I looked over at Ian and saw him grin. I wouldn't say he likes me, but he likes watching me, I know it. So I put a lot of greasy crap on my plate and went over to sit down.

"Maybe it's just a different kind of diet," I said.

Garnet stood up like she was shot. "It's Sunday brunch, after all, Ian. How about some champagne?"

She didn't wait for an answer, she just vamoosed, van-*ished*, into the kitchen.

"So what's the story?" Ian asked me. "Garnet says you had a magic evening last night."

I just looked at him. I wasn't going to give him the satisfaction of an answer. Then I thought of one. "Yeah, well, she said you were *working!*"

"Did Grandma really go out?" Debbie asked him.

"*Yes, Grandma really went out!*" She hates when I imitate her.

"Did he show you a nice time, Grace?"

"Listen, kid, I'm so hard up, *any* time is a nice time."

"You worried Garnet quite a bit."

"Daddy, here's your name in the paper!"

"*Where?*"

And that was all I counted for, Pearl. Has it ever been any other way?

Garnet came back with another armload of silver, a great big tray with a silver ice bucket, and five glasses. And a bottle of champagne.

"It's ten in the morning, Garnet."

That is one true thing about Jews, Pearl. They don't like to drink.

"It's Sunday brunch, darling."

I could see by the whole set of her face that she *wasn't going to let me get to her*. She just *sets*, like a big egg. She's not going to *let me get to her*, you know what I mean? You could say, Pearl, that's not the most tantalizing look in the world, when your own *middle-aged* daughter looks at you like that.

"Ma, I want some!"

"Ma, I don't want any!"

Disgusting little creeps.

"This isn't the first champagne I've had this weekend," I said to them. "I had two bottles last night. Probably a better brand than this."

"Far-out," Ian said. For a guy with a hair transplant, he has a wise mouth.

"To the good life," I said, and waved my glass around at them. I made it sound like their life was cat food, and they both drank up.

"That *is* good," Ian said over the table to Garnet. (Did I hear something sad in his voice?)

"The good life," she said to him. Another Mother for Peace.

Then she looked over at me. "Mother, there's just something I'd like to *say* to you, right now, so I won't start thinking about it and then resenting it, and then it would come out in another way."

Debbie started squirming again. David took a whole link of sausage in his mouth and started chewing for another round of Look.

"You really worried me last night."

"Yeah?"

"It's one thing if you don't want to do something, but to just . . . run off like that without telling anybody, well I . . . worried about you, Mother."

Ian was reading about himself in the "Calendar" section of the *Times*.

"*Yes?*" I said.

"I just wanted you to know . . ."

I gave her a look.

"I was worried about you."

Pearl, you won't believe it, but life is really like television at times. Because *just then*, all the doorbell chimes went crazy.

"Who can that be at eleven in the morning? Ian, did you have a tennis date?"

Ian looked over at me, and I wiped my mouth with a napkin. I always look nice in the morning.

And you know, and I know, I was *dead right*. How is it, Pearl, we always knew? Like you knew when Duane was going to call you up, and he did? And I knew when my sister stood up Fran that he was going to stand there, in our little living room, in that beautiful tweed jacket and his yellow sleeveless sweater and look over at me and give me that terrific smile and say, "Well, Grace, it looks like we've got our *own* selves to look after. . . ."

"I know it's early, and I'm terribly sorry for intruding like this . . ."—he was wearing another of those short-sleeved sports shirts, freshly laundered, and a different gem and lanyard this morning—". . . but I realized this morning, Mrs. Jackson, that I didn't have your telephone number. . . ."

Ian was standing up again, and Ed went over to shake his hand. Nervous but confident, is I guess what you'd call him.

"How do you do? I'm Ed Cochran. Again, you'll have to excuse me . . ."

"It's nothing, it's absolutely nothing. It's a pleasure," Garnet said, sitting in her chair like the queen of the PTA. "Leticia, get another glass, will you?"

For a minute I saw it all through his eyes.

Yellow curtains, pink carpet, flowered wallpaper, the two little children of the house in their karate bathrobes, hubby in his terry cloth, Another Mother for Peace in her morning gown which matched the carpet, and outside, all the *green stuff*, trees and ferns and birds of paradise, and hummingbirds flying and swooping through those big sheets of spray which came from all the sprinklers (which I guess the gardener had come by to turn on in the morning). Every drop from the sprinklers caught the sun, and the birds were going crazy out there, flying around in the shower. The sun came in and caught all those silver dishes on the sideboard. It was wealth *and* color.

I looked over at Garnet. I had to hand it to her.

"We were just celebrating," Ian said, waving his glass. "I hope it isn't too early in the morning for you."

"Champagne!" Ed said. "Well, isn't that nice."

"Won't you have some eggs?"

Now she had a *reason* for that stupid little blue flame under the chafing dish.

"I was so pleased at the opportunity to meet you and your mother last night. . . ."

"But you were *bad*," Garnet said, "to take my mother away like that! Don't you know we were supposed to stay the whole weekend?"

Ed chuckled. (Honest to God, Pearl, he *chuckled.)*

"Well, Mrs. . . ."

"Evans."

"Mrs. Evans, I'm afraid I don't see *you* there this morning, either."

Garnet looked hurt. "The Sunday session doesn't start until noon. But I don't know what to do." She tried a little joke. "We lose five hundred dollars if we don't go back. . . . I don't know, we might have lost already."

Ed did something in his chair. First I thought he was having a stroke. Then I realized he was trying out a bow. A *bow*, Pearl!

"It was certainly worth it to me," he said. "Since I had the opportunity to, as I say, meet your mother."

For a second they all stared at him. I didn't say a word, Pearl! I just smiled over at Garnet.

"Well," Ian said. "Well! What do you *do*, Mr. uh . . ."

"Cochran!" Ed said. "I'm retired now, of course, but for years I was an engineer. Then I went into business. I was a glazier." He saw that none of us had one clue of what that was, so he said, "Glass? You know? For buildings? I did the glass for the Bonaventure Hotel."

Ian looked impressed. "That's a lot of glass."

"Now, of course, I don't do much in that line, but I try to keep up with what's going on in real estate, and I have my investments."

Leticia began to take away the plates.

"Hasn't the recession been hard on that sort of thing?" Nobody ever said my daughter could ever keep her foot out of her mouth. But Ed looked smug. "Not if you have the *right* ones," he said. "The recession has been nothing but good for me. No, I spend about two hours every morning on the phone with my broker, and I make sure I have the rest of the day for fun. I love exercise and being outdoors. I suppose you could say that's what I do now, I try to enjoy life. I *do* enjoy life."

Pearl, if you could have seen their faces!

Because I happen to know that almost every bit of Ian's money is tied up in this house. And that the poor sucker, even if he is fooling around, puts in his fourteen-hour days. And that Garnet may not get anything *done*, but she *works* all the time. Plus the fact that underneath Ian's hair transplant and nose job is a bald businessman. I mean, I *found* one, Pearl! And I brought him home.

Then Eleanor Roosevelt put her foot in it again.

"Mother loves golf," she said. "Don't you, Mother?"

I looked at her, and she turned another color.

"Come on, Ed," I said. "How about taking a girl out for a drive?"

"Sure thing! That's what I came over for! That is, if you don't *mind*, Mrs. Evans."

"Oh, she'll be able to handle it. Won't you, Garnet! What should I wear?"

"I thought we might drive up the coast and have lunch at the Santa Barbara Biltmore." Then he looked sad and nervous and about a hundred years old. "Of course, I see now you've had breakfast. Maybe you don't want . . ."

"I never eat breakfast. *They* do, I don't. And I haven't been to the Biltmore for years. You wait a few minutes and I'll be right down."

I got up and swished out of there! Because what I *didn't* say before, Pearl, was that Garnet wasn't the only one with a fancy housecoat. I had a blue one, they'd given it to me Christmas before last, *bright* blue. So I looked pretty good, and I was the one with the date!

What did I wear? Dark brown gabardine slacks, my brown loafers, a white overblouse, and a camel's hair jacket Garnet gave me for my birthday. Clothes I'd never wear in Coalinga, but I *had* them, in case. And I came down right away, because I never wear makeup, as you know.

So I stood in the doorway, and watched again, a little bit different than it was an hour ago! The kids were gone, the dishes were cleared off, and the three of them were talking about whether or not it was a good idea to buy a condo in Laguna Beach.

I just stood there until he noticed me.

And, Pearl, *you* know me. I *used* to be beautiful, for all the good it did me. I'm not beautiful now. Not since Fran. But I can look good! I can look clean! I don't know what it is! But I *can do it!*

So when the poor sucker looked around, I did it. I only wished the kids were there; Ian and Garnet weren't enough. I *could* say, even Ian looked at me like I was something, but that wouldn't be true. He did have a smile somewhere in there, though. He did admire me.

As we walked out of that room, after the good-byes and handshakes, and promises to get me home on time, ha-ha, and promises to get together for lunch sometime soon to talk that deal over, because it was a shame not to put more of your money in real estate *now*, now that the market was down, I turned around to take a good look at the both of them.

They'd already forgotten us.

Ian was looking, by himself, out of the window. The sun had gone behind a cloud; I don't know what he thought he was going to see out there. Garnet had reached for the bottle and was pouring herself the last glass of champagne.

"I'm going to be working the rest of the day," Ian said. "I won't be home for dinner."

"Oh. Well, then, I think I'll just go back to that seminar."

The light was definitely out.

After all that, we were just two old people walking down the driveway to his car, two old people getting in.

We drove down San Vicente to the beach.

Since it was Sunday, everybody and his brother was out, in jockey shorts, or those baggy pants, or just in clothes like *we're* wearing, running up and down that middle strip of grass, or sitting like a bunch of insane jerks right in the middle of the street having picnics, sitting on army blankets eating apples while the entire city of Los Angeles runs past them or around them, even though the sun isn't even *out* anymore, and anybody with any brains would be home playing poker or watching television. No, they're *out* there, leading what Garnet might call the *strenuous* life! And even on each side of the street, the other half of Los Angeles is out walking its stupid dogs, the weirdest set of mangy dogs I've ever seen in my *life*. Just a set of made-up God-on-a-rock, rich-bitch dogs. Then Ed spoke up.

"Looks like they're having fun, doesn't it, Grace? Maybe we could do that sometime—come out here and have a picnic."

Do I have to tell you, I was speechless?

We turned south on Pacific Coast Highway off San Vicente, because there didn't seem to be any way to go north. So there we were—I guess you'd call it *his* neighborhood—driving down past those flossy retirement hotels on the inland side, the El Tovar, and the Georgian, and ladies richer than a foot up a bull's ass. With their Clorox hair and their walkers. I was going to say something, but then I thought for once, I might not.

"Hmmm?"

He was looking over at me politely, waiting for me to answer.

"I only asked, did you grow up around here?"

Didn't I tell him all that last night?

(And if I did, what did I tell him?)

"I grew up in Pasadena." A good address, Pearl! Little does he know!

"Home of the Rose Parade!"

"I was in it once."

"You're kidding!"

If it weren't so rotten godawful sad, it would even be funny, wouldn't it? He thought he was out with a fucking Rose Queen. Just like I thought I was married to . . . Lord Byron.

"In the old days they didn't have floats like they do today. They just had little wagons coming down Colorado Boulevard. And little girls from school with roses in their hair."

"My! Pasadena must have been beautiful in those days!"

Raining all the time, right? My mother dying. The roof leaking. No food in the house. I thought—just for laughs—I'd say something.

"We didn't have much money. . . ."

He laughed. "Don't I know it! The Depression made it tough on everybody. I couldn't go home some of those nights, I just couldn't face Madeleine and the kids."

He gave a big, gusty sigh. "Sometimes, Grace, she'd know how bad it was, and she'd ask if there was anything she could do. The bills always came to my office, and I told her to go on just the way she'd always done—not to hold back on anything. I kept her charge accounts open. I told her not to scrimp on the kids. But she'd make up these meatloaves, she'd say she found a new recipe. I came home early once, and caught her doing the dusting. She said she'd sent the maid home with a strep throat. *Hell*, Grace, I knew we hadn't had the maid in months. . . . Of course, you're too young to remember all that."

The hell I was.

He turned right and headed back down the ramp that goes down the bluffs to the beach, so that we were going north again, this time by the water. All the way down that ramp he kept saying, "Boy! Isn't *this* beautiful! Look at those mountains up there, Grace! Aren't those a continuation of the Santa Monicas?" And, "Aren't those the Channel Islands out there? No, I guess you can't see them from here. But I'm sure that's Catalina! Or is it a cloud bank? What do *you* think?"

"I had a house once, way inland, where on a clear day you *could* see Catalina."

He made the turn down onto the highway and into the fast lane. He was a good driver.

"My work has brought me into contact with many people, but never one like you."

I checked to see if he was kidding. It didn't look like it.

"Where did you go to college?"

I had the answer ready for that. "I got married in my first year." (My first year of Sawyer's Business College, but I didn't say that.)

He didn't want to hear about it, and I didn't blame him.

"Your daughter, she's very nice. And they have a lovely home."

"Mm."

We'd run out of conversation. It's a hell of a thing, when you're old, to have to go through things like this.

"Say, *Grace!*"

"Yes?"

"What are you thinking?"

I gave him a big smile. "I was wondering if they dance up at the Biltmore. I was thinking I haven't gone dancing in a long time."

He concentrated on his driving.

I thought: What the hell, tell the truth for once.

"You know, I don't live like my daughter, I want you to know that. I live up north. I live in Coalinga."

"You told me."

"Ed, I used to be poor. We came from a poor family."

He looked dark. "Your daughter, doesn't she take care of you?"

"No."

"That's a crime."

I thought I'd try again.

"My mother died at home. I was the one who took care of her."

He gave me . . . well, Pearl, I can only say it was an adoring, sappy look.

"What a wonderful thing for you to do. How old were you?"

"Twelve."

"You . . . you poor little thing. And yet . . . when you think what Kübler-Ross is doing now . . . you were able to give your mother that experience so many years ago."

And as far north as Zuma he gave me the talk on this woman who thought it was *high style* to die, who thought the most fun thing in the world was to rent a hospital bed and stick it right in the middle of the living room and then to sit around and play canasta with this dying person until he gave you a big smile and died.

"Did you do that with your wife?"

"No. I . . . I didn't have the guts."

I have those memories, Pearl. They aren't my favorites. Even you and I didn't talk about them much. My mother, sitting up in bed in that dark old house, dying. They didn't have Kübler-Ross then! They just had my mother rolling up pieces of paper into paper cones and coughing into them; saying to me *be careful* when I took out the basket to the incinerator. And I'd stay there in the cold mornings, putting matches to the newspaper underneath those cones, and when the smoke came up, I'd step out of its way. Only, some days I'd put my hand into it, and feel my mother drifting away. And once a week she'd ask me, so sad, so apologetic, would I help her change the sheets? Because it was so far for her to walk, around the bed. And she'd tell me how to make square corners. And I'd come home from school on a cloudy cold day, knowing, even as I was walking, how bad the dampness was for her.

To go in that house, and the lights were out to save electricity. It would be ten degrees colder in there than it ever was outside. There wouldn't be a sound, and I'd go down the hall thinking: Well, maybe this is it. The door would be half open, I'd step around it, and there would be my mother. Usually she'd be smiling, in a sweat, but still alive.

"I did all the work," I said. "Because in those days there wasn't much money. My sister had to get a job. My brother was a black sheep."

"My father was a minister," he said. "I told you that. But he only gave the sermons. I suppose he spent a lot of time praying. It was my mother who did the work. In El Paso once, a little Mexican baby died in her arms. It was a heat wave, you see, and the Mexicans always bundled their children up. So they died quite often of dehydration. When she was older, I tried—so did my sister!—to get her to go on a vacation. But she wouldn't go anywhere without my father, and of course, he wouldn't go anywhere."

We were heading up the coast. The clouds were out all over everything, but it was a clean day and the colors were black and blazing. We were at a signal waiting, I was thinking: How much farther to Santa Barbara? I was thinking: When do I get a *drink*, a drink for God's sake? I was even thinking a little bit about Sandy, because I know dope addicts are supposed to love cloudy days, because the sun hurts their eyes. Once, before he ran away, a friend of his came over to the house and said, "Good morning, Mrs. Jackson! This is a real junkie's day!"

We stopped for a signal. A car turned out of one of the canyon roads and turned right onto the highway in front of us.

"Say," I said. "Didn't that man look like my son-in-law?"

"Where? Dear?" he said politely. He was locked into the drama of calling me "dear." But I'd seen, I'd *swear* I saw, Ian—hunched over, with both hands on the wheel—and a scrabbly, spidery, usherette type of thing, disappearing down under the dashboard, out of sight, beside him. It looked like what it looked like! A nervous guy getting a blow-job while making a right turn, is what it looked like.

"What kind of car does your son-in-law drive?"

"A Mercedes, I think, a gray Mercedes."

But then, as he politely tried to scan the slow-moving traffic, it dawned on us both that every car on the highway was a Mercedes, either gray or beige.

Oh, I looked at all the guys in all the cars. If they were with their families, they looked like murder was on their mind. If they were alone, or with a girl, or on a car phone, there was some kind of *unseen* scuffle down there, which made you think of something *going on.* And they all looked like they'd been playing in the same bottle of hair dye.

So maybe I was wrong.

"Besides," Ed said, "what would your son-in-law be doing out alone? It's Sunday, isn't it? And we just left him at home."

He put the car in gear and drove slowly for fifteen minutes. We turned in along that pretty stretch of highway which still has the double line of eucalyptus on it. Santa Barbara coming up. There was a funny smell in the car; then I realized it came from those miles of flowers they've got up there, big gorgeous strips of flowers as far as the eye can go. It looks like one of those beach chairs we used to sit in in the thirties. Beach chairs for giants.

I was waiting for Ed, even though I'd only known him for less than twenty-four hours, to start up with, "Oh, how beautiful! Did you ever see anything like it! What kind do you think they are, anyway? What about you, Grace? What's your favorite flower?" But he was thinking of something else.

"Look, Grace, something you said a while ago has been bothering me. When I was young, my father, as you know, was a minister. He was very strict. There were many things . . ."

He peered through the windshield, hunched his shoulders, and then took the whole thing from another tack.

"You know, I could have married many girls. *(That's* not what I want to say!) Well, Madeleine. I met her at college. Mother and Father had their doubts about her, but she was of our faith. She . . . Madeleine was no stick-in-the-mud. We were the first people, the first married couple I knew, who gave a cocktail party. But we never drank in front of my parents. We never drank in front of *her* parents either, but then we found out that they never drank in front of *us* . . ."

I wished I could think of a way to ask him what fifty years ago had to do with now. Twenty I can see, but *fifty?* Then I remembered I'd been driving alongside the world's biggest ocean with a strange man, thinking of my mom. Or did I call her that? It seems like I remember her calling me . . . Gracie? Grace Note? But I don't remember what I called her.

By this time we were just south of Santa Barbara. Those terrible rich bastards! When I think, Pearl, that I live in a twenty-square-foot apartment, and these people, I can't think of it! It makes me sick! And I began to wonder. Am I dressed all right? If I'm not, I'll say I'm sick! I'll get a headache! I'll faint! I don't have to put up with this! I don't have to take it! I put my hand under my breasts, to feel what my stomach was doing. Sure enough, it was hardening up, I can *feel* those knots. I opened my mouth to gag. Then I was going to tell him to pull over—if he did it right away, maybe I wouldn't faint. We were off the freeway now, in Santa Barbara. Everything began to go black!

He pulled over to the side of the road. What *was* this? Where was the hotel? Then it occurred to me, what a *fool* I was! After all I'd been through! I didn't even know this man! I hadn't seen his wallet, I wasn't even sure about his name! Even if it was his right name, if anything was wrong with him you could bet money that Garnet and Ian wouldn't remember who he was or what his last name was or what kind of car he was driving. Come to think of it, this street we were parked on didn't have *one building in sight*. And I may not have been around that much, but I'm smart enough to know Santa Barbara is a city. There was no point in *screaming*, Pearl! Because there was nobody around. My knees began to shake, my heart began to pound. Not *again*, Pearl! I couldn't stand it!

"My father, Grace, you know, it's too soon to tell you this, and I don't want you to think the worse of me, but I have to tell you now, before things go any further. He never told me the least thing about sex except he wouldn't let me go to . . . well even when we were down in Texas, we had dancing school. But Father wouldn't let us go. He said . . . well, he said strange things would happen!"

Mother, I thought, why did you let me be born into hell?

"My father told us it was a sign of the devil to dance." *He* was shaking almost as much as I was. "He did it for our good. Maybe he believed it. But he told us both that dancing with a girl was the best way to get her pregnant."

Out of all those dancing lights you get when a migraine is starting, his head came into focus.

"What I'm trying to say, Grace, what I tried to say to you last night, is that before we go anywhere, you have to know something. I don't dance. I never have and I never will."

Just old, that's all that's wrong with him. And who am I to make any noise about that?

My head cleared enough to see past him out the window. Eucalyptus. I forgot that in other parts of the world besides Coalinga, they've got trees. I found myself looking at one particular tree trunk. It had what looked like a mushroom or a fungus on it. I squinted my eyes at it, trying to see.

"Even Madeleine couldn't teach me. She was lots of fun. A good woman. But she'd heard enough of the same things herself."

He laughed. "When I think of what my kids do now! When I think, just of what I hear on the radio, on those rock stations! They *sing* about things I'd never think about doing in my life."

I couldn't figure out what was going on with the tree. That *knob* was writhing, or *moving*, or something like that.

He was blushing. "Do you know, Grace, what I heard the other day, while I was driving? A song that was—do you know how we grew up with '*moon*-and-*June*'? This song was rhyming 'worm-and-sperm.' What are they thinking about now, Grace?"

The knob shook itself and flew away. It was a butterfly about eight inches across. I liked it better when it was a knob.

"Grace?"

I couldn't think of much to say to him. It got quiet in the car.

"I know you . . . well, you talked about dancing, and you were in the Rose Parade—you have so much, you're so peppy, Grace! And you have such a fine family. I'd . . . like you to meet my sister, but I should come out and say it. We're sticks-in-the-mud, compared to you."

I knew how I could set him straight. That I used to go out with a boy in Pasadena. And that our idea of a date would be, he'd bring over a jar of olives and watch me eat it. But why should I set him straight? Does it do any woman in the wide world any good at all to set anybody straight?

"I don't dance, Grace. Does it make a difference?"

"I'm getting hungry," I told him. "Let's go have lunch."

We drove straight toward the Pacific and into a world you could say I'm not used to. The eucalyptus got thicker and the air turned kind of pink. There were plenty of those overgrown butterflies in the air. There was the hotel, right by the beach—I'd never been here. I remembered with Fran, before we were married, we'd sneak out of the house away from my sis and go to a crazy little motel with a string of poinsettias outside. . . .

But never here.

The doorman opened my door and held out a hand. I guess he was used to hauling old ladies out of the passenger seat, but I bared my teeth at him and he pulled his hand back like I was going to bite. I got out all right, and stood under that awning waiting for Ed to pay up. (Why couldn't he have just used the guest parking like everybody else?) I looked around; I wasn't going to take any shit.

A sign said, "In keeping with our respected tradition, we have no air conditioning." So it was about eighty degrees and smelled of fish. It *did*, Pearl! Couples were walking back and forth, holding on to each other's arms, very slowly. Ed took hold of my arm—*he's* the one who needs support!—and walked me down into the cocktail lounge. Then he lowered me into a couch. We were back in the twenties. Needlepoint furniture, murals of Junípero Serra, all you needed was a grand piano with a Spanish shawl. Everyone was in couples, and everybody loved it.

"May I get you something from the oyster bar?"

"Yes, certainly," I said. "Thank you very much."

It wasn't all old people in there. Maybe only one-half. And they made it seem like it was the *right* thing to be, old, that they'd spent their time getting rich so that they could be here now. The younger ones didn't know how to do it. They wore white resort clothes and talked too loud.

How do you think *I* felt, Pearl? Like a person from another planet. Like the Rose Queen.

Then I began to notice the music. It had been playing all the time. "Nola." Then "Kitten on the Keys." Oh! *Why* don't they play "Perdido"!

Ed came back with two plates of raw oysters. The double martinis he'd already ordered were on the table in front of us. They were taking the pink light of the ocean, shimmering.

"This is the life, isn't it?" He said it as if I was the one who might know.

"Yeah, yes," I said. "Sure."

We both took a long drink, and sat back, and sighed. The place had some kind of high-toned convention, a dinner meeting, because over at another set of couches a bunch of jerks were talking about the Middle East and sophisticated drilling.

I looked at Ed. Was he listening or not? Maybe he was, because he said, "See that ocean, Grace? You wouldn't think there's oil underneath, would you? That there's money to be picked up right underneath the waves?"

We had a couple more. We sat and watched the sun turn everything dusty rose. That used to be my favorite color, but you never see it anymore. All I'm saying is that the ocean, without the sun ever exactly coming out, was the color of the roses on my old couch.

He had enough sense not to talk much. I just listened to the music, and then, I don't know, maybe I'm making too much out of it—you know, Pearl, how we'd make so *much* out of everything, how if someone called, or didn't call, or made a grab at us, or didn't, or called us into the office, or didn't, how we could talk and *talk* about it? Stretching it out like a pieces-of-eight salad? So maybe I'm making too much of it when I say the music changed. The tune was the same, or it seemed like it—but there was a *rush* that brought shivers all over my arms, I couldn't figure it out, but I felt happy.

The piano player got up and waved around at everybody and waltzed out. A couple of geezers put bills in his hand. But the music kept playing! And over at a side door there got to be a little congregation making an exit. All around us the old couples were getting up, or at least trying to.

"What is it?" Ed said. "What are they doing? Shall we go and see?"

And so we got up and joined the crowd. Forty rich old couples groping along to another room, to another kind of music, where I could hear, now, a lot of violins. I saw the young oil creeps sitting there watching us with a sort of contemptuous smile on their faces. I almost turned around and asked them: What the fuck do you think makes *you* so smart? If *you're* so fucking smart, why don't you bring down the fucking price of *oil?*

Oh, Pearl! You know I'm not easily impressed. You know that about me! But I have to admit I was *pretty* impressed. Like, if the room we came out of was where we *were*, this was another *place*. A big courtyard with something flapping and blowing up over our heads (Ed said later he thought it was old parachutes), and all over the yard a portable dance floor shined up to a high gloss, and all around the floor, tables with umbrellas and more champagne buckets than Carter has pills. I had to admit, life is full of surprises. And all over the floor, like they were all part of the same body, those geriatric cases, once they had staked out their tables and their champagne, *in one movement* sailed out onto the floor, dancing their brains out. Sailing around, these creaky ladies in a lot of silk, old enough to make you and me look like the camp fire girls.

And, I don't need to say it, each one of those frazzled broads had one dapper little guy, all grayed *out*, with shiny little dancing pumps and a dark blue suit. And next to these dancing greasers, Ed looked like Buffalo Bill.

I hauled him to a table, I made him order up some champagne. I tapped my foot under the table and hummed along while he turned dead white under his freckles and hung on to his gemstone lanyard.

"*Well?*" I barked at him. "Are you, or aren't you?"

"What?"

The poor dumb jerk.

"Are you going to ask me to *dance?*"

"Grace, I told you."

"There's a first time for everything."

"No, really, I don't."

"There's nothing to it."

"I couldn't possibly."

I drummed on the table. "Did you ever think of . . . telling your dad to just *stick* it?"

"Grace, I realize you're . . ."

I got up and took his arm.

"I want to *dance*," I hissed at him. "And I can't do it alone."

He got up like a whipped dog, and we stood on the edge of the polished floor. All around us these couples were swirling, about a hundred collected years of dancing lessons coming to life out there on the floor.

I could never afford lessons, sucker!

"Take hold of me!" I snarled at him. He was limp, he was suffering, but he did it.

"Now step *forward* with your *right* foot, see? *Now* with your *left*. Now with your right and *brush*. It's *one*, *two*, one-two-*three!* Hold on to me, you're doing it, you're *doing* it. It's *easy*, get it?"

The poor bastard didn't know what hit him.

I pushed him around like the lady in charge of the concentration camp, and in about twenty bars I could see him more or less coming back from the dead and counting with me under his breath.

"One, two, one-two-three."

"God," he said. "If my father could see me now."

"Ed," I told him, "just stay there and count. I'm going to *move.*"

I left him shuffling and counting, and whirled out in a turn. The room reeled around me. I saw tables, salads, old folks, champagne, the beach. Back against the wall, a still life, a photograph, what did they used to call them? A *tableau vivant.* A guy in his fifties. I saw the inside of his leg, and a girl's hand on it. Then a shrimp salad, and another couple, and came in close again to Ed's gemstone.

"Golly," Ed said. "This is fun. I can't believe it. I never knew it could be fun. Would you like to do it again?"

He had a kind of convulsion, and this time he threw *me* out. The room whirled. I was a long way from Coalinga. I saw an artichoke, the walls, the open side of the courtyard in flat stripes; lawn, sand, dark blue ocean. The couple against the back wall was further into it. She was chewing on his knuckles like they were short ribs.

"Gee, Grace!" Ed could hardly talk, he was puffing too much. I thought it would be a shame if he died just when my life was looking up. But he was dead game, and he tossed me out again.

Ah, Pearl, you were there, why should I say it? Just another turn was what it was, one of life's shitty little turns. Across the room the man looks up, like in "Some Enchanted Evening," from having his pud pulled and his knuckles rubbed down, and there it is. I noticed his transplant, his Julius Caesar bangs, and then I noticed him. My son-in-law. Across a crowded room.

Everything went black. Because I can faint when things go wrong.

Through spots in my eyes, I saw Ed, all concern, back at the table now, pouring me a drink. I tossed it off and said something rough. "I guess I wasn't in such good condition as I thought!" And excused myself to go to the powder room.

The Santa Barbara Biltmore has a long, dark hall. Its floor is that red Spanish tile, the kind that used to be in my house and Fran's. The hall was as long and dark as a tomb. I saw my reflection in a mirror. I heard my heels tapping along. I wished I had a cigarette to take out and *bang* against my purse, but I quit smoking years ago.

There's something in my heart, in the pure front of my chest, I can't stand it, Pearl. I hate it, it hurts.

Don't they ever get *tired* of it?

Don't they ever get tired of laying pain out over everything like aluminum siding, or the kind of crappy carpet you'd buy from some prick on Channel 9?

He was waiting for me by a potted plant. He said, "Well, Grace, you know why I came here."

I just looked at him.

"I've tried everything. I can't tell her. You've got to tell her."

Then, damned if he didn't say, "You're not going to *tell* her, are you?"

"If you want her to know, *fuck-eyes*, you're going to have to tell her yourself."

I went into the women's, and when I came out, he was gone.

It's not as if we didn't dance all afternoon until the band went home. It's not as if we didn't take a walk on the beach, with people looking at us like we were the king and queen of the senior prom.

It's not as though I wasn't even *nice*, you know?

Even that same night, when he took me back to the Georgian, escorting me past his neighbors, into the elevator which smelled of penicillin and perfume, and into his apartment.

He opened the doors to his balcony and I got yet another

view of the terrible ocean, and I thought: All right. You want to see if you can do it a few more times before you die.

He was happy, if they can even feel happy, if they even know what that means.

Why not?

If you keep your eyes closed, why not?

I was even nice then.

7

Sunday afternoon, April 26

I don't know why I should be surprised that it happened to me again. In fact, I'm not surprised. I tried to take control, to "show my mother a good time." It ended up the way it always does. If you're going to say *be specific*, don't say it! I'll say this—I don't know what a good time is, but whenever I even consider it, my mother knows all over again that I'm a fool. Because she knows there aren't any good times, or if there were, that they stopped in the thirties. All she knows how to do now is to laugh at people who are looking for them.

What if I wrote here that during those good times she always talks about, those times when she was still married to my father—when she *was* beautiful, she always connects her good times to being beautiful—one of her best good times was to switch me on the legs until her switch broke? Or that she would keep after me to do my long division until I'd cry, and then she'd switch me for crying? Or that I wouldn't make my bed right, and she'd switch me? Or, the worst thing, that she'd "talk" to me for hours about what a problem I was, and

I swear, I don't remember doing anything—I'd go out in the backyard sometimes and bang the screen door, but when you compare that to being an addict? Or a thief? What seems worse to you? Actually, maybe slamming the screen door is worse. But, I was going to say, the talks she used to give me were so frightening. Because—*please* don't read this to anybody—she'd move her eyeballs around when she was talking. She'd ask me those questions nobody's meant to answer. "Can you tell me why you did it? Why you did it?" And of course, I wouldn't know why I did it.

I feel very silly writing this. I guess I'm just a little upset. Nothing really happened except I took my mother to a seminar and she found a nice man. Why should I begrudge her that? The kids are out, and Ian is working, so I have a chance to catch up on my homework. (I'm doing very well in history, and I can really see that my French is getting better.) And my term paper in this class is coming along. So I guess I am keeping up.

Oh, my mother used to get after me for my homework. I know it was my fault. I can't imagine someone like you, for instance, if you had six pages of long division to do for arithmetic, filling in all the answers with zeros, and even working out the problems with zeros, and then hoping that nobody would notice.

All I know is, in that remake of *Invasion of the Body Snatchers*, when Donald Sutherland asks the girl if she can still do that funny thing with her eyes, and she does, it ruined the whole thing for me. I was relieved when the Body Snatchers took over. Everyone seems to overlook the one thing about the Body Snatchers. They may take away love and individuality, but I never knew anybody with too much love and individuality anyway. I kept thinking, if that woman married Donald Sutherland, and then if they had some kids and she rolled her eyes at them, made them *twitch* that way, that would be worse than the Body Snatchers, that wouldn't be human either. (And after the screening, that woman was even there. Ian introduced me to her. I couldn't say anything to her. Ian was disgusted with me, and I couldn't blame him.)

You asked us to write about our childhood when we couldn't think of anything else to write about. I feel funny doing it! I've been back in school long enough to see that even here, the kids are divided into two kinds, the kind that had a happy childhood—they are the cheerleaders and the football players, and just the plain kids who talk to each other in bunches after class—and the kids who had unhappy childhoods, and of course it still shows on them. They wear funny clothes, or the same clothes day after day, or they do things wrong, like cut their own hair, and it's different lengths on different sides.

The women in the Encore program are not supposed to have childhoods. I heard a woman just a little bit older than me introduce herself in class. I won't mind if you think of me as a grandmother, because I am one, she said. The teacher never called on her again.

The thing is, I can't get over it. I can't figure it out! Am I just making a big thing out of nothing? I can't believe that. Or was my childhood so different from anybody else's? Does anybody else besides me believe that if I do anything—fall in love, or have a broken heart, or hurt somebody, or pick up a deck of cards, or even eat avocado and crackers (a real favorite of my mother's)—that something will happen, that I will be (the only word I can think of), doomed?

I see all those normal? ordinary? people talking after class, and I can't believe that they feel the way I do.

I know that Ian, my husband, loves his parents. He doesn't make a big deal about it, he just does. Some afternoons he'll drop by his parents' apartment, just to see if they're okay. They won't even ask him to do it. And other times he will *really ask* me if I can't fix something with his mother's recipe. I can even say, I think I can really say, please don't laugh at this, that my children love me. If they do, it mainly comes from my not *doing* anything at all; just taking Davie to his karate lessons twice a week, and then putting his white jacket in the laundry without being asked. (Debbie doesn't like me all that much. I can't explain to her where I'm "coming from," because she wouldn't understand, even if she believed me. And if she did, she'd only think I was complaining, trying to get attention.)

I think this is a very bad-humored entry, and—I guess I already said why. I took my mother to a consciousness-raising seminar, about how to learn how to manage money and have a good time doing it. (She could use information like that, she doesn't have much money, and I know she can't count on much from Ian, he's very close with a dollar, except for his own family.) But naturally, she wouldn't listen, she only made fun, like she does of everything, everything! And then the last straw, as far as I'm concerned, she managed to meet a man, and run off with him before the seminar was four hours old! Can you believe that? It brought back a lot of things for me.

I might as well come out and say it. I guess I'm jealous. Because I've only been out with—I might as well say I've only been *with*—two men in my life. One of them is the man I think I've already mentioned in this journal. The other is Ian. My husband. My mother used to be beautiful. I never was. But I *can* say I've never jiggled my eyes at my children!

When I say "run off," naturally I don't mean exactly that. She was home before morning. And when her friend came by, he seemed very nice. But she managed to take everything I like and everything I do, and make it into nothing important again.

I'll only just say this. That when the kids around here, or the teachers, begin to talk about their vacations, all I do is begin to get scared. Because summer means fall. Fall means Halloween. Halloween means Thanksgiving. And Thanksgiving means Christmas, and those memories are . . . they are the worst days of my life.

I'm sorry. I'm not crazy. I'm not even neurotic. If I were to look like anybody, it would be the ordinary people in sweaters who talk outside of class, but I don't believe it.

You asked the class to write more about their own childhoods, to see how it might tie in with what we can give to the classroom, if we ever teach, or to the children we will come in contact with.

I don't know where to start. I don't know why you would want to read this. I was born in Beverly Hills. Ian likes that because, by accident, I got to be part of an aristocracy, but all it *really* was, was that our doctor worked out of that particular hospital.

I was an only child, until later. My father had been hit by the Depression. It's hard to know much about this, because my mother never talks about what it was really like, and my father has a hard time sticking to the truth. (I suppose everybody does.) My father worked in PR, I think, or advertising, or something else. But everyone talked about how he worked for the *Daily News*. I barely remember that paper, but I know it was part of a great Los Angeles tradition.

I grew up in a ramshackle part of town. I have a memory of the sun always shining, and pigeons everywhere. It really was almost the country. I was always climbing a tree in the backyard, and once, out on the lawn, I saw a snake.

I should say that my mother kept everything very clean. She worked hard all day. She was fond of saying, about a day, that *she'd never sat down*. Our neighborhood had little clean houses with patches of grass. On Sundays the men would drink beer. That was before television. There is a story that the way my father met my mother was, he came by somebody's house to get something, and there was this beautiful young girl, out on the front lawn in a pair of shorts, drinking beer, and that was my mother. (Another story is that my mother's sister stood him up, and there they were.)

We lived in a way that I think few people do today. My father went out and worked, my mother stayed home and cleaned house, and I went to school. I don't know exactly how they stood it. *I* have periods of awful boredom, but here I am taking courses again, and a couple of times I've let them have UCLA extension courses in my living room. Some of my friends are in dance class, or even learning to roller skate.

In those days, for my parents, there didn't seem to be those sorts of things. On summer nights we'd take a walk around the block. Once we had a friend—whose friend, I wonder? He got drunk, and took a beach umbrella and jumped off the garage with it. That was the most amazing thing I had ever seen in my life. During the war, I can barely remember, we had Sunday Dinners for Soldiers. Later on, when I saw the movie with John Hodiak and Anne Baxter, I realized I should have been twenty and *met* one of those soldiers. But I was only three.

My mother was a plain cook. Sponge cake with chocolate butter frosting. Why am I writing this? Who *cares!* But what I am trying to do, I think, is get some sort of "a handle" on two different things. (1) What it was really like then. The best I can do is remember the family of the sailor in *The Best Years of Our Lives.* Do you remember Homer? The boy with no arms? Sitting out in the backyard and talking about nothing? Except then you add hard-drinking newspapermen like Matt Weinstock and Gene Coughlin (and even now those names mean a hundred times more to me than Robert Redford or Paul Newman; Virginia Wright means more to me, for magic, than Barbra Streisand or even Gene Tierney). A lot of whiskey and a lot of card playing, and then my father's idea that there was *something else* out there, something that he wasn't getting. Maybe that's what it was like. (2) What became of it? I can never know whether it was "happy" or "unhappy," because it went by so fast. Everyone loses everything. My mother lost her mother when she was twelve. Our life was awful enough for my father to leave it when I was eleven, and good enough for my mother to keep on crying about it for the rest of her life. But all I remember are the irrelevant things, like my father building a brick barbecue in the backyard—a little one, and we'd have hot dogs. And he told my mother, "Your sister would make a big deal about this!" One of the few mean things he ever said. . . .

Once, in the old house, at night, my father and I were acting silly. It was a Sunday. We always wanted to go somewhere, but Mother thought it was too much trouble to "get dressed up." She thought she worked too hard. Maybe she did work too hard. My father wanted to go out for Mexican food. He was clowning around.

"Please, Grace, let's just go out for an *enchilale.*" (Instead of enchilada.) Every time he'd say it, I'd laugh. She was already dressed up, it seems to me, because I could hear her high heels on the linoleum. "Can't we go out for an enchilale!" Every time he'd say it, I'd laugh. My mother was very high-strung, even then. So, my father left. People do it all the time now, but then it was something.

My mother would say he took the "good times." I would say he took away the reason for things. If someone were to ask me, "What does that mean?" I'd have to say I don't know. Because it's still hard for me to see the reason for things.

Earlier this week, my mother made fun of my housekeeping. I had been helping Davie, who has a contest at school as to who can bring the most canned goods labels. The class that has the most labels gets an extra field trip. So, on Wednesday, because I didn't have any labels for him, I went into the cupboards and took off all the labels. Then Mother came in and pointed out that now I didn't know what was in the cans! Davie started to laugh, and I wanted to kill my mother. But she was absolutely right.

I used to be a terrible housekeeper. (I don't even think "housekeeping" is the right word. I didn't know how to "run a house.") After we bought this house, for two years, I kept thinking there were things that needed to be done. I took an exercise class instead. I had an extension class in philosophy taught in my living room every Tuesday morning. I found the wonderful gardener I think I've already told you about. I bought a rug for the living room that cost six thousand dollars. But still Ian would come home and say things like, "Garnet, I'm sorry, I can't live like this." And then, during the last section of the philosophy course, the teacher said, "It was so nice of you, Mrs. Evans, to let us have the course here when you've just moved in." But by then we'd been living here two and a half years. I looked around the living room, and all around the edges of that beautiful rug there were cardboard cartons that I still hadn't unpacked. I saw that in the dining room there wasn't even a table. Because I'd bought another beautiful rug for the dining room, and it looked so nice in there, with the trees outside the window, that I'd just put off buying a table.

And then I'd wonder sometimes why Ian wouldn't bring home people for dinner!

I finally had the sense to hire an interior decorator, and he said the rugs were perfect, I just hadn't gone far enough. So now the house is beautiful. And why can't my mother see that things could be a surprise? That it might be nice, if you were all getting along with each other, to go out in the kitchen and open a can, and see what kind of soup you were having for lunch?

I know what I'm doing is useful. Yesterday morning I went up by myself to the roof and sawed the big eucalyptus branches that scraped the shingles. I know I saved Ian money. But he's right when he says I can't take hold. I know this house should be air-conditioned, for instance. It's an old-fashioned house and it needs it. It already has central heating, so it would be practical! And it gets so hot and even smoggy in the summer! But then I hear the president talking about saving energy. Or Ian tells me I spend so much money on the house. So should I go ahead and do it? Last summer I spent time crying about it, and I still didn't decide. You hear so many things, you don't know what's true. I won't even tell you what it was like when we found the ground squirrel in the basement. Do you know they have super squirrels now, they eat pesticide and still go on living? And I hate to think that every ground squirrel I see is probably carrying the plague.

I suppose I should talk about what it was like when my father left. But everyone talks about that now, and everyone seems to think it is more or less okay. So what am I supposed to say, that it was *awful?* And that it was no one's fault, not his fault or her fault or my fault? Or that I have a brother who is an addict, and that's nobody's fault either? Did you see that special on television the other night about the decline of the family? (It's the kind of thing that Ian says is ruining the medium. He says if *Gunsmoke* ran fourteen years and *Barnaby Jones* ran all those years, why change the balance with a lot of things that pretend to be more than they are?)

The point of the show was that almost anything you could stick together could be a family. But there were places when I had to get up and leave the room. One family was a poor waitress who worked hard to raise her daughter. They were in awful shape. The mother was much nicer than mine (but of course, they were on television) and the girl was much sadder than me, but there was a picture of the two of them in a big double bed, all alone, watching television. They looked so awful. They looked like someone had beaten them up. And that's *now*, when things are supposed to be better.

You have only one friend in the world, and that is your mother. Mine hates the sight of me and always has. Once, when they put my brother in jail about seven years ago, the parole officer called me up. I tried to cover for him, and pretty soon the officer got snippy, I don't blame him. But he said finally, "Why do you think he would do such a thing?" Things like dealing, stealing, pushing drugs, getting beat up, landing in jail? I got fed up with the questions finally and said, "Well, his mother hates his guts and she hates mine too, what do you think of that!" And the parole officer finally hung up.

You say to be specific and stick to the facts. I was born in Beverly Hills, and grew up in Highland Park. My parents divorced. My mother and I lived alone for eight years while she worked to support me. My mother remarried—a man I never knew very well, and didn't like very much. Can I just say here, he burned my baby pictures? My mother had another baby, but before it—my brother—was a year old, I'd left home. (We'd moved to Coalinga by then, and I hated it.) I graduated from high school when I was seventeen, worked and went to junior college here in LA for two years. Then I married my husband, Ian Evans. We have been married nineteen years. My husband has worked for years very successfully in television, but he wants very much to go into feature films. We have two children, Davie and Debbie. Not much, is it?

Those are some reasons I will never get a divorce, never, never, never. Those nights my mother would go out on dates and leave me alone, and never get a sitter, because she couldn't afford it. I would be so scared, so scared when I was alone, that I'd cry from it. Once I was so scared to go down the hall to the bathroom that I wet the bed.

But finally my mother got a steady boyfriend, which is another reason I'll never get a divorce. (Where do these men come from, after you get a divorce?) You don't see them if you're single or married. I know I've never yet met another man in my life like Allan. But sometimes, when I go down to the student union to have coffee by myself, I can spot them, I think I spot them in the cafeteria, by themselves, having lunch. They're pale, usually, and have sandy hair and freckles and chinos and nylon windbreakers. They'd never go back to their high-school reunion because no one remembers their names. They're like a bunch of sad coyotes, waiting for the pretty girls (and the plain girls!) to go through their first marriage, so they'll be so beaten up, that they, the girls, will finally have to go out with them—these men.

Some women, and men, talk about the money, but those are the reasons I'll never get divorced.

Why am I writing this, when I have a good life now? I might say the whole reason for my life now is to cancel out the one I grew up with. But even now, when I look at the living room after the decorator got done with it, or at the dining room, now that we really have one, I remember, right after my mother was divorced, that a "career girl" came to live with us, a woman about thirty-five years old, and she gave a party once. I was so thrilled, so excited, because no one had been around our house for, it seemed like, years. This woman bought cartons of Ritz crackers, and jars of

Kraft cheese spread (are *you* old enough to remember those cheese spreads?). She made a very big thing out of it, and three women came. Afterward there were all those cheese jars, with knives in them.

So no wonder women take up with those men like Allan.

What I'm trying to say is, my mother was a fiend. So what do you do in the world if you know there are fiends in it? Ian always makes fun of me—he says people used to chase him home from school because he was Jewish, and it wasn't any big deal, that he always had to carry a couple of half-bricks in his schoolbag. I always say that at least when he got home, his mother let him in! But then he says I'm exaggerating.

My mother hated that Allan. She hated him, like she hated me. Well, what I mean is, she hated everybody! Now, how am I going to turn this in? How am I going to expect a decent grade on this?

After my mother had been dating that poor man for about five years, she decided she was going to like another man. Naturally the other man was drunk and mean and dumb. (As if, if it couldn't be my father, she wasn't going to let life give her anything good.) She decided to like this other man. She started giggling again! For the first time in eight years. She sent him a valentine. (To the bar where he drank, and he got it, and he knew who it was from.)

One night my mother got dressed and said she was going out. I asked her where. She said it was none of my business. For two solid years, every night of his dumb life, that Allan had come over and sat on our couch and corrected his papers, or else taken us out to restaurants where the dinners were so big I couldn't eat them and then Mother would get furious at me. (Even now, I wonder, my God. Hadn't she ever heard of a doggie bag?)

Every night of his life he'd come over.

So tonight like every other day of *his* life, he came over. But my mother wasn't there. She'd left me to tell him. What was I supposed to tell him? I told him my mother wasn't home, and that he should go away. Then I went to bed.

About midnight I heard someone at the back door. All those other times alone, I'd been scared, but this time I wasn't scared. I went to the kitchen door, and there was Allan, trying to break the lock. I think it was the first time I'd ever looked at him as anything more than something like that television program *The Incredible Hulk*. Just the hulk who sat on the couch. But through the screen door there was a lot of moonlight, and there he was. He was in worse shape than I was. "Oh, Allan, I said, go home."

I went back to sleep, and it seemed like only a few minutes later that my mother waked me up by sitting on the bed. I could see her in the moonlight, and she was smiling so sweetly. She said, "Garnet, wake up! Allan's almost killed Dick with a crowbar. He hid under the stairs of the apartment and tried to kill him!"

I know you won't believe me when I say I haven't seen her smile so happily since.

The next day Allan called me up to say good-bye.

By this time Dick had already moved into the apartment with a lot of bandages around his awful head. While Allan was talking, I asked him, "Do you want to speak to my mother?" Dick sat up on the couch like a mummy in his bandages, and my mother gave me one of her famous looks. So I said good-bye to him and that afternoon he swam out into the Los Angeles River—it was raining, did I say that?—and got counted as a flood statistic for that year.

Needless to say, we didn't talk about it, or him, again.

What goes without saying in all this, is that my mother was very beautiful. My mother believes the world is ruled by beauty. She may be right. I have pictures in my mind, my mother as a young woman, and extraordinarily beautiful, not like Ian's starlets, but as something red and glowing, with long, curled hair. A big, powerful, mean customer! But she is only five-three. She would dress up in V-shaped gabardine three-piece suits and march off to jury duty, or go down to the Traveler's Aid to help the soldiers. She'd go play golf. She'd argue with the butcher for meat. She'd try to teach me to ride the bicycle. All the time her hair would be cleaned and curled. Sometimes when she stayed home to do the wash she wouldn't look good, but when we'd take the 5 car downtown to have lunch with my father, she was a beautiful woman.

If you've noticed me in class, you might put me down as "beautiful"; everything that money can buy helps me. Good jewelry, good haircuts, silk shirts. Without them I'd be plain, I think. But my mother is *beautiful!* And it puzzles my mother, to this day, it drives her crazy, how it could have happened that I turned out as I did.

I look back to when I was a little girl. There was a family there, something like they have on network specials. My father sometimes did layout work at home. The smell of rubber cement, the clear look of it and the newsprint did something beautiful to the kitchen table. I suppose we were poor. My father once opened up the funny papers in church. What I'm saying is, and I'm sure you get this in journals from time to time, perhaps from older students, the whole thing was a lie.

So when I look outside at the sprinklers, or see Leticia mopping in the kitchen, or open the cupboards and see all those *CANS!* Well, what in the world do Davie and Debbie think? I have never switched them. Do they look at the kumquat trees out in the side yard, with the Mexican tiles set into the garden wall, and do they—I don't know how to put this—do they *sink into the time* until they don't know where they are, and *that's a family?* Do they feel safe enough? Even though I'm not very beautiful?

After a while, my mother remarried. The man whom Allan almost murdered with a crowbar, poor Dick. (You can imagine the mean fun my girlfriends and I made of that name.) Dick wore ribbed undershirts. He had ingrown hairs in his neck. I look at Ian now, so clean, and he can be so kind. He wears his hair in Aaron Spellings bangs (yes, I know, I should never let him see this entry), but I look at his clean, shaped brown hair and his perfect cashmeres, and the way he keeps himself in shape, and sometimes I really do think, *is that a man*, the same as that person my mother married? They must be mutually exclusive.

When I think of a color for my stepfather, I think of sowbug gray. Pocked and damp. With little narrow, soggy feet. What if I said he had a damp hole in his head, and that was his mouth? Because that's what he had. He had no books. He had no pictures. He was poor, and ugly, and had no style. He is what you can see now, down at the student union, another horrible coyote, waiting for a disaster.

I know that when he and my mother and I lived together, first in Los Angeles, and then in Coalinga—so that he could be close to his work—the sun didn't come out for several years. We lived in a duplex, a gray stucco duplex in the old part of town, with central heating that you stood on to get dressed in the morning, and all over the house was a smell, a smell of his gray suits that were too old.

He'd told my mother that he was in oil, but the oil business has many bad jobs, and he had one of them.

The main smell came from a thing I can't describe, a wooden thing, a contraption for hanging clothes, wet clothes, *in the house*. If I never washed again, I'd never have one.

Even the backyard of that duplex was a nightmare. (If I'd been my mother, I would have gotten therapy, I would have gotten help!) A gray incinerator, where we still burned the day's trash. A clothesline, a circular clothesline identical to the one in the yard next door. Sad old grass, and a poinsettia plant growing in the dry packed ground along the driveway. The sun never came out, and with a new baby my mother had to wash diapers, and training pants, and Dick's old socks. A couple of hundred yards away, the oil wells started. They never went away and they never shut up.

My mother forgot how to cook. We had canned biscuits. We had Mallomars. Every Saturday night my mother and poor Dick would buy steak and eat it on Catalina pottery plates with Durkee's dressing, while I stayed in my room, and the new baby lived in the dark in *their* bedroom. (I don't want you to think I'm fool enough to think the baby was having a good time, because they had awful fights in there.)

What I am trying to say, for the journal, for the course, is that sometimes, it seems to me, it isn't the people in the ghetto that are having the bad times, or the movie stars you read about that go out from overdoses. I am trying to say, me, us, them. Right here in West Hollywood or Inglewood or Eagle Rock or Coalinga, in one of those streets full of duplexes and two-story apartment houses, with lawns that start right up against the house, and go flat for a while and then *slope* that sickening one and a half feet down to the sidewalk, and all you see for miles and miles are trash cans and driveways and old poinsettia plants. Places with awful meals and laundry that never dries, do you understand? Places right in the center of Los Angeles, where the air is nothing but poison.

I'm not as stupid as I seem. I haven't told you about my children, and what I think of them. I haven't said anything about my husband, except that he's smart, and clean. I haven't said much about myself, except that I worry about my housekeeping, and a little about my intelligence. And aren't those proper worries? Aren't those what we're supposed to worry about? Professor?

No, I have written my journal, and been reserved enough. I *am* a little depressed! I may as well admit it. But! I have nothing to complain about. I want to be of some help in the world. Ian, my husband, doesn't approve, but he isn't really against it, either. I think he'd like me to be a starlet, but if that was really what he wanted, he could have married one. I'm too old now to go into Bullock's Westwood and buy mascara and those brushes and put blue all over my eyes. But I'm not afraid to talk to Jane, especially since she got her eye lift. I know I won't disgrace myself by saying anything too politically dumb. I can have the Fadimans over for dinner, and the dinner will even be good. I know the right caterer for our exact social class, and I'm in touch enough to know about the new Chinese restaurant on North Broadway. (Not what to order, I leave that to Ian.)

So I'm all right.

To hell with the rest of it! To hell with that darling actor who's an old guy now. Or those soup cans I guess I'm going to be stuck with forever unless there's an earthquake or a war.

But I might just as well tell you why I'm back in school, and it's not because I'm almost forty. I was never very beautiful. I had those big bones and liked to play volleyball. Everyone in high school decided I was a nice girl and had a good heart. They thought I must *know* something.

In high school, I had a girlfriend who was pregnant. I told her to go ahead and have the baby, *naturally*. There was a girl in a restaurant where I worked, I told her to go ahead and get married to this short-order cook. I helped Ian with his term papers in school and never took credit for them. I gave a lot of advice. My mother didn't like it, of course, but there was something wonderful in my position for a while, when I was barely seventeen, after I had left home and come back to LA. To be "kicked out," to "run away," all that—you have a wonderful freedom then.

There is a moment, if you are making an Orange Julius in the May Company basement downtown, if you are wearing one of two skirts you own and both those skirts are clean, if the people in the school where you go ask if you're planning to become a nun, if you're making an Orange Julius, and over in the rug department the rugs are rolled up and the poor guys are over there trying to sell them to somebody! But all you have to do is put the powder in with the ice and douse in some orange juice, and there's a family of poor Mexicans and all you have to do is line up the Orange Julius! And they drink it, and then you go home. Believe me, even if it's a five-dollar-a-week furnished room, and you use cardboard boxes tipped on their side for bookcases because you can't afford bricks and boards, and you never even heard of bricks and boards yet! You go home, and you're free. You're earning your own money, and you're in a state of grace, if I could use that word, because you're not hurting anybody, and nobody's hurting you.

Sometimes my mother, beautiful and mean, would come visiting down to Los Angeles. She'd come to the May Company basement and order a couple of Orange Juliuses, one for her and one for my little brother! I'd shiver and she'd laugh, and the other kids from behind the counter would say, oh, kid, she seems *nice*, and there was nothing I could say, but watch her, and the little kid, stand on the escalator going back up to the light, and all the stuff they had up there on the main floor.

Why don't I *get* to it?

Even when I was living in a furnished room, even when I was safe in LA, there would be Easter vacation, there'd be Thanksgiving. Even after I met Ian, there would be Christmas. Or even—there would be those long weekends, and my room would be clean and my laundry done.

There was no Highway 5 then, so I'd take the bus up 101. Or, if there was plenty of time, I'd go up Highway 1 along the ocean to see my mother.

I'd transfer and take the bus, past oil wells, into the town of Coalinga. They wouldn't meet me, I'd walk. They lived in a better house then.

A house on a street, a driveway, a garage. *He's* in there somewhere. Your mother answers the door and the shades are drawn, the whole place smells of cigarette smoke, there's a white cloth on the table. She laughs, she looks ashamed of herself. She'd say, "I don't know what's getting *into* me, I was hanging out the wash yesterday and Sandy dragged the sheets out on the grass. I got so mad, I hit him a few times, you know what he did then, ha-ha? He hid under the bed, the poor little thing, and he wouldn't come out for the longest time!" Or she'd say, "Dick *says* he's getting off hard liquor, you know what that means? That means a quart of vodka a day instead of a quart of bourbon!" Or she'd say—with that tone of voice, do you know what I mean?—she'd jiggle her eyes and say something so hopeless. "*No matter what I do, no matter what I do, there will never be a day when I don't have to get up and fix breakfast for him! And get the kid off to school!*"

I say, "*I* could come up here, Mother! I could come out here for as much as a week. I could do some of the work, and you could . . . *rest*, you know?" But she looks at me with a terrible look. "No," she says, "you couldn't, and it doesn't matter. It doesn't matter, it doesn't matter! Because it doesn't matter! Because no matter what happened, I'd know that I'd have to go back to doing it all over again!" The tears are streaming down her face, and she looks like she'd bite if you got too close to her. "*I have to do it forever!*"

A few years later when I was up there, I think I was married by then, Sandy was in the living room watching Soupy Sales. My mother said to Sandy, "You make me sick!" So you could see why Sandy wanted to run away. Well, I had done it! He was only a year younger than I had been when he decided to do it. I gave him good advice! I said *do it!* It *can't* be worse than what you have at home.

But he was beautiful. And there was no *way* he was going to live in a furnished room with cardboard boxes full of books for company.

Sandy came down to LA and he found his furnished room. It was in West Hollywood; he did well from the start. I was too dumb to ask where he got his money. He hung around the house a lot, but Ian was working sixteen hours a day then as a story editor, and the kids were small.

My mother was making a perfect fool of herself, calling on the phone long distance and saying, "What's wrong with Sandy, I know he's on *top!*" Ian and I were smoking by then, being sophisticated and listening to the Stones. Then one afternoon my brother sat on my couch and told me he shot acid into his foot. When I looked at him, all I could see was poor Dick, so when Sandy said, "I am not what I was," what could I do? I didn't even know what he was. When there were harder drugs, I agonized about whether to tell Mother. Finally I did, and she looked at me with her look.

"Didn't you even know *that?* Don't you ever know *anything?*"

No, I don’t, I mean it, I really don’t, which is why I’m back at school. So that, don’t think I’m a fool, the next time I give advice, at least

Forget it.

It’s late in the afternoon, and I haven’t done my laps.

8

I wouldn't tell him when he asked me what was wrong. I wouldn't tell him what was wrong, why should *I* tell him what was wrong? *He* knew well enough. If it wasn't him doing it, he *could* have been doing it, you can't tell *me* he'd been married to that cluck of a wife for thirty years with*out* doing it!

So even though he asked me for three solid hours, I wouldn't tell him. Why should *I* tell *him?*

Even though he asked me, "What's wrong, Grace?"

Even though he said, "We were having such fun, Grace."

Or, "Is it something I did, Grace?"

Or, "Do you have a headache . . . dear?"

When I heard that word, "dear," I *twitched.* How could he? Isn't it bad enough what they do, without them pretending to be nice about it? That to me is the real insult, Pearl. I know they think we'll buy anything, any crap they invent. I admit, I've bought bushels of it in my life, but that last little kicker, that they invented crap *and* they expect us to like it, that's the last little hunk I just can't swallow.

So I sat. I couldn't dance anymore.

They went on from three to six exactly, and then they vanished—all those old geezers suddenly began to limp out the door. Some of them went back to the bar, but most of them drove home, down the driveway in a string of elderly Cadillacs, all polished to hell.

It should have been fun, Pearl!

But it wasn't any fun, you can't have any fun!

They won't let you have any fun.

I didn't talk to him, except to tap my glass every half-hour or so for another drink.

But you know? He didn't get mad, the poor simp.

He didn't shrug or sigh or say,

"Well, if that's the way you feel about it,"

Or, "If you're going to be *that* way,"

Or even, "Well, I've had it! I've had it with your headaches and your tantrums!"

Once, when he said, "Was it the way I danced? I told you I didn't dance very well," I almost told him.

But I was so mad, Pearl, so sad. I could have knocked his fucking block off.

It made me sick. You were lucky never to have children, Pearl, I mean it. Because suppose you have sons? Suppose they grow up? You know what they *are*, you know what they do. You know what they do to the world. But suppose you have daughters? You raise them to suffer and die. And we'd been dancing about it. My head ached. I felt like I was going to throw up.

The sun was going down, I looked at the ocean and thought: I'm glad *I* don't live near the ocean. Think of the junk in it, think of the sharks and the kelp and the jellyfish, the worms, the snakes. At least you know where you *are* by the oilwells.

Ed said, "Well, it's getting dark." He gave a sigh. "I guess I'd better be taking you home."

I couldn't face it. I couldn't face going back there. So I told him.

First he said I was mistaken.

Then he knew I wasn't. I think he felt worse about it than I did.

I started to get mad at him, I said, "And you don't know

anything about that sort of thing, right? Oh, no, of *course* you don't. . . ."

But I saw from his face he *didn't* know anything about it!

But after I'd told him, of course, there was one more person in the world who knew.

Finally he said what really got to me. "Oh, I feel terrible about this. I don't know them, of course, but they seemed so nice. This just makes you lose some of your faith in the world."

"You can say that again," I said, but I began to cheer up. Because—the hell with the rest of them—*I* was going to be rescued. And there is something *to* that, you know?

When I was all alone in that apartment I was sharing with my sister, no more than seventeen, an *orphan*, Pearl, and Fran came over for a date with her, only she was out with somebody else, *naturally*, and I opened the door to Fran in the hall, in that great-looking striped shirt and his yellow sleeveless sweater. He asked for my sister, and I said, "She isn't here," but what I really said with my whole body is: I'm alone here, I'm all alone here, don't you see it, my parents are dead and I'm the only one left! And he said, "Ah, would you, if you're not too young that is, would *you* like to, ah, take a ride and maybe have a beer?"

Or before that, the cute guy in high school, driving up the gravel in front of our house, and he comes to the door with this crazy bulge in his pants, and it's *olives*, Pearl! Because he knows I love olives and we're too poor to afford them.

Or years later, after Fran had gone, down in the Help Me Bar, and the only road ahead is an abyss! Sitting in the back of that place, which—you know it, Pearl—was located in the exact center of Nowhere. Sitting with a career girl of forty whose name I forget. And up comes this pale little guy who's obviously taking his life in his hands doing this, and he says, sweat breaking out over the freckles over his upper lip, "Um, can I buy you a drink? If you're not busy, that is?" And that takes care of the next five years.

Or—in another bar, maybe that's what went *wrong*, Pearl—that wiggy, handsome face, and by the time I'm bored to death with Allan, and this heavy-lidded guy whispers, "If I were a gopher, I'd go for you!"

They save you. They give it to you so they can take it away. At least, I see how it works.

Congratulations, Grace. Saved by an idiot, but saved by the bell. Believe me, I didn't know I still had it in me.

He asked me if I wouldn't eat a little something, and I said I thought I could eat a sandwich. Maybe just a chicken sandwich. We staggered just a little as we went into the dining room, but we got there. We didn't talk much. I guess I was letting the situation more or less sink in. And I guess he was too.

After dinner, like I told you, we took a walk in front of the hotel and watched the moonlight on the ocean. Don't get me wrong! It wasn't romance! I could almost *feel the air* closing down over me, like a big fur coat with safety locks.

Poor fool, he was walking until he felt sober enough to drive. Or, God, who knows. Was he apologizing to his wife?

He made a mistake taking me back to his place, we should have stayed in Santa Barbara, but they always want to show you their *place*, right? It would have been a mistake anyway; we were too old for it. But I can remember being too young for it, and too fat for it, too thin for it, too pregnant for it, too sick for it, too mad for it, too bored for it, too sad for it. I can only remember about twenty times in sixty years when I've been *for* it, and as I remember, those were the worst mistakes of all. Sex is the *worm*, Pearl. (As if you didn't know.)

Anyway, it's a small price to pay.

Next morning, he bounded out of bed, ran over to the French doors, opened them wide, did some deep breathing. "Look at those trees, Grace! Look at that ocean! I tell you, we really *do* live in God's country!"

But I could only see the edge of a palm tree, some sky, no ocean at all. I could see his skinny shivering butt in his thin little pajamas. He kept *talking* to me while he was looking out of the window, I caught about one word in three. He was shivering away.

All of a sudden he said, "Just one minute, excuse me, Grace." He belted across the room and into the bathroom, where he started flushing the toilet like mad, but of course I could hear it all anyway.

He came out all steamy and wild-eyed and fully dressed.

The poor guy.

Oh, Pearl! *What have we come to!* Going down in that elevator with two women in walkers old enough to be dead already. I thought of what Fran and I used to say to each other when we'd see some awful creep back in the Depression: *There I go in ten years!* I was going to nudge Ed and say it, except we didn't have to wait. We were there already.

He took me to the International House of Pancakes. I saw our reflection as we stood in front of the glass doors. Nice old folks.

He had soft-boiled eggs. What can I tell you? I played with a piece of toast.

He was happy, Pearl. He kept grinning. Did he wear dentures? His teeth were awfully good. Who did his shirts? They looked great. I'd opened his closet while he was shitting away in the other room, and there were eleven shirts, all perfectly ironed, no laundry tags. But his apartment smelled old.

"We have the whole day ahead of us."

I looked at him and smiled. The restaurant was hot and smoky. It was making me sick.

"All the time in the world, dear."

There wasn't one thing wrong with him.

"Don't you think you ought to call . . . your daughter, though? Grace?"

"I don't think so."

"Poor kid. It's rotten luck for you."

"Do you think we could get some fresh air?" Because I couldn't breathe, I was going to faint, I was going to throw up.

"Of course."

We walked along the pier for a while, I felt better. He held my hand, or tried to. He was so tall and skinny that I felt like Spanky McFarland, the queen of short and fat. So I yanked my hand out of his.

Then he looked so sad I thought: *Why not?* What *else* is my hand doing? Why should I be picky?

And *then* he looked like he was in seventh heaven. Pearl, doesn't it ever seem like a *crock* to you?

"I thought, dear, that . . . since we have the whole day to spend together, that . . ."

A whole day. And after that and after that. Whole days.

"Well, first of all, what would you like to do?"

I shook my head and smiled at him. I'd only said maybe fifty words so far this morning. But once you get them started, you don't have to say anything for five years or so. (And if only you didn't have to listen!)

"If there's nothing you really want to do, we *might*, we might go and spend the afternoon with my sister."

Give me a break!

"Because, Grace, she means more to me than anyone in the world."

I didn't say anything.

"I know it sounds a little dull, but she's stood by me for a long time. I'd like her to know that . . . I've gotten lucky."

The poor guy. I think he had to go to the bathroom again, he was jittering around the sidewalk. We were off the pier by now, back up on the strand, walking along cliffs, looking at the ocean. It was a little colder than I would have liked, I was getting an earache. *He* was in heaven.

"So, is it all right, then?"

I just looked at him.

"That we go down to see Edith?"

I nodded and smiled. I needed a drink in the worst way, but it was only ten-thirty in the morning.

"Great!"

Then he peeled into a Standard station. I was right.

But it was too early to visit his sister. It was too early to do anything. And it was too cold to go back out on the pier, and neither one of us mentioned going back to his room.

So we went for another drive. He was mad for his car, believe me.

You could see he thought it was time well spent. Because he was on his first day of an *affair*. And we were getting to know each other.

You know how *that* is! He never stopped talking. I mean, he never stopped talking. We drove inland this time, on residential streets past pretty houses, while he said, "See this gem? Have I told you about it?"

I nodded my head yes.

"Madeleine gave me a . . . gemstone processor. It was one of the most thoughtful gifts I ever received. Because you not only have the finished product, but you are able to stay with this one aspect of nature . . . this . . . *rock*, through an entire process. From the earth—I usually look for fossils and rocks up there in Old Topanga Canyon—to the washing and the sorting. After you put them into the machine, it turns day and night. You *hear* it, the actual polishing. You can stop the machine, reach your hand into that cage, and pull out something. It isn't a precious stone yet, it isn't even valuable, but it isn't a rock, either. You are *making* something from the most unpromising beginnings. It's a wonderful experience, Grace.

"Hiking," he told me, "are you interested in hiking?" He didn't wait for an answer. "It's the most wonderful, calming experience. You get up in the morning—don't worry, I wouldn't take you far!—you can stay at a motel, say, at the bottom of Angeles Crest, then you drive up, get out of the car and *walk* for four hours. I'll tell you the best part about it. When you're above the smog. To be moving around up there, in the clean stuff, it's wonderful."

The mountains reminded him to be serious. We couldn't rule out a worldwide catastrophe, no thinking person could, so he was proud to say that from the very beginning he'd been conscientious about instructing his sons in the art of survival. He didn't believe in shooting your fellowman, but shooting a *bear* to live on, or even a squirrel or a dove, well, that was a different thing, and if his sons were lucky enough to make it through the first part, and if they could make it to the Rockies—the *far* side of the Rockies—he was reasonably sure they could make it. Because he'd spent weeks with them in the summer and winter, camping out.

He was too happy to go on with that line of thinking for long. He just wanted me to know he'd been a good father.

"You know what's fun to do, what we could do sometime? It's something I've always wanted to do. And don't tell me it's corny, Grace! Those television marathons. You know, where they raise thousands and thousands of dollars in just a few hours, and they have those banks of people answering the phone? I've always thought it would be fun to do! I've phoned *in* pledges, but I've always thought it would be fun to be the person on the phone. You'd be part of something bigger than yourself, don't laugh, Grace."

I wasn't laughing. Believe me.

"How about photography?"

I tuned out for that one totally, and I guess he noticed, because after about a hundred hours of developer and his own darkroom and how he'd love to take a picture of me and Garnet and the grandchildren, he started asking.

"Are you hungry?"

"Would you like to . . . freshen up?"

"Would you like a drink before we get there?"

But I had enough sense to know it wouldn't be the smartest thing in the world to go rolling into his sister's house reeking of Four Roses.

So I shook my head *no*.

Driving east on Santa Monica Boulevard had taken us dangerously close to Brentwood. He noticed, just in time, at least I think he did. At Barrington he turned right and doubled back to the coast. But he avoided San Vicente and the runners and Garnet's neighborhood. He stuck to Wilshire. There was hardly any traffic. It was beginning to warm up. You could tell he thought it was a beautiful day.

"Skiing," he said. "Now, there's something I haven't done in years. How about you . . . dear?"

I had a *picture*, Pearl, of Fran up on skis in his thin little sleeveless sweater and two dollars in his checking account and a head full of dumb *ideas!* I had a picture of Allan stuck at the top with a class full of English papers doubled up in his scrabbly hand. Or, God help the poor bastard, Dick drunk as an owl, up on skis and pointed straight down. I also thought of my mother dying with nothing to eat in the house but toast.

"Not in years," I said.

About eleven blocks from the coast he turned north off Wilshire and began to slow down. I got a sinking feeling.

"Listen!" he said. "How could I have been so absent-minded? I *know* what we can do! We can travel! Do you like to travel? Now, don't *laugh* at me, Grace. It's not like skiing. Lots of people our age go. We could go anywhere."

He pulled up in front of a house. It had trees all around it, and *pansies* in line across the front lawn. We were there. But before we went in, he took my hand. "I know I've been talking a lot," he said. "It's just that I want so much for us. I feel so lucky. I almost feel like I don't have a right to be so lucky."

He leaned over to kiss me, but I said, "Don't you think they'll be looking out the windows to see who you're bringing?" And he jumped back like he was stung. Then he grinned.

"You're right," he said, and he got out of the car and sprinted around in front to let me out.

But that's when I said, "Ed! Don't you think we ought to have *called* first? Don't you think it's a little early to be meeting your sister? Don't you think we ought to call *Garnet* up and at least tell her where I am? Don't you think we ought to get to *know* each other better?"

He stood between me and the house, in a quandary.

"Ed," I said. "It's barely noon yet. You know what we could do? We could go to the *races*. Couldn't we? Aren't we close to Hollywood Park? Couldn't we do that? Wouldn't that be fun?"

He wavered.

"Listen," I said. "Couldn't we just be together for a while?"

So we drove to a phone booth and called Garnet. I couldn't tell what she thought. And of course I went back to the house later, Pearl, but I stayed out of their way.

And I took Ed to the races. He won eighty-three dollars on a two-dollar bet. I picked the horse out for him. And can you believe it? The next day we went to a tennis match. And we got to be regulars at the Bellevue Bar. He beat me at ski ball down on the pier. We put in our time in his apartment and at one point in that week he looked over at me and grinned. "You know what, Grace? You could say it's like riding a bike. It *does* come back to you." He was right, too.

So it wasn't until the day after Garnet found out—I think it was right after May Day—that we managed to check out his sister. (By then, I didn't have the heart for the races.)

We walked up one of those perfect walks, sixteen bricks across in a zigzag pattern. Rosebushes trimmed into little trees. A lawn as green as Astro Turf. Windows so clean that they reflected the *outside*, so when you looked at them you saw clouds, and the car we came in, and the house across the street. And inside, not so clearly, you could see about a hundred yards of frilly curtains. Do I have to *tell* you, the curtain twitched?

Ed had a hold of my elbow, I don't know what in Christ he thought he was going to *do* with it, his hand had my elbow with his four fingers straight *up*. I tried to jerk it away from him, but every time I did, there'd be those four fingers again. And there we were at the door.

Chimes, Pearl. Garnet says one of Ian's friends is the doorbell king of California, that every time a doorbell rings that guy gets a little bit richer. He must have made a fortune off these people.

The door opened. There was a woman our age, and a husband behind her, and I could have been on Mars.

"Edith. Stan. Here she is. Isn't she a beauty? Grace, my sister, Edith, and her husband, Stan."

Stan came out from behind his wife and gave me a hug. Edith managed to control herself. She looked at me, opened her mouth and said, "Would you like to wash your hands?"

I said no, *no thank you.*

It got so bad for a second with the four of us looking at each other that Stan finally had to nudge his wife. "*Well*, aren't you going to let them in?"

She did, but she wasn't hot about it.

I'll tell you the kind of place it was. You *know* the kind of place it was! It had a grand piano in the living room, and a thick beige carpet. It was *clean.* It had family photographs in silver frames. Even supposing we could afford the frames, who do you imagine we'd put in them? Garnet, in her waitress uniform? Sandy in a *lineup?* Fran, walking *away*—you'd just see his back? Dick, framed artistically in puke? Allan, nibbled by the fishes? My mother . . .

It wasn't very funny.

Edith was nervous. She asked us to sit down. We did. It was a beige brocade couch. They sat in two chairs opposite us. Ed was grinning like a fool.

"What lovely roses," I said.

(That's because there was a big bouquet of floppy pink and orange roses in a sterling-silver bowl on the table. And between the bowl and the table, an ironed doily.)

"Stan raises roses," Edith said.

"Edith does the vegetables," Stan said.

"Oh, *Stan!* Don't make me sound like . . ."

"Do you know where I met Grace?" Ed said. "I met her at one of those kooky Hollywood seminars *you're* always saying I shouldn't go to!"

"My daughter dragged me," I said.

"I'm glad she did," Ed said.

Jesus Christ.

Edith said, "We'll have lunch in a few minutes."

"A soufflé," Stan said to his brother-in-law. "She's worried too. You know what happened the last time Edith did a soufflé?"

She looked like she wanted to kill him, but she was too refined.

"It's the eggs," she said to Ed. "He thinks that everything should be the same as it used to be, he doesn't realize we're working with cold-storage eggs."

Stan pulled his chair up closer to me. When he did it, I could see the two dents dug into the carpet by months and years of that same chair stuck into that same carpet. "I was raised on a farm," he told me, "and I think I would have stayed there all my life if it hadn't been for this *woman* here. I can tell *you*, *she* changed my life."

Ed was talking to Edith. You could see they liked each other.

Stan devoted himself to me. "I had always intended to be a farmer, and I'm sure I'd still be there now, except my father made the mistake of sending me away to college. That Edith! She'd lived abroad, she owned a roadster. I guess you'd be too young to remember that!"

(I saw Edith give him another look. Because she and I were the exact same age, of course.)

I smiled. I was trying to hear what Ed was saying to his sister. He was telling about me, that I was visiting my married daughter who lived in Brentwood. (Only he lied and said Bel Air.) Do the gods *laugh*, Pearl? Does the god of tuberculosis and whiskey and the Great Depression ever have a good laugh for himself?

A muffled *ding* came from out of the kitchen. Edith jumped like she was shot.

"Don't open the oven door in a hurry," Stan told her. "Remember what happened last time. Look at it first. Turn on the light in there and look through the door."

Mind your own business, asshole! is what I would have said to him, but she just disappeared into the kitchen.

As she left—and I *mean*, she was about to float into thin air—I said, "Is there any—?"

"No!" she said. "No, there's *nothing to do!* I'll be just a minute. There's . . ."

Then she was behind the swinging door. I looked into the dining room. More flowers on the table. Napkins in *rings*. I looked the other way, out onto the street. An old lady drove by in slow motion, riding one of those trikes. That's about the only thing Coalinga and this part of Santa Monica have in common.

"Still working her as hard as ever," Ed said to his brother-in-law.

"Harder! We drove down to El Centro last week. The peaches are already in down there. She worked three days putting them up. I kept some of them out for leather. I've been working on a new kind. . . ."

"Stan and Edith camp a lot," Ed said to me. "They make . . ."

I stopped listening. Just thinking, you know. What *our* families would have done with some of this—a brother and sister who liked each other *too much!* And a husband too chintzy to buy his own canned goods.

We went in to lunch. The soufflé was soft and puffy. There was watercress salad, one bottle of wine, and something about the way it sat there in lonely splendor, you knew it was the only bottle we were going to get. We sat down. And I do have to tell you that their table was carved, and had this border hanging down from it, so you couldn't cross your legs? They'd put in forty years of marriage, three meals a day, and never even got to cross their *legs?*

"Ed says you came from up north," Edith said.

Now that the lunch was safely out, she could let down just a little. Poor kid. I could remember the feeling, actually.

I told her I was a secretary to the Judge, while Stan and Ed talked about the recent basketball playoffs, the Dodgers in spring training, and the world situation. From their point of view, not one of those three things looked good.

I managed to give the impression that I'd had only one husband and that he'd died. (Well, one of them did!) And that my daughter was married, and my son was working. I didn't say working at what.

"I have a general secondary," Ed's sister told me. "And during the war, when Stan was in the Air Force, I substituted for a while. Well," she said to his disapproving look, "you said yourself there wasn't anything else to do! We were living in a garage then, can you believe it? That's how bad the housing shortage was. And *I* helped put together our down payment!"

"We could—"

"Come on, Stan," Ed told his brother-in-law. "Everyone knows my sister didn't have to work!"

"How about jury duty," I asked her. "Does he let you do that?"

Silence, while they tried to figure out if I was joking. Then Ed laughed, to tip them off. They laughed along with him.

"Just once," she said. "Back in the fifties. A malpractice case."

"He was acquitted," Stan said. "Edith is too softhearted."

"I don't know how you can say that!" She spoke right to me. "We weren't allowed to talk about the case at night, and I didn't!" She turned back to her husband. "Not that you didn't ask me over and over, just to get me to tell you."

To him it was one big joke. "Honey, I read about it all along in the papers anyway. I knew more about it at *every point* than you did."

He looked over at Ed and grinned. "Besides, I don't think women should have secrets from their husbands."

Don't ask *me*, Pearl! *Why*, after thirty years, does he have to put down the one job this poor woman ever held? *Why* does he have to laugh? *Why* does Ed laugh along with him? *Why* doesn't she take the rest of the soufflé and stuff it down his pasty old chest? (Because she irons his shirts, of course, but *why?)* And here's the best part! He likes her, he's proud of her, he's showing off to his brother-in-law. And Edith's looking put upon and flustered, but underneath she's telling me, *See that carpet?* See those roses? Hear that clock? See that *re-fine-ment?* (And looking at my polyester pantsuit with more than your basic doubt and disgust.) Because it's silk for her, and cotton and wool, and cotton shirts for her husband, and even if it means a lifetime at the ironing board, it's not *work.*

All the time, Ed's looking anxious through his chuckles. Will they be able to stand me? Will I be able to stand them? Can we have dinners together? If so, how often? Am I going to be dumb enough to light up a cigarette, or even shift my eyes around for an ashtray? Am I going to mention that I was *brought up a Catholic?* Are they going to scare me off with their truly AMAZING dullness? How many dinners a month will I stand for? Will I mention that I love to play poker, and suggest that we all get together? Tonight, say? But to imagine Ed, with his sweet face, playing poker, well, I can't, that's all.

Did I say *sweet face?* Shit. That's the kind of place I'm sitting in, Pearl, in this early-afternoon silence, and more good housekeeping and peace of mind and good taste than I've ever seen in my entire sixty-three years.

I clicked in again to a memory of Fran and me during the war, when he was dodging the draft and these folks were serving their country in a garage. We were out driving on a Sunday afternoon on Foothill Boulevard, and we got hungry, so we stopped at a chicken place, it looked like a pretty nice place. We read the menu, and down at the bottom it said, *No beer, no wine, just a lovely place for lovely people.* We got right up and left, but here I was again, in a lovely place for lovely people.

"Is it all right," Edith said, and she pushed back her chair as she said it, "if we wait just a bit for dessert? I thought we might walk in the garden. . . ."

We pushed our chairs back. I stretched out an arm to help her clear the table, but she said, "*No!* Don't bother!" She was back in a flash, and the four of us went out into the side yard.

She leaned up against him and they walked in front of us, more or less like one person, veering a little bit as one of them decided to stop and show us something.

I said it was a beautiful garden.

"We worried about it at first," Stan said. "We wondered if it was fair to plant so many things that other people would have to take care of when we're . . . gone. But then we realized. We were putting in things that—"

"That would give the most beauty." It was the first time she'd interrupted him.

". . . for minimum care. Very few annuals, for instance. But plenty of bulbs. And citrus. Most people don't realize that citrus is not just a California cliché. They stay green all year, most of them bear all year around. . . ."

"You and your grapefruit. . . ." Now she was kidding him! (In her very refined way, of course.)

He blushed. "I *like* grapefruit! They shouldn't grow this close to the ocean, but they do. I have a grapefruit every morning."

She looked at me and shrugged. She was really proud of him.

"It *does* beat inflation. We have the oranges and the lemons . . . and all the summer fruit. . . ."

Stan smiled. "Edith gets *quite crazy* when the apricots ripen. But we have jam for ourselves and all our friends."

I looked at Ed. Was this what he'd had with his wife? I remembered what Fran had said, how *despairing* he'd get, with his head in his hands in the kitchen. "Do I have to live in this *box?*" he'd say. "This crackerbox all my life?"

They showed us flowers, the late daffodils, the poppies, ranunculus. They'd built little paths around. It looked like a miniature-golf course. They had a little arbor with a vine growing over it.

"That's going to get too heavy in a year or two," Ed said.

The bees were buzzing. A few birds doodled along. Stan and Edith moved along at a basic snail's pace. I tilted my face up to get the sun and shade together.

The dessert was fresh strawberries off their own vines, and just as we were about to sit down, Stan and Edith gave each other the high sign. Edith sat down and began to talk in a shaky little voice, and Stan appeared at the door with a bottle of champagne in a silver ice bucket, on a silver tray, and four spotless crystal glasses.

"I guess we should celebrate?" It was Edith, talking to her brother, while he tried to look dignified. He smiled at her, and he had tears in his eyes.

You could see that Stan opened a bottle of champagne about once in a year. Ed finally had to help him with it.

Nobody could think of a toast, or didn't want to give one, but we all smiled, and finally Edith shrugged and laughed and drank. "Oh! It really does go in your nose! I keep forgetting that. . . ."

"The strawberries are delicious," I said.

The champagne loosened up Stan. He made a few mildly risqué remarks about what fun it must be for us to be starting over, and what was it like to go on a date? His face began to bead up a little bit, and his wife got up to draw the blinds. When he reached for the champagne, both Edith and Ed reached for it, Ed getting there first. He said, "Let me do that, old sport," and Edith chimed in tartly, "Ed's more *used* to it," but between their bickering, Stan didn't get a second glass.

We talked a little about children. And it was nice to say that my grandson was proficient in karate. Because Stan got to ask his wife, "What's that?" And Edith patiently explained to him, "I think it has something to do with kicking, dear."

After dessert I got up to help clear, and this time she let me do it. Her kitchen was small, and blue, and clean. She opened a cupboard to put something away, and I saw a mile of good china, good glass. And in another cupboard, jars and jars of home-canned goods.

"It keeps me busy," she said. "Actually, I like to do it."

"I never was much for that sort of thing," I said. "Not that I didn't want to. . . ."

Which leads to what I'd been trying not to say. "I was married twice. My second husband died, but my first husband left me. I had to work after that."

She gave me a hard, intelligent look. "The Good Book never said life was easy." Then she laughed. "My parents used to say that. It used to drive Ed and me *wild!*"

"You have a nice place here—"

"I think Ed's happy to have met you." She was holding the dishes under scalding water and then putting them carefully into the dishwasher. "He didn't always have the easiest time of it."

I wasn't going to say anything, so a couple of saucers further along she went on. "The worst thing, I think, is when someone just doesn't love you very much. There's nothing you can do about it, you see. You can be kind or not kind—nothing about the situation changes."

I wasn't even sure who she was saying didn't love whom, and I didn't think it would be too swift to ask.

"There's no one on earth kinder than Ed," she said. "I don't say that because he's my brother. In many ways, he's too kind. When Stan got sick, there was never any question, Ed was there. He'd come over to the hospital every day, he'd spend his time with Stan, they'd watch sports on television, but then, when it really counted, he'd come out in the waiting room with me. We'd talk about things in our childhood. This was last August. All the fruit in back was getting ripe, and Ed came over every morning at seven for a week and helped me pick and sort and can. He said he appreciated the chance, because he was lonely since Madeleine . . . but I'd see him outside on a ladder, reaching for fruit . . . I'm just telling you this so you'll know he's a good person," she said.

"Is he all right?"

She looked at me.

"Your husband? Stan?"

She looked out her kitchen window, out over the cool and spotless sink to the little orchard they'd made, and their dinky little arbor.

"Well, who knows? They always say they got everything until two years later, and then they say they were mistaken."

She let out a deep breath. "He's not in good health, no. He has high blood pressure, his heart isn't what it should be."

She gave me almost a mean grin. "Don't worry! I'm not the kind to go live with my brother! And I'm sure Stan will go on living for years. But it's hard. It's hard to even think about . . . some of the eventualities. For all of us, I suppose."

"Look, I'm not saying this means anything, but my daughter says . . . Aren't there *things?* You don't know me, but I mean, diets, hypnotism?"

She gave me a haughty look.

Well, *okay*, lady!

But afterward we sat in the blue living room looking at the

flowers that were red as fire between us, and spent the afternoon talking. They sat in their two chairs, we sat on the couch, because we were guests, and the dullest things they said to each other meant something. And Ed sat there beside me; something else was with us. Some sort of sick little child, some sort of retard, some baby with a rash that you're stuck with, that thing that you—Give me a break, Pearl!—the baby with a birthmark. The thing that you have to love.

The sun was going down, but nobody moved to turn on the lights. We talked, mostly they did—Ed and Edith—about their parents. Their old home, the things they did when they were kids. How Ed had insisted on soft bacon when he was little, how he'd called it "wrap-around bacon." How when Edith was seventeen she'd had diphtheria. "I was so afraid we'd lose you then," Ed said.

They saw each other as kids, and I could see it too, the good-looking, rangy, pale, freckled guy (too square for anybody like *us* to go out with), and the little girl who tagged along after him, for whatever reason got it in her mind that he was the *best*, and never, in fifty years, found a reason to change her mind.

Stan sat back and grinned at them both.

Pearl, I wanted to kill someone for not dealing us out a life like this.

Then Stan, who'd been watching with his head reared back, reared his head back a little more and began to wheeze.

Ed hurtled halfway out of his chair in less than a second. Long practice.

Edith put out a hand.

"No. No. It's nothing. He's just a little tired. It's absolutely nothing." She changed tone, the tone you speak to a sick kid. Or the tone you don't even let the kid *hear*, you don't let anyone hear it. "It's nothing, darling, come in, we'll lie down together for a while, it's nothing, darling. It's nothing. Darling."

She helped him out of his chair, and took him down the hall, and shut the bedroom door behind him.

Ed looked at me.

"She's very good to him."

"She's worried sick. . . ."

We said it both at once. "Do you think we should go home now?"

I really did think it was the best thing we could do. "Maybe we've tired him out."

Ed looked so sad. "I hate to leave this way. I suppose . . . the best thing we could do would be . . . I don't know. Why don't we get on our coats, and when she comes out, we'll be ready to go? I can't leave without saying good-bye."

We got up and went over to the entry. It was a tiny room with brocade wallpaper that caught the last little bit of light. A crystal chandelier chattered as we went by.

"I'll just get your coat," Ed said.

He opened the hall closet and stood looking at the coats, the parcels, the whatever, and then he began to cry. It came from under his throat, from some soft place.

"Oh, God," he sobbed. "Oh, hold me. Oh, God." Something like a fog? A rain? His tears fell down onto my face. I put out my hands, just to press his waist, just to hold him *together*, but . . .

Okay. It was like he spilled some water on my heart and it cracked and broke apart, and what was in there was so awful, I couldn't stand it.

I could have it now, if I wanted it. All that stuff. I could have it. But God is so fucking mean. I could only have it if I could stand the pain.

He felt something in me and backed off.

"What's wrong," he said. "I'm sorry. Are *you* all right?"

Two fools standing in a closet. I took a look at him. A last look. My foot started to jitter on the floor.

"*Nothing!*" It came out like a howitzer. "Nothing. I . . . I just feel a little *faint* is all."

He knew. He'd been dosed enough with bullshit in his life.

"What is it, Grace?"

"I need some air."

He put it in his computer and decided to believe me.

"Is it . . . something I did?"

"No, kid. Not you." I put my arm around him for the first time as a volunteer. And the last. Tried to feel, for once in my life, a man.

"I'm taking a walk," I said.

He reached for my coat and helped me on with it.

"I'll go with you."

"No!"

No.

9

April 27

My husband sucks on his tongue when he sleeps. I know, everyone makes jokes about snoring, about husbands snoring, and now, sometimes on the health pages in newspapers, or over the radio, they talk about "sleep-apnea," which is when they snore, and then stop. You have to worry about them dying, or going into a deep depression.

I don't know what to do about it. Ian's always had severe migraine headaches, so terrible that at one point I went out, about seven years ago, and bought us one of those hospital beds, king size. Do you know how strange it was to wake up in the night and see him sitting beside me in the night, this person, sitting up, and you had to look twice to see if it was asleep or awake?

Then his back began to bother him. He works under terrible tension. I remember that when his first series was in the planning stages, if ever I went by the bungalow at the studio to have lunch with him, his partner would be sitting on the couch and Ian would be stretched out on the floor on his back because he was in such pain. (That was when he was younger, of course.)

You could almost say that as the pressure went off him he cranked himself back down to a lying position in bed, but I wished he hadn't, because then he began to snore. I didn't know what to do. I'd poke him, but it made him angry. Then I'd try to pat him, but he said I was patronizing him. Then when he began to hold his breath between snoring and I heard those news stories, I got really upset. I kept after him until he went to a doctor. The doctor gave him some medicine, and he went back to regular snoring.

I don't know. It got so it bothered me so much that I started asking him if he wouldn't think of going to an antisnoring seminar. I don't blame him for being angry! There he was, working fourteen hours a day, supporting all of us, bringing his work home with him, and I know I've said before in this journal that I'm not exactly the queen of efficiency. And after a long day he would go to sleep and the minute he shut his eyes, there I was after him. I had to kid him into it; I said it was all right if he snored around me, but what if he snored like that on the casting couch? He said, okay, he'd go.

They taught him self-hypnosis and how to keep his glottis (?) out of the way. He griped about it, but he stopped snoring.

Everyone makes fun of consciousness-raising, but there's one place where it really worked!

Except, the thing is, other things started happening. I couldn't even say what exactly, except I bought him some acetate pajamas. (He said he wanted pure silk, but with the Cambodians suffering so much, I couldn't make myself buy them.) But the acetate made his nose run, and he started *swallowing*—in the night. I don't know what made me more upset, just the sound, or the idea that he was swallowing something that was toxic and might make him sick. Then that acetate! I thought at first I'd like the rustling sound it would make, but as soon as he'd go to sleep (especially since he got so preoccupied with racquetball), he'd make these jerky movements with his arms, playing racquetball in his sleep, and something about that sound made me crazy.

I bought a sleep mask, but it gave me nightmares. And I was afraid to buy earplugs, because suppose something happened to the kids in the night?

And he said I looked silly in my sleep mask. So did the kids. And I did.

All the things I talked about haven't happened *just now.* They've happened during nineteen years of marriage. These things would come and they'd go.

Maybe it's only been the last ten years. Ian says I'm never happy with anything. When he gets really upset, he says why don't I make the upstairs den over into a room for myself? Except he hates to spend money needlessly, we have so many expenses as it is. (And I never noticed him asking why don't I make the den over for him!)

Because the bedroom is mine too. I made it nice. It took work; he doesn't understand that.

When he started his new project—it's a three part mini-series, he won't tell me anything about it—I noticed Ian was doing some other things. When he'd be reading scripts, he'd start to clap his tongue against the roof of his mouth. Usually, every time he'd turn a page. At first I'd ask him, "What is it?" He'd say, "What is *what?*" Very upset because I'd interrupted him when he was trying to work. Because he didn't know he was doing anything.

You suggested today in class that we look to this journal for possible ideas for our term paper. I don't mean to complain, but it pointed out to me again the quality of my life.

Because I know, without him (or you!) telling me, that if I had something more of my own to do, I wouldn't be having these thoughts all the time. But the only thing that seems to work is very hard physical exercise, and don't you think it's a little strange to wake up in the morning and think: I'll take two yoga classes and play three sets of tennis so that I won't have to hear or see my husband in the night? Could I do a term paper on that?

I feel so awful saying this because I *swear*—I'd take a lie-detector test on it—that I love my husband. And my greatest fear in the world is losing him.

But here's the thing. About ten o'clock at night (because we like to get to bed early on week nights), when we're in bed and reading, it's like Ian isn't my *husband* at all. There isn't even any question of loving him or not loving him. I look over at him, except I try not to, and it's like those terrible close-ups they have of Ronald Reagan's chin on television. (Why that man didn't invest in chin lift, as long as he was going to the trouble of running for president, is beyond me.)

I look at Ian's chin and teeth and mouth, and they're alive. They have a life entirely outside our relationship.

Maybe it's the new dentist. If so, it's my fault. (est says we're responsible for our own condition, and really, I know that's true.) If it's the new dentist, then it *is* my fault. Because I heard of this new man; instead of anesthesia, he uses acupuncture. He doesn't use the water method of cleaning your teeth, and that's good, because I heard that causes heart disease. But to make up for no water, the man says you should floss five times a day, and that's what Ian's been doing.

Maybe I just made him too conscious of his mouth. Because now, at night, when he's reading, he flosses for a while. Then he very neatly balls up his floss and sticks it in a tray (not an ashtray, we don't smoke, just a little dish. All it's there for is the floss). Then he reads, and he sighs, or says, "What shit! With *all the writers!* . . ." But he doesn't finish his sentence. He begins, not really there, very *absently*, to run his tongue over his teeth. First he starts at the base of his lower front teeth, where his tongue would ordinarily be anyway, and presses with his tongue. The dentist told him that's where plaque settles, and I think he wants to move it on out before it gets a foothold. But then he gets more involved in his script (and I really do admire the way he can work, he has incredible concentration), and his tongue runs all the way around his upper teeth.

I can't help it. I remember I went with some kids down to Ensenada, years ago, when I was a freshman at City College. We went to El Rey Sol, I think it may have been the first expensive restaurant I ever went to in my life—isn't it strange, we wouldn't go there now, it isn't nice enough—and a man across the restaurant was sucking his teeth. The boy I was with said something like: If I ever get to be that age and do something like that, I'll *kill* myself!

Of course, he's that age now. I wonder if he remembers that, when he's sucking his teeth.

Finally, all I want to say is that my husband sucks his teeth, and then his tongue. I watch to see how he does it, I even try to do it myself—you know how sometimes when someone is cracking gum and your jaw aches, the only way you can fix it is by opening a stick of gum yourself?

I watch him out of the corner of my eye—and this isn't late at night, but early, when the kids still come in and out, talking, joking, sitting on the edge of the bed, asking for things. I'm always impressed by what a good, dutiful father he is. But then, when the kids leave, he starts doing it again. I try to imitate what he's doing with his mouth, but I can't do it.

(To be fair, he hates when my stomach growls, he can tell if I have acid indigestion. He hates when I lie on my back and my ribs stick up.)

All these things are what television jokes are made of, pure situation comedy, but what if, maybe, they're not jokes?

I try to believe, I do believe, that you can improve life, and that we should be happy. We're put on earth to do something, and why shouldn't we use our time to be happy? Isn't that the point of "California," or places like this university, where we can work, and change ourselves? For the better, I mean? Isn't that one of the reasons that Ian and I have worked so hard?

But what if Ian had stayed exactly where he was, over on the east side? What if I had stayed where I was, in Coalinga? Right now, he'd be watching television instead of making it, but he'd still be doing that with his teeth.

And I used to watch and listen to my mother eating Campbell's vegetable soup and soda crackers. I can't explain it, but it was the sound of no hope to me. Well, if I were doing that right now, eating that awful meal and making that noise, would my children care any more or less about me? Would my mother have any less respect for me? Would my husband sigh any more than he does now? Let me end with a little joke. Would I get a worse grade in this course than I might now, writing this entry, eating *la grappe* cheese and getting those dried skins in my teeth, drinking white wine, which skips my waist and goes right down to settle in my hips? Does all this, I mean, *all this*, count for anything at all?

April 29

Something terrible happened last night. David came into the den about eight-thirty. We were watching Ian's show, and the kids know he hates to be disturbed when he's watching it (even though they won't watch it anymore, they say it's corny). David was wearing his karate clothes and he had something in his sleeve. Debbie ran in after him, crying. He laughed at her.

Ian gave me a look, and I told the kids to quiet down. They did for a minute, but they stayed in the den. Debbie looked desperate. Davie pretended to let her corner him. I mean, he actually let her get him into a corner, a real corner where we had some family pictures and Ian's two Emmys, and our one and only piece of Steuben glass. (I know David's tricks! He wanted to give the appearance of standing still, and dodge Debbie until she ended up taking a poke at him, which, if he could dodge quickly enough, would end up destroying something of value.)

That's pretty much what happened, only worse.

David stood in the corner as still as he could. He was grinning. Debbie kept on trying to get at what he had in his sleeve. Ian's show was getting to the end of Act Three (which, I guess I ought to say, is the one which has to work in an hour show or the whole thing fails). I was sitting there, knowing something was going to happen.

Debbie hit David. She slapped him in the face; I've never seen her do that. David was so surprised that he just stared at her; then he reared back with his right hand and hit her back as hard as he could! I saw where his fingers left four pink marks on her face. (All I could think was that a Jewish prince isn't used to getting hit, ever.) Debbie tried to hit him back, and the Steuben glass (two pigeons in love) shattered to bits. Ian was ready to go into a rage, but then—I wish I could say it better—we all looked down to where what had been in David's sleeve was rolling, crazily, like it was drunk, across the hardwood floor until it hit the edge of the rug and then fell over on its side, bulge up. A diaphragm. Debbie, age thirteen, has a diaphragm.

The poor little kid began to cry.

Then David, for no reason I could see, did one of those awful karate kicks out from his hip and knocked Debbie down. She took a yellow ginger jar with her. The diaphragm just stayed there.

It was the look on Ian's face made me go over to David first. "You awful little boy," I think I said to him. "You go to your room right now."

But he grinned at me and stood his ground.

Debbie was on the rug sobbing—I can only say that these things *never happen* in our house—sprawled in the corner on her knees. Then, in a very irritating way, I must admit, she began to inch over on her hands and knees to get that really terrible-looking piece of rubber.

And Ian did the most disgusting thing. The most ill-considered thing. He had been sitting there in his pajamas and robe and those leather slippers men have. And he reached out with his foot, he's very tall, and covered the diaphragm with his foot. So cruel! He said, "*What is this?* . . . What *is* this, Debbie? . . . Debbie, answer me!"

Debbie looked at me, I guess to protect her. At first I didn't know what to say or do. I didn't want to take his side, but—how can I write this?—I didn't want to be associated with that rubber thing either. I really hated all of them then. I wished that I'd never gotten married and had kids. I really thought last night that I'd made a terrible mistake, when I was too young to know any better, getting onto an awful treadmill with a lot of people I didn't like very much, and that there wasn't going to be another deal of the cards.

Even my mother got another deal, every seven years or so.

The thought of my mother, maybe, made me react in a way that was equally ill-considered. I just began to scream. I went up and hit David. I hit him as hard as I could.

"*That's for you!*" I told him. "*And that's the end of your karate lessons! I'm not spending another penny, and I mean it!*" Then I went up and grabbed Debbie by her shoulder. I got a handful of hair along with it, and she—what's the word?—she winced in pain. Of course, that made me feel worse than ever. "Oh, just get up," I told her. "Don't slop around on the floor like that! That just makes it worse. Get up!"

She slumped down like she didn't have a muscle in the world, so I pulled her up on her feet. She's so young. I stooped down a little bit so I could look up, from underneath, into her eyes. "*What's the big deal!*" That's actually what I said to her.

You could see that she was going to try to weasel out of it—*they* would say, "shine it on"—make what happened into something else. "He hurt me," is what she told me. "He kicked me."

"*You idiot!*"

Was that really me talking? I felt like I was possessed. "You fool! Why did you leave it out where he could find it? Go into the bathroom! Clean yourself up! And get that hair out of your face!"

I could see by her face, that dumb kind of surprise, that I'd never talked like that to her before. "So he hit you?" I said. "Then *hit him back!*" I rushed over to where David was standing, but he ducked out the door before I could even raise my hand.

Do you know what Ian was doing? He was actually watching Act Four of his show.

I was still so angry that I wasn't afraid of him, or embarrassed, or any of the ordinary feelings I usually have about him.

"You could get your foot off something that isn't yours!"

He moved his toes over, keeping his leather heel where it was. Something about that—dominion?—infuriated me.

"Don't harm something that isn't yours! Don't you know any better than that?"

Someone had to pick it up, and it had to be me. So I bent down and picked up the poor squashed thing and put it in my pocket. "You don't have to look so righteous," I told him. "It's not as if I don't remember, even if you don't."

Actually, I wasn't being fair. How can men remember? Because *they* haven't been to have their diaphragms fitted, or their coils put in. Or—I had a tubal pregnancy once, and I remember the day I went into the hospital—it was the end of a life, and while I don't like to get sentimental, I have this whole son I never had. He would have been dark, and not liked sports, and I could have talked to him. Every year when that day goes by, Ian never remembers. But why should he remember? It wasn't *his* tube! So how could he remember, the pain and the embarrassment, of going into a doctor's office when you're young, young, and asking an old man for a diaphragm?

How can you expect anything else? I've done enough gardening to know that you can be pulling wet green grass out from a shade tree and everything is blue and green and damp under there, and you move no more than eight inches, you don't even have to shift your weight, and you're in blazing sun, pulling up dry rye grass, it's the same ground, the same weeds—but a different world. So how could you even expect him to

"Look," I said. "Do you want to talk about this? Don't you think we ought to talk about this?"

"No."

"What do you mean, *no!*"

He was glued to the set. I even watched it with him for a minute or two.

"We had to do that shot just twice," Ian said. "You wouldn't believe how well it went."

"Ian!"

"Look," he said. "Don't misunderstand me, Garnet, I'm not blaming it on *you*. I know *you* don't have any control of her. I'm just saying it's painful for me to talk about. Finding out my daughter is a slut."

What happened then only took as long as the fourth act. Just eleven or twelve minutes. Fifteen, if you include the commercials. I don't say I acted rationally, but I tried to stay under control. I picked up the biggest pieces of the broken lamp and put them in the wastebasket. (Because it would certainly cost more to repair than to get a new one.)

"Look, *you*," I said (and you must understand that Ian and I never fight), "if you don't remember, *I* do. What it was like before *we* got married. You weren't so picky then."

He started to laugh, and I said to him, "Listen, Ian, I'm not dumb. You have to think so, that's probably so you can earn a living. You have to be smarter than somebody, *why not me?* You know? But why bring your daughter into it! Because she's a human being, Ian, a human being! There's no point in ignoring her, and buying things for her, and then laughing at her, and then being disgusted at her, just because she wants to see what you're all talking about! Which is just sex anyway! I'm not against it, it makes a good living for you, but it's not dirty, Ian, it's not disgusting, Ian. There's nothing wrong with it, no matter what my mother says, no matter what you say, so . . ."

I was really upset. "You know what I want to do with all this? You know how I feel about you and your mean ways and your *television?*"

He was deathly pale. I've never talked that way before to him.

"I feel like *this!*" I ran over to the shredder and turned it on, grabbed it, and crammed poor Debbie's diaphragm right into it. The machine made an awful sound and then stopped. But the wire ring and that sad rubber were gone.

"I don't want to hear another word about it, Ian," I said to him. "And I never want to have another night like tonight."

He didn't answer. His mouth was open, and he was looking at the door. My mother had come in from an evening with her friend. She was looking at him. Suddenly I felt really good! I felt, *for once!* in control.

"Well?" she said. "What's wrong? What is it?"

"Nothing, Mother," I said. "We were just talking about the kids."

And I walked out, leaving *them* to think something over, for a change.

Which is why, when I get this entry back, I'm going to have to *burn* it, like someone in *Mission Impossible*, because I took the shredder to the repairman this morning. I haven't seen a tradesman look so funny about anything since the dog had pups on one of our king-size sheets. He says it will take six weeks, at least, to repair it.

May 1

Today, in what I promise is my last attempt to please my mother, I took her to lunch at Michael's. Have you ever been there? I'm not sure if it's a place where professors go. (I don't mean just that it's expensive, although it is, but only that it doesn't look like professors go there.)

I haven't said so in this journal, but I do have some friends, and we make it a point to go to Michael's for lunch once in every two weeks.

Because that place is what the Polo Lounge should be but isn't. It's like . . . it's a vision of the good life that isn't all covered with palm fronds. And they don't have those pink telephones, or *any* telephones, and no show-business people, except Sally Struthers once in a while. No one ignores you if you're a wife. In fact, to go there if you're a wife is quite . . . all right, because it implies that your husband has lots of money.

The secret message there is that everyone is crazy about eating. They say Michael's has the best food in town, and because it's all the way out in Santa Monica, the people who are willing to take a few hours off in the day to go there have these secrets between them. That they have enough money, and that they'll kill for the hollandaise on the salmon, or those five light sherbets they give to you in tiny scoops for dessert. (And I like it because I've more or less discovered that having old money and being plain are almost the same. I look like a Pasadena matron there, rather than a girl from Highland Park. But I forget, you said in class the other day you were from Princeton, so those distinctions mean nothing to you.)

I hadn't seen much of my mother, really, since she met that man—I *still* don't understand how she does that—and since the unpleasant evening at home night before last. (Before I get to what I say here, I should record for this journal that I mended fences with Davie and Debbie. I apologized to my little girl for hurting her feelings, if I did, and drove her to my own doctor so that she could be refitted. And I told her how mature I thought she was not to be hurting her health with the pill. And that's all I said. Because one thing I've learned is that I don't know anything at all about men and women together. I haven't said much to Davie, but I try to forgive him; he can't help what he is any more than any of us can help it. I suppose the trick is to learn to like them for what they are.)

Salmon in that light white sauce, tarragon chicken, frisée

(a heavy, crunchy salad with salt pork and croutons), those are what we had for lunch. Barbara and Ruth came along, beautiful women my age with plenty of money and good manners. My mother, who looked very nice indeed. You could almost have said she was a new woman since she met Ed.

Michael's. Two rooms and a patio. The kind of pictures on the wall you respect. Hothouse flowers indoors, banks of low-growing fresh flowers outside. Men in business suits drinking soup with smiles on their faces.

Of course, I forgot, we were going there with Mother!

Mother had asked specifically to sit outside, but we no sooner stepped outside than she got a shaking spell and asked to sit inside. I suppose you know by now that I should never be surprised that my mother does anything at all, so when she insisted that we go inside, we did.

Once we were inside, my mother—that woman!—insisted that she wanted to see the view, that she should face the patio rather than I. Then she said she wasn't hungry, but again, I want to emphasize that I wasn't surprised. The best restaurant in Los Angeles on one of the most beautiful days of the year. Why should she be hungry? Barbara, Ruth, and I had champagne cocktails, my mother ordered a manhattan. It was all right, it really was. You have to learn to like them for what they are.

Barbara and Ruth teased my mother about her dates with Ed. My mother barely spoke to them. That was all right. Why should she like my friends any more than I like hers? I had another champagne cocktail, and they brought the *frisée*. I asked the waiter to remove the flowers from the table because I recalled my mother had an allergy, that was all right, that was okay. I saw across the room a clothier friend of Ian's. We meet at parties and I see him at lunch at Michael's quite often. I nodded at him and smiled, but he didn't smile back. I got up to excuse myself—I like to look at the pastry table before the entrée comes, so I can pace myself.

Upstairs in the rest room I noticed that I felt *good*, quite peaceful, the best I had in the four weeks since my mother had come to visit me. I was thinking that she actually had a chance of going away with that man, marrying him.

I came down the staircase, admiring the light coming in through the round windows upstairs, then stopping to look at the pastries. (It did seem to me that the waiters, those nice boys who don't like women, looked at me strangely.) I walked back through the restaurant, noticing what people were eating, everything beautifully colored and *light*, because that's the way they cook there.

I thought: I have come a long way from Highland Park, from City College. I know something about the world now, and I've shown that I can be kind to my mother.

As I went back to the table, the whole place seemed flooded with light, a beautiful place. Heaven on earth, if you could let it be. As I got back to the table, the three of them actually stood up for me.

My mother, the shortest of the three, wasn't nearly tall enough to hide what she was trying to hide. Ian was out on the patio with a young girl. I smiled at them all. "That's all right," I said. "I see him. Are we sure we want the salmon? It's very rich." And I saw that they had just brought a new chocolate mousse out from the kitchen.

It was all right, really. I had another champagne cocktail, but I do have to tell the truth here, the endive from the frisée stuck in my throat. It has those awful power-saw edges on it. Ruth and Barbara, how calm they were, new women, fine women. I'd had them over to the house, I'd met them in discussion groups, I'd sat with them through endless dinners where our husbands talked shop and we had talked about . . . nothing really, because what was there to talk about?

But they always knew how to laugh and have a good time.

Not a trace of pity on their faces. I caught the eye of the schlock clothier, who couldn't look away. I grinned at him and winked.

The only one, I suppose, by then, who didn't know that Ian and I were in the same restaurant was Ian, and, I suppose, the girl. But what did it matter? We were in a new world. The salmon came, I ate it, really, it was okay.

What I couldn't stand in all of this—the scared faces of the girlish waiters, the staunch calm of my friends, the clothier with guilt written all over his face—was my mother's face.

See? she kept telling me, without even opening her mouth. This is what life is really like.

After my sixth champagne cocktail I still wasn't ready to believe it.

And she had the bad manners, when the dessert came, to tell me she'd known it all along.

I wanted to tell her she didn't know anything.

But instead I picked up my lemon mousse (I *am* a nice person, I swear it. I hadn't ordered the chocolate), and fully aware that this was an anticlimax from the shredder incident, I walked over to their table quietly and reasonably and asked her, "Have you tried this? It's really quite good." And smacked her with it, right in the face. Then I dug both my hands into her hair and pulled. Ian stood up and said *pugh!* Something like that.

"You idiot," I told him. "I'm so sick of being stuck with an idiot!"

The waiters crowded around to get the three of us out.

I still had my hands in that girl's hair. I remembered some aikido imagery from the prosperity seminar I'd gone to, I thought of ticks, of gila monsters, of things that don't let go.

They carried us outside, but I didn't let go. I thought of a tick swelled up with blood until she can't take any more. I felt something loosening, and made my hands tighter, until I realized that it wasn't my fingers letting go, but part of her hair. Outside on the walk there were parking meters and passersby, but, no, I didn't let go.

By that time I'd begun to talk to her, reasonably, the way I tried to talk to the secretary at the auto club to complain about their atrocious road service. "It's not that I'm mad at you," I told her, trying not to break my concentration, "I'm not really mad at him, either, I've just *had all I can take*."

She was screaming, a very high dumb shriek, so I don't think she heard me.

I saw the meters, and the face of one of the waiters, who,

showing he had some balls for once, really did try to put a stop to it. I made my fingers into sharp little teeth that wouldn't let go. I saw that by a fluke Jody Jacobs had been there for lunch and that she had her notebook out.

Ian's head passed by my eyes. He was reaching for the other girl. "Darling!" he said, and that did it. I gave two yanks and left her with two perfect bald spots over her ears. Let her try to pass it off as this year's Bo Derek haircut!

Then I thought of Ian's leather slippers, and I went for him. I rubbed that frizzy blond hair on his face, I scratched his cheeks, I tried to take the buttons off his shirt, because I'd given him that shirt for Christmas. I blush to say what I told him, but I wasn't screaming. I just told him that he'd better be watching out for herpes. I took a lot of skin off his face, but frankly, not as much as I would have liked.

Then it was all over. All over. Jody had gone either for the phone or back for lunch. The waiters must have remembered that there were orders coming up. The girl was sitting in Ian's Mercedes, her hands covering her bald spots as if she were having an Excedrin headache. I noticed I had no more hair and blood to rub on my husband, when he broke and ran, dodging as if he were in a football game, ducking—did he think I carried a gun, for heaven's sake. He slammed into his car and took off, in first.

There was no one out there with me. The sun was behind a cloud. Barbara and Ruth had gone home, I guess.

I looked through the windows in at Michael's. Everyone was back in there, eating lunch. What surprised me was that my mother was gone. (Then I remembered her friend lived right around here.) I looked around for a while, walking up and down the length of the sidewalk in front of the restaurant. I suppose I was a mess. One heel was off a sandal, and my stockings were in awful shreds.

I walked, limped, down to the Santa Monica Mall, bought a Pepsi at a drugstore, went back to the car, waited around for a while, and then drove home.

After I came home, I gave Leticia the weekend off. I tried to send Davie and Deb over to their grandparents'. The kids said no, they wanted to spend the night with their friends. I don't think they even noticed anything was wrong. They packed up little carryall bags and left.

Debbie, I think I saw, turned back out on the lawn to look at the house, since usually I ask them to kiss me good-bye and they won't. And this time I didn't.

After they left, I came here, in the den. I pulled the blinds, but left the drapes open. The last of the light came through the slats for a while, and then it left and it was dark.

10

Saturday, 5 P.M., May 2

Since yesterday afternoon I've spent a good deal of time on the phone. Ian called last night, about ten, and said that he'd been working so hard for so many years that he feared for his health. That he had to cut back for a while, and in view of that, he was thinking of a trial separation. Then he said a couple of other things. One, that it shouldn't bother me too much, because I haven't looked at him, been interested in him, in years. Then he said that he felt he might use this situation "creatively," that there was a ninety-minute teleplay or even a feature film in the situation we were going through. I didn't have the heart to tell him they'd done it a few times already.

Before that, I called Mr. Cochran's house and asked Mother if she'd mind staying somewhere else for a day or two, that Ian and I were trying to work things out. She was calm, polite, even—but it seemed to me I could hear in her voice the proverbial rat leaving the proverbial sinking ship.

I sat in this chair all night thinking. Was it true I wasn't interested in Ian?

Then this morning, about eight o'clock, I started to call my friends. Because, to me, the worst gaffe in this town is when someone asks you how your husband is, except he isn't your husband anymore.

So for about six hours I was on the phone. I cried only twice, and the part about Michael's makes a nice story.

I can just see you reading this! Another Brentwood matron and her divorce! I'm not a fool, I know the kind of life I have! A woman who spends her time in restaurants. A woman who worries about pleasing other people who don't like her very much. A woman, really, very short on problems! I am not sick, and never have been. My clothes are good. Ah, and I have nothing to complain about! *Right?*

The one thing my friends wanted to know—wives, like me, threatened by the earthquake—was how I knew, and when. "Really," they said. "Not *when* you saw her, but before that. Didn't you know before that?"

I remembered a "friend" of my poor mother who came to our house when I was eleven and said, "Oh, not you and Frank! Because you always were so good together!"

At least, no one said to me, "You and Ian were so good together."

But they did ask me when I really knew. They're asking what I did wrong. Because if they know that, they can keep it from happening to them.

Because being "attractive," or gentile, or going back to school is definitely not the answer. Because, look at me!

Because, keeping house doesn't do it (we all have those sweet girls named Ofelia and Leticia to do that), and cooking doesn't do it, because we're all on a diet, or should be, and "listening" doesn't do it—I don't know why, it just *doesn't*—and being "sexy" doesn't do it. The sexier you are, the quicker they get tired of you; they just get *sick* of you, like fruitcake. Children don't do it, because when they're *ready to go,* no child on earth could keep them in your house.

I personally think beauty has the chance of keeping them

around—I mean a twenty-four-year-old woman (assuming the husband is fifty) who doesn't like sex, and looks bored all the time, and doesn't like kids very much or at least won't bother with them, a girl who only laughs when she's playing pinball, I think that woman has a ten- or even twenty-year chance, but none of my friends, my acquaintances, have that or are that. Even the younger ones, the second wives or third ones, took some of those false steps, those wrong turns, like having children, or pretending to be interested in what their husbands do for a living, or letting themselves be seen after they had their brows lifted or their breasts injected. Or got "too excited" in bed, which I really believe is the wrong thing to do with men you are married to.

But what do I know?

Why do some people get cancer and some people don't? They can say it's stress, they can say it's cells, they can say it's chemicals (I personally think it's hereditary), but all anybody ever really knows for sure is: Some people get it and some people don't.

I knew from the very beginning! I knew when I met Ian! I knew when his hair began to fall out. When he started taking two showers a day. When I got a bill from a doctor I never heard of and Ian said it was his prostate. When he told me I needed eye shadow. When he told me I had a natural beauty and didn't need eye shadow! That time I wrote about, when my mother saw him with somebody in the Nate 'N Al's. When he'd turn away from me when he was asleep. When I gained weight. When I lost weight. When he bought a new shirt. When he'd walk past the kids without saying hello. When he'd be kind to my mother when she didn't deserve it. When he told me it didn't matter! That I didn't have to do that fancy entertaining if it upset me, that that's what they had the Bistro and Chasen's for! I knew when after we got that terrific refectory table for the dining room, and nobody sat at it. I knew from the beginning.

How I knew was a certain look Ian gets, and I've seen it with other husbands. I see it at parties, and I think: *Oh, boy!* And then I read about it in Rona Barrett the next week or month. I see it everywhere. What they do, what Ian did, before he ever took the chance in broad daylight and took a girlfriend to Michael's, is just to turn away in his chair, almost exactly three-quarters away, and look something like three-quarters out.

You can't blame them. I can't blame him. To be out of living rooms and karate lessons. To be out and gone, to slide through and out of it.

Seeing Ian at Michael's is like having cancer. I think of driving down to Tijuana and across the bridge, past all the cardboard houses, out toward the ocean, with the wind blowing, toward the new bull ring, which isn't so new anymore. Now that Ian's rich and busy, we never go there, and now that he's eating lunch with somebody else, we'll never, never go there. But what I'm saying is, I think of driving out Second Street in Tijuana almost to the beach, to Dr. Contreras' clinic, and see, it's all white stucco in the sun, and they have trouble finding people to mow the lawn or even water it, but you go in there and take a lot of laetrile and you don't even have cancer anymore, it's *gone!:*

What do men want, I wonder? Don't they know even Marin Jenson eats food for breakfast and says dull things? I think they know that, and that's why they look for the shift in the air, that break, that place, where they could slide out, and be gone.

Saturday night

I just want to say I'm scared. I haven't seen him in thirty-two hours. I really did think he would come home tonight, but he didn't. I feel sick. I don't care where he is, I can't stand this. I'm scared. I don't have anyone to call. I'm going to die.

I'm sick. Don't worry! I'm not going to turn this in.

Sunday night

Now I'm going to think it, I'm going to say it. If *I'm* boring, if I'm a dud, if my mother shakes her head at me, what does that make Ian? I'm going to make myself say it. Ian can be a very boring person. He's very vain.

He's always picking up his slacks off his knees and giving them a little shake. He's *prissy*. I can say that. And if he could choose me, what does that make him? His last two pilots have been the most terrible ripoffs, and he doesn't even notice it. He thinks he had the ideas himself. But somebody else already had the ideas and already took the risk and already made the money. The big money.

Writing this journal has made me see that it's easier to criticize than to *do*, to write, to really have an idea. Even while you're having them, you see all the sadness of your little ideas. So if Ian has the idea of a woman marathon runner, or an older man falling in love with a young girl, or three beautiful starlets living together at the Studio Club, well, at least now I don't have to pretend to be impressed by those ideas. I don't have to pretend they're his.

A little divorce. A stupid little speck of pain in West Los Angeles. My mother could feel something about hers, but mine's already been done better by Mazursky and Tucker. Actually *they* did it once for *Blume in Love*, then Mazursky went ahead and did it *again* with his *Unmarried Woman*, and they all got a nice round of Oscars and made a lot of money.

I want you to know, I'm *not suffering!* It's against my religion. I have nothing to complain about.

It's eleven-thirty at night. The kids are asleep. They came home this afternoon. I'm wearing a flannel bathrobe. I don't feel right in the living room, so I'm sitting in the bedroom. The kids know, but we haven't talked about it much. I can't say they've been nice, but I can't say they've been awful. Tonight they fixed dinner. Guess what they did. They opened up six of those cans without labels and put them in Chinese bowls and we ate them with chopsticks. Garbanzo beans, canned string beans, tomatoes, chili, creamed corn. It was almost fun.

Don't get me wrong. I spent most of the day crying. But I keep waiting for the real anguish to set in. That anguish is just hanging around outside the window . . . actually, what's really outside the window is a fair-sized kumquat tree, in bloom.

Monday night after dinner

There's plenty to write about; I've had a busy day. After going to your class, I began work on my possible term paper: "Careers or Their Alternatives for Women Past Forty." Little did I know, when I chose that topic . . .

I went to see the Red Cross. Can you believe it? They said I could help when other people gave blood. Or, they said, *I* could give blood once a month. They said they always need women for volunteers.

I checked out the Democratic party. I already had a ticket to a fund-raising lunch. Do you know who they had as a speaker? That man who back during the Afghan crisis sat in front of that Sidney Greenstreet scene in Delhi and said on television, "*This . . . Means . . . War!*" I wouldn't have remembered except he told us about it again at lunch. It was the high point of his life. He *still* thinks it means war. He's just waiting around for it, and he's going to be very disappointed if it doesn't show up.

Afterward a man told me they discourage women workers, except just before elections.

I have to admit I came home after lunch to watch *General Hospital.* They get so much fun out of their disasters. And I really was interested to find out, even before all this happened, who was the father of Monica's child.

In the afternoon, I guess I should say it, I went to see a well-known psychic in Glendale. I have money, so I didn't have to see one of her staff. I got to see her. She took one look at me and said my aura was disturbed. Kind of a nasty gray green. I had to laugh. My *face* was gray green! I told her about my husband, at Michael's. She smiled at the idea of the lady with the bald spots. I told her I thought my heart was breaking. She looked between my ribs and said no, it wasn't breaking, but I could visualize some epoxy, if I wanted. I started to cry, and asked her *really*, what could she do for me? She looked out of the window, she has an office right there on Brand Boulevard, which must be the most depressing street in the whole city. The street, the dents where the car tracks used to be, the brown linoleum on the way up here on the stairs, the yellow of the walls in her own building. But she told me she can see through walls. She looked out the window and said sitting on the earth was good for you, and taking hot showers to wash off the bad energy worked pretty well, but the best thing, she said, was bathing everybody in a burst of white light.

God help me, all I could think of was the Democratic lunch. The only white light I could come up with was the hydrogen bomb. All the bombs built like (excuse me) penises, and how excited those men get at the prospect. But I knew what she meant, of course. You just get the energy, she said. You start it in your solar plexus and continue it out. Then you wrap your friends up in it. Your enemies too, if you can. She wasn't even looking at me, she leaned her arms on the sill and looked out at the traffic. "That's really all I know," she said. I gave her an extra twenty-five dollars and she raised her eyebrows at me.

So that's been my day. *Another Brentwood Matron.* Without a husband. Tomorrow I see my lawyer. Which reminds me, I could be a lawyer! But what if—in the words of my husband's business—I just pass on all of it? Women are not the only ones to live worthless lives, professor! My husband, with his endlessly stupid show that not even *he* likes to watch! My gynecologist, and you know how he spends his days! That worthless politician blowing up the world because he can't think of any other thing worth doing except haranguing women at pathetic lunches.

The men at Gold's Gym, lifting weights, and keeping fit.

Fit for *what!*

For the record, I am not suffering. My *looks* may be suffering, but I'm not! I will leave you with this. About six o'clock tonight I went to get my eyebrows waxed and started to cry when the wax hit my skin. To save myself embarrassment I told the girl I was going through a divorce. *Another Brentwood Matron.*

"Oh, kid," she said. "Oh, gee, that's terrible. I got a divorce once." She pulled off the cheesecloth and the wax. It hurt really badly, and I could feel my eyes more or less drowning in tears, spilling over and going down into my ears, just like in that old dumb song.

"Yes," I said, and it was really hard to keep my voice steady. "Did you suffer a lot? How long did you suffer?"

"Oh, kid," she said. "It was a drag." She grabbed the other piece of cheesecloth and wax, and yanked it off my skin. I couldn't stop crying.

"I felt bad," she said. "For about two weeks."

She made me look in the mirror. Actually, she'd done an almost perfect job. As I'm writing this, I can feel a lot of smooth brow. If I could get rid of everything as easily with just a little sharp pain,

Well.

Wednesday A.M., *May 6*

As I guess you know, last night was the Academy Awards. It's been four days, five days (four months? five years?) since I've been a "woman alone." Ian is gone. It's so strange. I've been reading Joan Didion. Getting a bead on how I'm supposed to feel.

I must admit, the idea of me going down the drain with a male gigolo type and wearing a silver lamé dress made me laugh. I haven't gotten out of my bathrobe except to drive the kids to school and come to class for the last five days. But what really made me give up on the whole thing was the part about her shopping! How she bought for a huge family because she felt so bad. We're still using up those cans with no labels. I don't think I really told you, there were over two hundred of them.

I think the kids are fine. You say to be specific, so I will. Yesterday afternoon we went to a Little League game with Davie. Debbie and I really yelled, we really wanted him to win! We didn't have to go straight home, so we got some ribs at the Colonel's and ate down by the beach.

And this morning Debbie said she needed some new clothes. Before with Debbie, when she needed clothes, we always went to Saks or Bonwit's or we had an argument about Fiorucci, because I don't like to buy that kind of thing for children, and settled on Heaven. Well, we had a talk about money, that we'll still have enough, probably more than enough, but that for the next few months we'll have to be careful. I remember *my* mother and how she cried when she told me the same thing, but then she went out and *bought* me, without being asked, that blue-and-green-plaid dress with the Peter Pan collar from the Broadway. So in the same breath I asked Debbie, "Do you want to go shopping?" And she said, "How about Pillars?" I don't know if you know Pillars, but it's a store for seconds, expensive stuff and schlock all mixed up, I didn't even know Debbie knew about it. We went there and spent the whole afternoon trying things on and actually laughing. I ended up buying her some skintight leopardskin punk-rocker pants, seconds from Fiorucci. I could never have done it if I'd had to show them to Ian.

I've been thinking, I am on a vacation. I thought I'd feel bad about the Academy Awards, because for the past eleven years I've always gone with Ian; he's always been able to finagle invitations. But it came to me that the two days before the awards have usually been my two hardest working days of the year.

I spend the day before over at Jax, picking out a dress and getting fitted, then I'm back at the Beverly Hills Hotel getting my hair done. Here's the worst part. We've never used a limo to go to the awards because Ian hates them, he thinks they're pretentious. (Or maybe he thinks we don't deserve one.) So, I admit I wait until the last minute to pick out the dress, but sometime before I go in for the second set of alterations and my hair, I'm out in the backyard washing the Mercedes and coating it with wax. It's crazy, but in all these years, Ian would never use a commercial car wash because of what it does to his wheels. And we've never begun to be rich enough to afford a chauffeur.

So for the first time in eleven years I'd be watching the awards on television. We turned on the set in my bedroom. I got into a clean nightgown and combed my hair. We made up a big plate of tuna sandwiches. Davie was studying for a geometry test, he had a friend over who knew geometry to help him study. They set up a card table beside the bed. Debbie climbed in with me.

We tuned in early to watch Regis say hello to everybody as they went in. I remembered awful nights, when Ian would loiter, or downright stop, in front of the Pavilion or the Santa Monica Civic, refusing to go in until Regis called him over. I'll never have to go through that again.

I kept waiting to feel some pain, but I didn't. Then I felt Debbie beside me tense up. And I saw Ian go in, not so eager to talk this year. I saw him, with one of those awful little starlets out of your (my) bad dreams, with ringlets all over her head and a big chest and a babyish droopy mouth and the beginning of a double chin. She wasn't the girl from Michael's. And I wondered if that was who my mother had seen in Nate 'N Al's.

What I saw with her was a sad, nervous-looking guy whose evening clothes looked as though they'd been rented. He held on to the girl as if his life depended on it.

I was afraid of what was going to happen next.

But then Debbie said, "She's not as pretty as you, Mom." I was so happy I almost cried. I'm not sure if I can say why, but I got a sense of the *continuity* of it. The Invasion of the Body Snatchers, backwards. This little pod, my daughter, might be turning into my friend. I looked over at her. She'd just had a bath, and I admit that may have influenced my feelings. Her face was tight and pink and her mouth was pressed together. She's such a tough, terrific little kid.

Davie said, "Are you kidding? With those bazoombas?" His friend sneaked a nervous look at me, and then relaxed when he saw I wasn't upset.

I bit into a sandwich. (No, I'm not going to get fat, but it really is fun to eat sandwiches in bed!) I don't know if I've said, but this week we seem to be living mostly in the bedrooms and the kitchen. There are quite a few things around here we really don't need. I've already been thinking about how we might live, or where, if this "separation" really "happens," which I guess it's going to do. The good furniture I'll take out of here, and the junk I'll leave for Ian. And whether we'll be able to afford a small house at the beach.

As I say, the boys were at the card table and Debbie and I were in the big bed. We settled back to watch the awards. We got to laughing quite a lot. Audrey Hepburn looked really terrible! Bernadette Peters was falling out of her dress, and Davie's friend said he knew for a fact that she had herpes. I don't want you to think we were really making fun. But I had always been afraid of them before. Now I saw them another way. Audrey Hepburn as a tired woman whose husband had left her. Bernadette Peters, something like Ian's girlfriend, very pretty, but with that chin! They had breadth and depth and energy, but their bodies weren't perfect, any more than mine, and for every winner there were the four losers, and for every loser, people who weren't even nominated, and for every one of them, lots of people who didn't even care.

On the other hand, I kept saying to myself: Get *on* it, Garnet! You can't make a life out of eating and sleeping and watching television and fooling around with the kids! What would Ian say? What if he's been right about you all along? What about the Man from the Seminar? What would he say?

What if you could, be, or do, or have anything you want?

I watched the awards and I started to smile. I kept thinking, there are all these people, getting the awards they've worked so hard for. When Bruce Dern lost, I *saw* him trying to act like a good sport. To see him trying for sweetness, it almost made me cry. All I can say is, at about the time I realized I'd never be going to the Dorothy Chandler again, for the awards, or maybe, conceivably, for anything else in my whole life, I finally saw those people as

I finally saw those people.

And I really wanted for every one of them to win.

Then we heard a terrible bumping in the front of the house. The kids looked at each other. I saw Davie considering whether or not he was going to have to be brave. God help me, I thought, what if that's Ian? That means I'm going to have to take him back. Then I knew what it means, to have your heart sink. A terrible, familiar step came down the hall. The whole house shivered from it. The four of us sat looking at the door. It opened, and it was the one thing worse than Ian standing there, don't laugh.

My mother. And she was very upset.

She looked around. *Oh, my God, she said, oh, my Christ! What's happened here?*

I took it all in the way she did. In just five days, the porch light out, the Mercedes gone, the lawn unmowed, the flowers in the living room dead, the bike in the hall, the parcels of laundry half-open, half put away on the dining-room table, the kitchen with mustard and mayonnaise and onion peels on the sink, the card table with its terrible look of being cheap and temporary, the half-eaten sandwiches, the middle-aged abandoned woman spending what's left of her life with her abandoned kids. This is it. This is what I've been waiting for all my life.

I saw my father leave, cool, and disgusted, plain as day. I saw Ian, imperfect copy, leave right after him. I'd have to explain it all to Mother. And she was already mad as hell.

"Come on in, Mother. Sit down. Would you like a sandwich? I don't think we have anything much to drink except milk. Who do you want for best actress?"

What my mother said when she came in.

"Oh, my God," she said. "He's done it, hasn't he?"

"*Mother*," I said. "How are you? We've been a little worried. I wasn't sure I should call you over at Ed's. Well," I said, sitting there like a wimp, a very big wimp, with crumbs in the bed, and the ruffles on the bolsters a little bit limp and greasy, the kids suddenly looking a lot like what they *were*, slope-shouldered, with too many teeth and too many braces, and neither one of them with near enough chin. Davie and Debbie both, for all their O.P.'s and Sasson pants, have hefty behinds. What I'm trying to say is that there was way too much flesh in that room. Someone who *liked* us might have said we were "vulnerable," but I've really misrepresented my family situation if I've ever given the impression . . .

Okay. Something so *weird* must have happened to my voice that I noticed all the kids were looking at me, and my mother was standing in the doorway looking around at all of us and nervously moving her foot, not tapping it but *moving* it like I know she does when she's ready to blow.

"It's been a long enough time *coming*," she said, and her voice was like a hacksaw.

I never said my children were very bright. Davie asked me the other day what the *Mediterranean* was, and Debbie didn't want to give Leticia a digital clock last Christmas, because the numbers weren't in Spanish. But they had sense enough to be scared. They began to look around the big room.

I'm not like those wives who say, "Oh, I did everything,

down to the architectural *drawings*," no, I didn't do anything but buy things, and work hard, but our bedroom is huge and rich and very beautiful. Separate reading lights shine down out of the ceiling above the bed, as if Ian and I slept in a giant 747 made out of mattress—and we did, you know? Except we flew to different places. The television closes itself behind antiqued cupboards, and the kids were eating at a card table so they'd stay away from the other side of the room, where a tiny love seat and two matching chairs pull up in front of a tiny fireplace, because, yes, we do have a fireplace in our bedroom, along with a chaise—and our food, our dip, our chips, our junk food, our sandwiches, our crumbs, were at least spread partly out on a white wicker bed tray, with napkins (paper, I admit) embossed with the family name.

She was standing in the door. The kids drooped all over the room. Everything was just a little bit dirty.

"Christ," she said. "It took him long enough. But it isn't as though you didn't see it coming. Christ, even *I* saw it. It didn't take a genius to see it coming."

The kids began to look around the room, like they were blind. See *what?* See *what?* They'd already seen their dad walking into the Academy Awards.

"Well, Mother." I didn't know what to say.

"And they say Jews are good family men!"

Up on the screen three set decorators got the Academy Award. Didn't they even know that nobody cared? That the other people down at the Pavilion could hardly get their arms up for one sad clap of applause?

"You didn't even finish *college*," she said. "At least you won't have to go back to business school like I did. Working eight hours a day at some shitty typing job."

They gave a special award to the Museum of Modern Art in New York. A tired-looking guy accepted it, and a woman who looked as if she'd given the world of art too much, and not gotten near enough back. She gave a long speech.

"But you won't be taking any more of your *extension* courses," my mother said. "You won't be going to any of your *parties*. You won't be any SHARE lady anymore."

Of course, I'm not a SHARE lady, but my mother read an article about SHARE ladies once, about Hollywood wives with nothing better to do, and she hasn't let up on me about it since.

"You're going to have to move out of this *house*," she said. "Let's see how you like *that?*"

Debbie looked up. She was scared. I can't tell you how I hated to see that.

"*Will* we have to move, Mom?"

I knew if I told them what I wanted, a big, drafty, clean, two-story house at the beach, no carpets, just a lot of flowers and throw rugs—I knew if I said yes, she'd start to cry and not stop for weeks or years. I remembered the one-bedroom apartment Mother and I had once, off Melrose, a place that looked into another one-bedroom apartment. So small, so sad, that finally, when there was that terrific snowstorm—the only snowstorm I've ever seen in Los Angeles—I walked out of the apartment house and it wasn't until I was clear out on the street that I saw the city was completely white.

I ignored my mother and looked over at Debbie.

"Oh, I thought . . . sometimes I get a little *tired* of this house. It's *nice*, but you know? It's a little *on the nose*. A little like the Spelling house, you know? I'd thought something a little more like the way Jane Fonda lives. . . ."

"Doesn't she live in a *pig sty* or something?" Davie asked.

"She's up for an award, mo-mo!" Debbie said to him. (In our house, "mo-mo" is short for "moron." The other person answers back "ron-ron" to make it *right.)*

But Davie was back watching Donna Summers singing "I Will Survive." Maybe it wasn't. Actually, I remember, it was "Last Dance." (I guess you're right. If you start looking at the world, it really does become a mirror. Everything out there is an index, or a clue, if we can just figure it out.)

But what I was thinking is this. The Spellings are nice, they really *are* nice! But wouldn't *anybody* rather be Jane Fonda? I had, with my own mouth and my own mind, kept my daughter from the bad things in the world, maybe not forever, but for the next fifteen minutes.

My mother was furious. It's not safe to contradict her. She's spent sixty-something years getting that across.

"You think you're pretty smart," she said. "But do you know how *old* you are? Do you have any idea of the kind of settlement you're *really* going to get? Do you think Ian hasn't been putting his money in Swiss banks? They *all* do that! Oh, he cares about the kids *now*, but in a couple of years when he has some with his new wife, he won't give a *shit* about them! He won't care if they live or die!"

She certainly had everybody's attention.

But all the time she was saying it, I had this funny feeling. I was Wonder Woman, fending her off with my bracelets. I'd had fears, these fears, you know? That when Ian left, I didn't feel any pain, because I was dead. But now Mother was saying these awful things that I *knew* hurt me, because they always *did* hurt me, and here they were, not really hurting me.

I tell you, I got so excited, I got so *high* off that, I hardly knew where to look. Someone else ran up from the back of the auditorium, up on stage, and got his award. My God, I thought, I can do anything. I *know* it's a general statement, don't tell me that in the margin! I can be free.

The kids were looking so terrible by this time, I did what I'd never done or dreamed of doing. I laughed right at her. I laughed out loud. "Oh, come *on*," I said. "There's plenty of money for all of us, and I don't belong to the SHARE ladies. I've told you that before, about a couple of hundred thousand times."

"You don't know what it is," she said. "You don't know what it is to be alone."

The kids looked scared.

"Oh, I don't know, it might be kind of nice. I thought I might take the kids to . . . Bali!"

"Bazoombas!" Davie's friend said.

"*Stupid*," she said. "You're so *stupid*—there's no point in talking to anyone so stupid. The kids are going to leave you, just like Ian did. You'll be all alone. A woman where I work died all alone at night. It was over a long weekend, and do you know how long it took them to find her?"

"Eight days," I said. "A little over a week. You told me already."

"Eight days," she said, tapping her foot, jiggling her eyes, "and she'd had her electric blanket turned up to high. You can't imagine how it *smelled* in that house."

"Look, Mother," I said. I could see that maybe we wouldn't be talking much after this. I might be losing my husband and my mother too, in less than a month. "I can't even tell you *how*, exactly, but I know exactly what I *want* to be doing from now on. I want to have a good time."

She looked incredulous. Literally like she couldn't believe her eyes and ears. Then she said, "*You!* Are you kidding? You can't even ride a *bike!*"

"I'll learn," I said.

"You can't even play *poker.*"

"I'll pass on that."

"You can't even dance."

"I will!"

"There's no point in even talking to you!"

"Maybe not."

Then my mother looked very crafty. "I understand what you're trying to do," she said. "In your own way you're trying to cope. And, well, I admire you for it. But there's no point in repressing your anger. You can get *cancer* that way. No, really. You can."

Was she really even fighting me? Was she just trying to protect me? Was she trying to do for me what I hoped I'd do for my kids? Anyway, it was her last try. Because her best friend had died of cancer. *That* was so bad we didn't even talk about it.

But I had my vision. Maybe it was the movies, maybe it was just California. I thought of what I'd heard about biofeedback, sweet people on *Sixty Minutes* making electric trains run with their brains alone. I thought of the Contreras clinic, harmless folks chewing apricot seeds and playing gin rummy on the lawn.

"Oh, well," I said. "I'm not going to worry about that."

"I can't even *talk to you!*"

My mother was raving. And not that I was sure I could

make a habit of it, but I loved her then more than I ever did in my life.

The kids were glued to the screen. The Big Ones were coming, and I was curious too.

"You're a fool!" my mother said. But I didn't answer.

She stood in the door. She stood there a minute, and vanished.

Jane Fonda walked up for her award. I started to cry, and the kids looked over at me. "Isn't that just *great?*" I said. "Isn't that just *great* that she got it?"

I got up and went out on the bedroom balcony. It's a little one and it hadn't been swept, naturally. My feet crunched on peppers, and leaves of a pepper tree brushed my face. I heard the Best Actor from inside the room. He was so happy. I remembered John Wayne from a couple of years ago. I'd never liked his work, but I was sorry he was sick, and even then I'd loved it when he said, *I'm going to be around for a long time yet*. Maybe he wasn't, but I will be.

11

You know me, Pearl, I'd like to be able to say I met him by accident. But you know it'd be a crock of shit if I said it. So what if I say that after I walked out on Ed, I had to seriously consider my situation. I was "retired." All the places I could think of that were waiting for me were places I'd die to stay out of. I could see them as well as I see you now.

The fluorescent little crappy box where I'd typed so much of my life away. The other little box where I slept. That pink thing of Garnet's. In a family full of black sheep (like Sandy, like my brother, like Fran, *I* was in danger of becoming a black sheep). Oh, I know what I was *supposed to do!* Work one day a week on a Welcome Wagon! Take a part-time job baby-sitting. (Because old folks get along so well with *children*, and they both need *love*, don't you see?) Even take up yoga, like I supposed Garnet would be doing soon.

I wasn't so much of a fool as to say I didn't *know* what I was walking out on. The chance of a lifetime. Even I knew that. You couldn't say he was a bastard; you couldn't even say he was a bore. You *could*, but shit. He was actually a pretty nice guy. (That's all I'm going to say about it.)

"I'll just be gone for a few minutes, I feel a little faint, I'm going to get some air," I told him, and I stepped out on the front porch of his sister's house twenty blocks back from the beach in Santa Monica. Square City! All up and down the block, houses which were new and silly forty years ago (the kind that when you got married Pearl, Fran stuck a fire-cracker in the new muddy lawn and mud went all over the front-room ceiling!). Now those miniature castles and stuff had lawns like fiberglass (a cannon wouldn't make a dent in those lawns), and perfect trees, and the right kind of flowers. I walked down the little concrete walk and turned around and looked at Ed, standing there on the porch. Money in the bank, a lanyard around his neck, and a good heart in his old chest. Living in a world . . .

"You're sure you don't want me to come with you? Dear?"

"No, I just feel a little faint. I need a little air. Dear."

I gave him a wave and a bright smile, turned at the end of the little walk, and out, to the right, onto the sidewalk. I took a last look at his brother-in-law's roses. And then walked, slowly, as if I were feeling a little faint, up to the next block, and turned toward the beach. I remembered that a few blocks over, there was a rent-a-car place.

Walking and running, scared to death he'd find me, I made it up to the big cliffs by the Bellevue. I checked out the ocean in the late afternoon. I took off my sandals and walked in bare feet along the palisades, past the Georgian, where all those rich people slept on the porch with their mouths open. I bent down and rolled up my slacks so I could walk better, still scared to death I'd look up and see his Ford LTD sliding along beside me.

"Grace?"

And I'd have to say something nice.

It wasn't until after I'd rented the car—boy, I *hate* to drive in the city, or out in the desert on those lonesome roads, or on freeways with all those cars; I hate to drive *my* car, or *borrow* a car, or *rent* a car! It wasn't until I was in the car, and made a right turn in traffic turning north on Pacific, which, as I remembered, *had* to turn into the Coast Highway, that it more or less dawned on me. I was doing to Ed the exact same thing that Fran had done to me years before.

The other thing I noticed was that I was driving along the coast, and if my memory didn't fail me, Coalinga was definitely inland from LA.

That was because I didn't know the city anymore!

That was because I didn't really know how to drive!

The tears started streaming down my face.

Where was I going to go, Pearl? What was I going to do? If I was going to drive home, I was going to have to take San Vicente. That was going to take me past Garnet's house, and she didn't want me there! Then I'd have to take Wilshire and turn onto the San Diego Freeway. I'd get stuck in the worst of the rush-hour traffic! I knew, crying or not, that if I took it north far enough, out across the valley and over the Grapevine, if I avoided the Bakersfield turnoff and stayed on Highway 5, in a few hundred miles I'd be home.

So I made a U-turn in traffic, and another, until I was on the Coast Highway going north. That way, for a few more hours I could put off going home.

I owned the furniture in my apartment. I had five thousand dollars in the bank. I had the pension, you could barely live on it, but along with Social Security, you *could* live on it. I had a nine-year-old car up in the carport. I hated to drive it, but I could drive it. I had two kids.

Other than that I didn't have anything.

I couldn't even muster up a thought. I kept a grip on the wheel and stayed in the slow lane.

It took me maybe two hours to get as far as Santa Barbara, and I took a chance and took the off ramp—making another left turn in traffic!—heading south again, looking for a motel.

Then I got excited. I saw my hands on the wheel of the car; the knuckles were white. Believe me, this time I wasn't thinking of tea dancing at the Biltmore!

I went into a crappy little Motel 6 and signed for a room. The man looked at me funny.

He asked me, "Any luggage?"

I gave him a *look* and said, "No!"

Then I got smart and said, "I just came in on the *train* from Pittsburgh to *Los Angeles!* And they *lost* my luggage, can you imagine?"

But he was back looking at the TV.

I went out and bought a bottle and some cheese and crackers, and stayed up in bed until after Johnny Carson.

The next morning, I had some coffee, got in the car, got some gas, and left. The air was foggy and sweet.

I tell you, Pearl, it all came back to me! The motel in Carpinteria with the Statue of Liberty in front! The other little place with all the succulents, and the crazy lady who spent her time covering her whole motel with murals. The times when Fran would take me on hunting trips with him, up to the "wilderness" behind Santa Barbara, and I'd go with him, begging to come back this way by the Coast, so that we could stop at one of those goofy little motels. I saw we were just one of many couples, too, you know?

I'm not saying this was a gorgeous trip! Because no one was staying in the motels now. All the traffic was over on the freeway. These crappy little towns were *out of it*. But every once in a while I'd *see* something, and it would bring back the trips up here, or *down*, to the racetrack in Del Mar, or over the border where he always got into trouble, drinking himself sick at the "world's longest bar," or once when we sailed in the Wrights' boat down to San Diego and then—how did we get there?—we ended up over in Tecate, drinking and singing Mexican songs.

What *happened* to all of that? is what I was going to ask him. You bastard! Where'd you *take* it? Because I'd gone thirty years without seeing a glimpse of it, once.

I drove through Grover City, Shell Beach, all the way to San Luis Obispo. A lot of crud had come in around here, I admit it. Tract houses like I'd lived in with Dick. Oil wells sticking up out of a perfectly good ocean. All that *condo* shit.

I drove through the place the first time, that's how out-of-it the town really was. I didn't notice until I got all the way out, and on the road to Big Sur, that I'd gone too far. You know how I hate to take chances when I drive, but I made the turn and came back. Then I saw the sign, "GAVIOTAS," just a chintzy little thing, stuck up by a McDonald's golden arches. I got out and found a pay phone, braced the book against my stomach, and picked out his address. Then I went to a gas station, pretended I was lost, and looked up his street on the map. *Then* I drove in to a *forest of tract houses.*

I was ready to cry again, because I *knew the man* I'd been keeping track of for thirty years, in all the telephone books in Southern California, and he wasn't supposed to live in a place like this.

The tract was the kind that didn't have through streets, so I passed the same set of houses over and over again. The lawns weren't mowed, or not enough of them were. One house in every three had those rust stains on the sills. The streets had hundreds of kids in them, all playing with their pukey little Frisbees, all skidding out in front of my car with their fucking stupid skateboards! Or playing their stupid ball games, getting ready to break some windows and get grounded for it, and the real little kids had their red plastic trikes, paddling their fucking little feet off. The *wives* were all out on the street *talking* to each other, all their hair up in curlers and their behinds like tractors.

And every living-room window had those cruddy tieback net curtains.

Shit City, and no mistake.

I even passed the house I'd thought he'd lived in all these years, not once, but maybe two, three, four times. Peach-colored stucco, with dichondra in front, a bougainvillea, a palm tree growing at a funny angle over the driveway, a three-wheeled plastic trike, some gazanias, and—the last time I went by—a wind chime in this little alcove by the front door. The streets here were the names of streets we used to live on. Cypress, Micheltorena, Argus, La Monte. And even though the map said I should be *out of there* already, I'd take the same stupid turns again. Cypress, Micheltorena, Argus, La Monte. I couldn't find where he lived.

Finally I turned right and not left, onto a street which went back down to the freeway. Maybe, maybe, I should just forget it, turn inland the next chance I got, go on home.

But it was too late in the day for me to get to Coalinga before nine or ten at night. And I don't drive in the dark. So I decided to find a motel for just one more night. Get some rest.

Before I found the motel, I stopped into a Lucky's. Because I needed a toothbrush and some paste, and some shampoo. I needed some Woolite and some panty hose. I needed a bottle and some cheese and crackers for tonight.

I hate Lucky's! I hate Vons and Alpha Betas! I hate Zodi's and White Fronts and Two Guys! I hate all that *so much!* I hate the steam irons and the distilled water you have to put in them and those terrible little plastic jump seats they have, to stick their kids in when they . . .

In the aisle, looking for shampoo, I couldn't get by. There was this old fart, picking up the Head and Shoulders, then he'd look at it. Then he'd put it back and pick up the Breck and look at it. Then he'd pick up a *jar* of something and look at it. He had a shopping cart with a kid in a plastic jump seat wedged in the front part. The kid was awake but out-of-it. But he had another one, a thin, dark little customer, who kept dancing around like she had to go to the bathroom. "Come on, Daddy, I want to go *home!* I *hate* this, Daddy, come on!"

But Dad kept studying the shampoo.

"Just a minute, Jeannette! We've got time enough. It's important to know what you're paying for."

The kid saw me, but you could see she was the kind who'd rather see her father embarrassed than do anything about it. So she gave me a terrible face and lolled her head back at the geezer there—the kind of guy who lets his sweater go so long between trips to the cleaner's that it goes *up* in the back. . . .

He's reading about *shampoo!* My life is ruined, finished, over, and he's spending his life in the fine print! I started tapping my feet then, I guess, and drumming with my fingernails on the rim of the shopping cart. Because if *he thought* that I was going to *back down* that aisle, and get something *else* while he devoted himself to his *shampoo!*

Something in the old guy's back got stiff. He straightened up like he was listening to something—the siren announcing World War III. He turned his head and looked at the kid.

"Jeannette! Are you doing that?"

Jeannette shook her head no.

The guy looked down at the kid in the plastic thing, but *he* was dead to the world. He looked around at all the crud under the fluorescent lights, and then he turned around and took a look at me.

"Grace?"

"Fran?"

"Frank," he said. "Well, for God's sake. Grace, how are you?"

I felt like I was going to faint. This time I really did.

"Well," I said. "Aren't you going to buy a girl a drink?"

"Oh," he said. "Gee, Grace, I haven't had a drink in seventeen years."

I couldn't think of what to say to that.

"But I could buy you some coffee, though."

"I don't drink coffee," I said. Then damned if I didn't recognize what he was wearing. Faded to a clean old beige now, it used to be Fran's gorgeous, sporty yellow sleeveless sweater.

"*Fran*," I said. "Jesus H. Christ. The great American author."

He looked at his kid. "Jeannette, this is . . . an old friend of mine, Grace . . . What is your last name, Grace?"

"It doesn't matter," I said.

We stared at each other while people began to pile up their carts on either side.

"Well," I said. "See ya."

"No!" he said. "No, Grace, wait a minute. I live right around here, come on over for a few minutes, I . . . gee—I guess, I'd like you to meet my wife."

"Is it that . . . ?" But I'd forgotten her name!

"Nah! No, it's a very nice woman. I know she'd like to meet you."

And while I picked up my shampoo and got my panty hose, I could hear Jeannette whining from the other aisle, "What's *she* coming over for? You said you were going to play ball!" And Fran saying, "Sshh! She'll hear you."

It was the stucco place with the wind chime. It was about four o'clock in the afternoon when we got there, and a cloud had gone over the sun. There was a kind of raw wind going on, the kind of weather, the kind of afternoon that when Fran came home when Garnet was a little girl:

"Hi, honey, how are you?"

But he would have come in the back door, through the kitchen, and wouldn't answer.

"Fran?"

But he'd go straight through the kitchen, into the dining room, to the sideboard where the whiskey was, and pour himself a stiff drink.

"Would you get me one too?"

But he would be out of the dining room by now, in that little living room, sitting in the green chair by the radio, staring at the last of the light which came in through the glass curtains.

"Fran?"

But there wouldn't be an answer. And I'd look at the kitchen . . . *spotless*, with a bowl of oranges on top of the refrigerator, and spotless oilcloth on the kitchen table, and the spotless Gaffers & Sattler stove which I'd spend a whole day, sometimes, taking apart and putting together again. I'd look at Garnet hunched over the kitchen table, working in her color book, and if she was good, she could turn on the radio and listen to *Captain Midnight*, provided she kept it down, so it wouldn't disturb Fran. I'd look in the dining room where the table was set for the dinner that cooked in the oven. I'd think of the clean towels and sheets, rough dried in the sun, hand-cranked through the wringer of that old washer, I'd think of the ironed pillowslips that I'd taught Garnet to embroider, I'd look at the glass curtains, *spotless*, because I always had a set drying on the rack out in the garage.

"Fran?"

And I'd walk into the dining room and pour myself a drink of my own.

And go on out there with him.

"What is it *now*, Fran?"

But he'd be sitting there in total despair.

"Please, tell me!"

And maybe, maybe, he'd grind it out. "This life, this life, this awful, stinking *little* life. . . ."

And I'd look through the curtains out to the front lawn, and the row of palm trees that would be swaying in the cold wind. Maybe I'd be dumb enough to say:

"Have you lost your job?"

And he'd look at me with hatred.

"That's all you can *think* of, isn't it?"

I'd be smelling over-browned potatoes, and I'd say:

"Don't you feel well?"

And he'd look at me and smile, and shake his head as though the whole thing was hopeless, absolutely hopeless.

"Is it something I did?"

(But I knew goddamn well all *I* did was spend six hours out of that particular day ironing his goddamned shirts. Twenty minutes to a shirt. And then pick up the kid from nursery school, and then shop, and then start dinner.)

Sometimes he would tell me: "Don't you *know*, can't you even *conceive*, that there's more to life than this crackerbox?"

This little yellow house, so clean you could eat off any place in it, a crackerbox?

So I'd stare at him. I wouldn't know what to say. It was the best place *I'd* ever lived in, is all I knew.

Then he'd start asking the questions.

"You don't even know, do you, there's a whole life out there!"

Well, we always went to Virginia Wright's New Year's Eve party.

We went to the races a lot.

We'd take Garnet out to the movies.

We played poker once a week.

"Don't you understand? There's *life!* There's literature! There's *art!* There's travel!"

Sometimes three or four couples from the *Daily News*—we'd all go together to rent a cabin for a long weekend up in Big Bear. . . .

Then he would say it. "I could have written a novel, Grace. A *good* novel, I know it."

"Well," I'd say. "Why, for *Christ's sake*, don't you *do* it?"

But he'd look at me with hatred.

"Sure! After working eight hours a day. And an hour trip home on the streetcar, you want me to sit down and *write a novel!*"

And just about that time Garnet would come out, walk right into it, and say:

"What's for dinner?"

Or, "When's dinner?"

So he wouldn't have to say it—that *we* were what was keeping him from everything he wanted—he would only have to look it, and say, like there was a giant tank rolling over him, "Come on, Garnet, come on over and sit beside me. How's it going, kid?"

And maybe, only later, as we would be getting undressed for bed, would he explain it to me kindly, *again.* "You know what Dostoevski said, don't you?"

Well, *Christ*, by that time you'd better believe I knew what Dostoevski said. But Fran would go over it with me again. He'd explain it sadly and kindly. "It's not your fault, I know that. But Dostoevski always said that wives and children killed more artists than the cholera."

I'd be in bed by that time. Sitting under the bedside lamp that I'd hammered into the wall, because Fran didn't do that sort of thing, looking down at the chenille spread, thinking that I'd certainly gotten it white, but that the new soap had left it pretty stiff, and I'd say, "Well, why don't you *write* something, then? If you can't write a novel, maybe even a short *story!* Or did we kill that too?"

He'd pull on his pajamas like he was God on a rock.

"If you write it, I'll even type it, okay? I'll send it off for you, okay? Or did we kill the post office too?"

By that time he'd be in bed, and as if nothing had happened, he'd reach over to have sex. I'd look over at Fran's heartbroken, handsome face as he pulled his pajamas down over his rump, and my answer to him *and* Dostoevski was: *You make me want to puke!*

You make me sick, you know that?

And I'd roll up in a ball as hard as a rock, and sleep.

Then he started writing, of course. I typed the stuff for him, and sent it out.

I'd get into bed early every night—because what was the use of sitting in the living room? *He* wasn't there! I'd sit up in bed and watch him write. He'd be smiling, he'd be creating, with two fingers. He looked so good in his long-sleeved shirts. He looked so good in his yellow sleeveless sweater. He looked so good in his wavy hair and his mustache. He was so funny, when he was funny.

Except he was full of shit.

He made me want to puke.

And after six short stories he left me, and I started finding out about the women. Because he left some of them too, and they called me up to check it out.

I found out I was lucky to know how to type.

I kept track of his address.

But even though I kept looking in the card catalogs of every library I went in for over twenty years (and I read a lot now, even more than I did then), I never saw Wickendon, Francis.

He stood in the alcove by the door.

He said, "Come on in. Gee, I hope Norma's home, I'd really like for you to meet her."

I stepped inside the house, and the first thing I noticed was, the place was very clean.

Then I noticed the old watercolor of the man with the fish between his teeth that we used to have over the piano.

I noticed the *other* watercolor of the little Japanese couple holding hands. "*You* don't need this, Grace," he'd said. "You never liked it from the day I bought it."

"Take it, you miserable fucking bastard, take it! If you don't take it, I'll break it, I'll burn it, I'll sell it!"

So naturally he took it.

I saw the little print of the cathedral of Chartres. Well, he'd had it when he married me. It was one of the reasons I'd loved him so much! To be so handsome! To be a newspaperman! To have a pastel of a cathedral on your furnished-room wall!

I looked down at the end of the living room (not a whole hell of a lot bigger than ours used to be), and in the dark of the late afternoon I saw some green and gold in the bookshelf.

"The set of Mark Twain," I said. "Twenty-six volumes."

He looked so pleased that I remembered. "Twenty-five. I lost one somewhere. Come on in the kitchen, Grace. I think I can find you a drink. Gee, I can't believe this is happening! Norma'll be home soon. She'll be really amazed to meet you."

I took one last look at the living room—that little ashtray shaped like two gold hands! That little stork made out of gray metal! Ah, you left me the house, you bastard, but you took everything that made it wonderful to me.

He was shorter than I was now. He was careful when he walked.

"Is that really your same old sweater?" I said.

"Oh, yeah. I hate to give it up. I really love it."

He'd put the little kid down in the back bedroom somewhere. It raised hell, and then finally quieted down.

He went over to the stove and looked in the oven. Something in there was cooking. It smelled pretty good. Then he reached up in a cupboard and measured out some rice.

"Since Norma's working now, I try to do most of the cooking."

I was looking around the kitchen. It was pretty, much

prettier than ours used to be. About a million cookbooks over the sink. Funny sayings and notes, stuck with magnets onto the refrigerator. A Japanese paper lantern over the table. Some bullfight posters. And it was clean! Something was screwy about it, though. It looked like the house of some people who are getting ready to grow up, they're on the *verge* of growing up, but they haven't grown up.

The rice was stowed away. He looked up at the kitchen clock to see if he was pretty much on schedule for dinner. "What can I get you, Grace? Beer? Wine?"

"Hill and Hill blend," I said, surprised. "What else?"

"I'll see if we have any."

He poured me out a drink. And we sat in his kitchen while I drank it.

"You're looking very well, Grace."

"The legs are the last to go," I said.

He got up to turn on the light.

"Norma ought to be here pretty soon," he said.

"How long have you been married?" I asked him.

"Eight years now."

"What'd you do in between?"

"I was married. Nobody you know. It didn't work out."

He didn't ask *me*, why should he? What did *I* ever do that was interesting?

"What about the writing? Did you ever do any writing?"

Already by this time, the age, the old man, was falling away. He looked pretty good to me by now, still young, still handsome! Elegant, and with a tan, and the most beautiful eyes in the world. How he *could* look. Now he leaned back in his chair, lit a cigarette, inhaled it, looked around the bright yellow kitchen.

"Actually . . ." he said, then gave it up. "No," he said.

Norma came in a few minutes later. She stared at me.

I was so *old*, it said all over her face. But I stared back. Because she was just about Garnet's age, and that's not young.

She was pretty, though. Short, and dark, with a head full of dark brown curls. She had a tan too. It looked like they both spent a lot of time at the beach. And you will never believe what she said to him, Pearl, after she'd finished being polite to me: "Hello! How are you? Isn't this a coincidence? I've heard so much about you . . . *No!* Really good things, and of course I know Garnet very well, she's such a nice person."

The first thing she said to Fran (after she'd checked the rice, and the meat in the oven), the first thing she said before "Where's Jeannette?" and "How's the baby?" was "Did you get any writing done today?"

Fran looked over at me and said, "A little. But of course I met Grace here . . . I got a little sidetracked."

She sighed.

He looked at her and shrugged and laughed. "Ah *come* on, kid! Gimme a break."

"Of course, it's hard with the kids," she said. She looked like she felt awful about it.

"Well," I said, "you know what they say. Actually, it was a Russian who said it first, I think. *Wives and children kill more artists . . .*"

Pearl, she didn't crack a smile. She bought it, hook, line, and sinker.

She was very nice. She talked about her job. She said she was sure the little kid would wake up soon. She asked Fran if he'd remembered to pay the electric bill. Of course he hadn't, so she let out a lot of breath and said she'd take care of it after dinner. She apologized that she hadn't remembered to offer me something to eat, and pulled out two kinds of crackers and two kinds of cheese. The exact kinds I like.

"This is a nice house you've got," I said. "How do you keep it so clean when you're working?"

"Saturdays and Sundays," she said, and smiled. "Listen," she said, "would you like to stay to dinner? There's plenty."

"No," I said. "Thank you a lot, but I've got to be going now."

But I couldn't get up. I was looking at the refrigerator door. There was one of Fran's poems up there. It must have been a birthday card to her, something like that, he'd done the picture too. His drawings were so funny! His printing was so wonderful! He always made anything, everything, so wonderful!

I stood up. I wanted to tell Norma something, shake hands with her, clap her on the back. "Garnet will be so surprised," I told her. "That we met like this. She thinks the world of you."

I wouldn't let them walk me to the car.

I got in and started to drive. Well, what else was I supposed to do? I had to go back to LA to return the car.

I had in mind going to see Ian's parents. They lived in Santa Monica. They'd always been nice to me. They'd give me some coffee. Then I'd decide what to do. (Was I going back to Ed? Well, to tell you the truth, I took a little longer walk than I thought. Two *days*, to be exact. . . .)

I took 101, the freeway, south this time—the hell with the pukey little Coast Highway. I got straight in the middle lane and drove.

South, toward Brentwood, Santa Monica, the valley. Away from wind chimes and bullfight posters and tieback curtains and unmowed grass.

It had been years since I asked him, "*Why'd you do it?*" But here I was in the car, holding on to the wheel with both hands, asking again, like a total sap, a total patsy, "*Why'd you do it?*" Because that watercolor of the guy with the fish and the Japanese couple, that pastel of the cathedral at wherever, those were mine too! Those years made them mine too! Those kids could have been mine too. (But I have to admit that made me laugh. Maybe he could *keep* the pictures!)

"What good did you get out of it?" I asked him, out loud. "You caused *all that heartbreak*, *all that suffering*, and what did you get out of it? Another fucking *wife*, another set of fucking *kids*."

That's when I started to cry. Not for now, but for all of it. For all my heartbreak and suffering. For all my heartbreak in the night. For Garnet coming home after school, sweaty and wrinkled, with a big stupid smile on her face, and all I could say to her was, *Do you have to be so clumsy! Do you have to shake the furniture when you come in!* And then at least have the satisfaction that someone else in the world was crying, along with me.

For Sandy, dancing alone every afternoon in front of the television. For Dick, throwing shoes, because I couldn't love him. For . . .

What it was, was this: You couldn't get out of it by leaving your wife. ("You can't get out as easy as that, you bastard!" I told Fran, out loud in the car.) You couldn't get out by wanting your husband to die, and waiting until he did. You couldn't get out by driving away your kids, or running away from your parents. No, you'd have to stop *eating*, is what you'd have to do, you'd have to stop wearing clothes. I could understand those TV documentaries in the sixties about hippie freaks who not only wouldn't eat meat but wouldn't cook anything. I could understand those hermits who hang out in the desert and eat locusts. Because you don't have to cook locusts, so you don't have to have a kitchen, don't you see? Because the minute you have a kitchen, I don't care if it's a fucking pot stuck in a fucking *fireplace*, then you've got to have some fall guy cleaning out the ashes.

I hate to drive at night, but I made good time. By now I was hitting the San Fernando Valley, which is a nest of that shit. A worldwide scam based on that one thing. The pot, which needs the stove, and then the food, and then something to keep the food from spoiling, and then one of those fucking floors that somebody gets to keep clean. And pretty soon you've got leftovers spoiling in the refrigerator, and a cupboard full of soup tins with no labels on them. Your husband's gaining weight and hating you for it, *so of course he leaves* because he can't think of any other way to lose twenty-five pounds and he thinks he'll puke if he sees another pot roast cooked with a can of mushroom soup mixed up with onion-soup dip and wrapped up in foil! Then he reads that foil causes cancer, and that cinches it.

I thought about my Apple brown Betty, made with Grape-nuts and a loving hand. "Shit," I said to Fran. "I really mean it!"

But I was getting hungry.

It seemed perfectly sensible to drop by Ian's folks'. We'd always gotten along pretty well, even though they were Jewish. And they'd been married close to fifty years, they were bound to have some food in the house.

I made the right turns, I found the right street. They lived close to downtown. On Normandy, above Wilshire. Not so far from where I used to live when I was single.

But it had changed. It was a terrible street. I pulled in between two cars, and got out. Big white two-story duplex apartments all up and down each side, shining in the moonlight, and even after fifty years, sixty years of being a neighborhood, nobody around there had had the sense to plant any trees. Just dinky box hedges, and hydrangea, the hydrangeas your kids send you every year when they don't want to come over.

But clean! That grass—there wasn't a peep out of it! They'd mowed it until it didn't dare grow. I went up on the porch. They live on the ground floor, and the lights were on. I looked in the window.

They'd already had dinner. They were sitting in the living room watching television. The lights were bright. Ian's mother likes *beige*, so they had beige walls and big beige brocade couches, and thick beige carpets. The couches had plastic covers on them, and from his chair to her place on the couch, from her place on the couch out to the kitchen, they had those clear plastic runners across the rug. I could tell they'd had dinner because the dishwasher was rumbling over a *Starsky and Hutch* rerun. The lights were on in the kitchen. There were serving dishes coated with foil out on the sink; there was Tupperware, and the end of a roast swirled up in clear plastic. (She was waiting for the things to go down to room temperature before she put them in the refrigerator.) Do I have to say what the kitchen floor looked like? Liberace could have chipped away little pieces of it and had it mounted into rings.

I decided to go somewhere else for dinner. (It was a dumb idea anyway.) I drove back down Wilshire into Santa Monica. It was a shopping night, the stores would be open until nine.

I kept thinking what a pretty place Santa Monica was, so much prettier than Coalinga, and thinking that the next big quake, this pretty little town was going to take a dive smack dab into the ocean.

I had some idea of taking a walk on the pier—do you remember, Pearl, when we'd go out there on Saturdays, when you and Fran and Duane and I would go out there? I had some idea of getting my fortune told. . . .

It was jumping in downtown Santa Monica. I had some idea of parking on the street because I was afraid of driving out on the pier in case of the quake, but there weren't any parking places, so finally I went into the parking lot of their one big department store. I walked through the store on my way to the pier.

Henshey's Department Store! Say, this wasn't so bad! This was like the places I used to take Garnet when she was little! This was like a real department store instead of those stupid *shopping centers*.

I walked through the book department, and the jewelry, and the candy—*good* candy, not that Sears Roebuck shit. I walked by wigs and purses.

I got to the notions. I remembered I needed some safety pins because the hem on one side of my slacks was coming out and I didn't want to sew it until I got home. So I found the pins.

Then I thought, what the hell. I might as well get some thread and a needle, who knows exactly when I'm going home?

Then I saw some of those things that lengthen your bra straps. I got some. My bra had been cutting into me like a bastard.

Then I saw some stuff that hardens your nails. I'd been having trouble with one nail, I decided to get some.

Then I saw a lady buy a little wooden circle hoop, to hold embroidery, and some cotton.

"It's for my granddaughter," she said. "I think it's a nice kind of useful present, don't you?"

Then I saw a lady trying to exchange a satin stocking

holder. "I don't want my money back," she said. "It's not that. It's just I got my daughter green, and she wanted salmon pink."

I saw a woman, maybe forty, buy some padded hangers. "They're for a friend of mine," she said. "They're a thank-you gift."

I saw a woman with a plastic bag full of empty plastic bottles. "My sister's going on a trip," she said. "She's been saving for it for a lifetime. Don't you think this will be good to put her perfume in, and her cold cream? So she won't break anything?" She ended up buying a whole plastic bag, hanging from a hanger, with separate partitions for the perfume and the cream, and also for a nightgown, and places to keep the dirty underwear separate from the clean.

Not one goddamn thing—except the thing that hung from the hanger—cost more than five-ninety-five.

My God, Pearl! If I had the money I've spent on notions!

I thought of how they put the notions counter on the ground floor, always near the entrance. I saw heartbreak, and suffering. Women wanting to give their children love, and settling for a pink padded box. Women who'd made it as far as they had by embroidery, and they only hoped to God embroidery would work one more time, women . . .

Then I saw something that made me so sad.

A little counter, right in the center of notions. Between the pocket calendars and the Snoopy notebook paper I saw a pair of ceramic praying hands, made out of cream-colored china. They cost exactly five-ninety-five.

Was it Arbogast, out at the office, out at the school, who had given me those exact same hands?

"Oh, kid," I said out loud. "I'm sorry."

Thinking about the buttons and the snaps, the bath salts for people who were allergic, the pinholders for people who didn't sew, the small change smuggled out of grocery money or Social Security; thinking about the women with their little bits of satin, I began to cry. *Again.*

I *cried*, Pearl! I cried so hard I couldn't stop for dinner. I couldn't go into a restaurant looking like that. And I was afraid to go into a bar by myself. I wanted a drink but I couldn't go into a liquor store to buy a bottle, because where would I get the glass? And you aren't allowed to have an open bottle in your car anyway.

I got out of there, fast. I skidded up, through traffic signals, to Montana and turned right. I drove to Ed's sister's house.

The shades were all pulled to the same length; they had little tassels hanging down. The lights were on, and someone had even turned the sprinkler on the front lawn. I wondered. Was Ed in there? And were they lecturing him: "Well, what did you *expect* would happen, with a woman you'd—admit it, Ed—a woman you'd picked up in a hotel?"

I thought of when I was a little kid and my mother got me a white silk hair ribbon that I thought was *it*. The first day I wore it to school I was a jerk enough to say to the girl next to me, "See my new hair ribbon?" And she said, "My mother says hair ribbons that come in metal barrettes are *common!*" I put my hand up to my hair, and felt the metal under the silk or grosgrain or whatever the shit it was.

"Yes, I'm common!" I said to them behind the shades. "And that isn't the half of it. But tell me the truth, Mrs. Whatever Your Name Is. Don't you think window shades with strings hanging down from them are just a little bit *common?*"

So, even though I hated to do it, I drove over to Garnet's.

The lights were almost all off in the place. Maybe it was because she was my daughter, but after only the few days since she'd found out, I could *see* the untidiness in the place, the way it was out of focus—the dead leaves under the hedges, the way the tin cans weren't separated from the paper trash, the fine greasy dust on the kitchen baseboards, the way she'd only learned enough Spanish to tell the servants they were nice—the whole smudged look of her, looking like she was getting ready to duck from the next person who came along to hit her. . . .

So dumb, I thought. So fucking dumb! *Never* could do the

right thing, *never* even learned to curl her hair! Never learned to have her nails done, never learned how to tell a joke!

Had Ian come back? No way, José.

You blew it, Garnet! After all the things I told you, you absolutely blew it.

I wondered where the kids were. Because she spoils them so! And I remembered the nights even when Fran was around, when I stuck Garnet in bed and said, "All right, that's *it!* If you come out for a glass of water, you're going to get *switched!*" And shut the door *absolutely tight!* Even though I knew she was afraid of the dark.

And when I went in, Pearl, she didn't want me.

"So *dumb,*" I said to her, back in the car. "So dumb you don't even *know* you're dumb!"

Needless to say, *I* wasn't so dumb. I wasn't so dumb as to fail to notice. That they were inside and warm, and had dinner and their own dumb good time. And whatever their good time was, they didn't want me in it.

Sandy, mean as he was, was the only one I could ever talk to. But he never told me where he lived, and Garnet wouldn't either. All I knew about my own son was, "close to City College"!

I started the car, got back down to Santa Monica Boulevard, and turned east. Through Westwood, through Beverly Hills. Miles and miles of rich bastards! Then some kind of sex mill. And miles more. Until I got to Vermont. You know, for a while Fran and I . . .

Never mind! It was awful now. Awful. Big ugly stupid blacks! Arabs! Everybody poor! What was I even doing here? I turned right, down by the college, and there were the most pitiful run-down streets!

No lawns or anything like that. Just big families of Mexicans out on their front porches, and cars parked up on the dirt where the lawns should be. Students halfway running to class, and layers of dust over everything. Two-story frame houses gone to hell. The smell of beans, and a lot of policemen, and the whole thing lit up like it was day.

I found a house I thought might be his. A little wooden thing like the kind Fran and I had in Highland Park.

Sandy?

If he lived in a place like that, would he live alone? Would he be with a girlfriend? Or with a family? Would it be a place for . . . drugs?

The door opened on the porch, and a yellow light went on. A Mexican woman came out and started watering potted plants. Even though her front yard was hard ground, it looked like she made up for it by keeping a zillion plants on the porch.

She must have been a hundred years old.

I looked up and down the street. It could have been a foreign country.

I locked both doors and started to drive.

I stopped for gas once.

I finally stopped at Denny's, where I could get some eggs. They made me feel sick.

I was stopped once by a policeman.

"My children," I said to him. "I'm crying about my children."

He said, "Just go home, lady. And be careful, okay?"

I never drive at night. I almost never stay up past six-thirty. I'm undressed, in my slip, asleep in front of the television by six-thirty!

But about now was the time I usually wake up. I took Highway 5 at seventy. "So what if I die?" I asked them all. "*You* wouldn't even *care!*"

They'd care, all right. They'd be delighted.

I got home a little after one in the morning. There was a huge full moon, and even though I'd given up being afraid, I began to be afraid. Pull my car into that dark garage? Get out of the car, go through the dark, open the door to my living room, that sad smell, turn on the light?

The worst thing would be, no burglars, not a mad rapist in sight. And Johnny Carson was off by now.

Of course, I didn't have to go home. I could go down to

Ida's. (With her knickknacks, her cooking, her kindness that drove me nuts. I couldn't go there. And if you don't know why, Pearl, by now, I can't tell you.)

I sat there, in the freezing cold, in the desert, looking at the apartment complex under the moon. It looked like another planet, and I'm not kidding you. It was *cold* in that car, and I never had gotten the radio to work. You can believe me, Pearl, when I say I'd come to the end of the road.

After about an hour, I turned around and drove back into town. She'd think I was nuts, but tough shit.

And I knew her address. It was only another apartment. I'd been there a few times before.

She answered the door. Edna Harris. The teacher I barely knew. The only one of the faculty who had hipbones you could see. Fifteen years younger than me, but living all alone anyway. She answered the door right away, without asking *Who's there!* She looked older than she usually does, with her gray hair down her back and her makeup off. She was wearing a dark green flannel robe tied tight around her waist.

"Edna, *please!*" I sobbed, I clutched her robe. "Please! I *can't go home! You've got to let me in!*"

"Well," she said, "come in, then."

"I haven't had anything to eat for hours," I said. *"It's been terrible!"*

She didn't look very impressed, but she did go out to the kitchen.

Ordinarily, even with it being Edna, I would have turned up my nose at her house. Because who does she think she *is? Just an old maid*, for Christ's sake! But here on the one side of the living room is a wicker basket full of plants and there on another side is a poster of Queen Victoria which says *"Even a Queen Can Get the Clap,"* and there's a cut-rate stereo from a cut-rate-stereo place and a lot of classical records, and over in the corner is her cello, because she and three other people here in Coalinga have the guts to think they make up a string quartet. Across from the couch are two white wicker chairs. And above them is some farfetched picture of a lady with a white face leaning back in some kind of posture and a guy is madly kissing her neck—I *mean*, come *on*, Edna! And little vases and bookcases and all that shit, and to my knowledge she's never been married.

"They've been pretty worried about you, down at City Hall," Edna said, and brought out some brandy and a bowl of nuts. (I guess I'm never going to get dinner.)

I told her my story.

My awful story.

She's heard most of it before, at parties, when I was drunk. But not about Sandy, or Garnet kicking me out, or Ed.

I will say this for her. She never tried to say, "Oh, but women raise two children all the time."

Or, "I'm sure the kids love you in their own way."

She listened until I finished up. She kept pouring brandy for us (she's the kind of person with an ice bucket!). Finally, about four in the morning she said, "Well, you're not exactly sure if you want to retire or not, is that it?"

"I can't go back to work! I can't go home!"

"How's your money situation?"

"My husbands left me *nothing!* Nothing!"

"Yes, but how's your money situation?"

How was I supposed to know that?

"You've got Social Security and a pension? And the apartment can't cost you much."

"But I don't *want* . . ."

"Listen, Grace. There's no point in your going back to work, when you've worn out your welcome."

She sat thinking about it for a while, sipping her brandy.

Edna, you're a good old gal, but why, on *God's green earth*, you think you have the *right* to sit there with an ice bucket in this crappy apartment like some kind of a queen!

"School's out the first of June. I was going to take a charter flight to Europe. Why don't you come along? You know, take a vacation."

"Edna, *have you lost your mind?*"

She looked at me. "Why?"

"I couldn't *impose* like that. I . . ."

"I was going alone anyway."

While I was thinking of what to say, she lit up a cigarette and gave me a hard smile and said, "Well, what are you going to tell me? That you can't afford it? Or you haven't got the time? Or some other crack-brained shit?"

12

"How could I do *that?* I just *told* you, I don't have any *money*, my kids don't take *care* of me, my husbands were nothing, I suppose *you* don't know very much about that—"

But Edna cut me off. She took out a cigarette like in the old movies, she pulled it and pounded it, looked at it, felt it, did everything but *hump* it, then lit it and stuck it in her thin little mouth.

"Cool it, Grace. You aren't the only one who got dumped by her husband. You'd think you'd know that by now. You're not dumb. They're even going to have a TV show—did you read that? A situation comedy called *The Dumpies.*"

"I like you all right," I said. "But let's face it. Why would you want to go anywhere with me?"

She laughed. "Why not? Grace, you're like the old cartoon. Do you know it? The soft-drink cartoon, about advertising? *No worse than any other brand.*"

"But traveling is hard *work. You're* younger! *You're* certainly able to take it, one way or another! But who's going to take care of *me* if anything goes *wrong?* Suppose I got sick?"

Edna looked bored. "Eat some chicken soup," she said. "Take an aspirin."

"I really mean it! What if I get sick along the way! What'll *you* do then?"

"I'd walk away and leave you," she said.

"I'm not kidding!"

"You think I am?"

There was a quiet. I looked around her living room. In style, but something funny there, like no one cared about it.

"Listen, Edna."

"*You* listen, Grace."

"*I* don't have to—"

Edna looked tired. "Sometimes I wonder why I stay in this town. I came here because of a guy. You even know him, Grace! But that was a long time ago. The kids I teach aren't smart. The men I go out with are married. I've wondered and wondered why I stay."

"So?"

"I kind of like it here. I'll put it more strongly. I love it."

"There's no place on earth I hate more."

"So, come along with me."

"Why should I *do that!*" I knew how to use that voice. But Edna could use it too.

"Because you've got nowhere else to go."

"That's not true! I . . ."

She poured herself a drink and looked at me with slanty eyes.

"You don't know what it's like," I told her. "You've never had children."

"Two. One dead, one run away."

"But you're a beautiful woman. . . . You must have had a good husband. . . ."

"I left him. For the guy who worked up here. It was a big deal, for a while."

"But *why*, for God's sake," I said. "Just tell me why! What's the suffering *for*, Edna? Because I mean, I can't *stand* it any longer!"

"You're standing it," Edna said. She poured herself another drink, and grinned. "I really don't know why I like you, Grace. But I do."

* * *

The flight was awful. I'd found out I was the fourth person she'd asked. She wasn't a whole hell of a lot more popular than *I* was in Coalinga. And she made me pay my whole way, even when I told her, I *told* her! Neither of my husbands ever paid me any money, and my kids didn't care if I lived or died.

I had eight Bloody Marys between here and London. I panic on planes. "Sometimes I think I don't care whether I live or die anymore," I said to Edna.

Edna just smiled. "Well, don't look at *me*," she said.

Later in the night, when the plane was bouncing around, I said to Edna, "My God! What if we *crash!* What will we do *then?*"

"Grace, you've got something . . . macadamia nuts . . . between your teeth."

The plane dropped fifty? seventy? feet. "I can't go through too much *more* of this." And I wasn't putting it on anymore. But Edna drained off the last of her second double martini and clicked back her chair and went to sleep. She slept real neatly, her mouth together, her eyes closed, with the lids twitching just a little bit, no more than that.

I was thousands of miles from anywhere. I was scared, Pearl.

An Indian guy sitting across the aisle said something.

"*What!*" I said to him, as though he were Mr. Lambrozini with a stack of things to be run through the Xerox machine.

"We are sliding on the air! It's quite fun, don't you think?"

"Oh, sure."

I still had a whole Bloody Mary in front of me. I drank it up, and felt the plane moving, and lay back to go to sleep. Because after a while, there really isn't a whole lot else you can do.

Oh, Fran, you poor bastard, I thought in London, you really should have seen this. I thought of all his love of books and how he went on to Garnet about Mark Twain and Herman Melville. Books were born here, Fran.

(What do you want from me, Grace? he said back to me, sorrowfully. I could have been a great man! But my father died! My mother was sick! My sister, you remember how terrible it was with her. My first wife and I didn't get along! *You* didn't understand me. No, you didn't! You really didn't! My third wife . . . well, she was a good woman, but what are you supposed to do with twins? And my fourth wife works like a dog. I could have been a great man! My mother said so! We had a picture of Sir Galahad up in the living room. Everyone did, in my generation!)

I was sitting in an English pub, under a portrait of somebody. Some jerk in armor. It could have been Sir Galahad. Edna sat next to me, she found some guys. It was an hour until closing. We'd already had a lot of beers. A terrible old man in a jump suit sat next to me.

"I only have the next five hours here in London. But I was hoping you could tell me how to spend it?" He was looking at my chest, and while his left hand held a pint of bitter, his right hand, in his suit, began to do something else.

"You really think you're something, don't you?" I sneered. "Just because you've got one of *those*."

"You American girls," he said. "It doesn't get past you, does it?"

He got up. Then, while I watched him, he looked around the pub and sat next to another woman, older than I was. I mean, she was *old*. She had those old weird legs and feet with bunions, and a flowered housedress. *Look at that, Pearl!* You can see how her heels are run over from a block away!

The guy in the jump suit sat down next to that crone and with one hand on his dick and the other on the table, asked her what must have been his five-hour question. Whatever it was she said, he liked it all right, because he grinned a toothless grin, got up, and came back with two giant beers.

Sex is the worm, Pearl! It is the *worm!* Did you know that when you rode with my daughter? Did you know that when you smiled, when you waxed your legs?

"Everyone in this place is over sixty," I said to a woman sitting next to me. "Is it always like this here?"

"*What?*" she said, and cupped her hand to her ear. She was my age.

I couldn't stand it anymore. I gave Edna a poke.

"Okay, Edna, I've had it! I *told* you I shouldn't have come, and now I *know* I shouldn't have come! It's all right for *you*, I guess, but I told you I shouldn't have eaten that—whatever it was—and that's *it* for me! I feel terrible and it's time to go home."

Edna fished around in a big patent-leather purse and pulled out our room key. "See you later," she said.

I tapped my foot. "I'm *sick*," I said. "I mean it. I think I'm going to throw up."

"Go outside, then, for a little air." The guys around her didn't even look up. But behind me a man said, "Like to play some darts, love?"

"Get away from me!" I said.

Edna said, "Well, Grace, it sounds like really you had better go on home."

"*You're not coming with me?*"

She began to look annoyed.

"*Edna*," I said. "I think I'm going to faint!"

"Put your head between your legs!" the guy behind me said, and somebody laughed.

I stayed, and I had a few more beers. But I didn't speak to Edna the rest of that night, or morning, or on the boat train to Holland, or when we got to that cheesy Japanese hotel in Amsterdam—so that when, for the *only time* in your life, you think you're going to see some *windmills* and some wooden shoes, all you get is a bunch of *cheesy Japs*, and decent bourbon is three dollars a drink.

Edna didn't even notice. For fifty-two hours she didn't notice. She dragged me to stupid fucking museums where all the pictures were of stupid Dutchmen you didn't want to see anyway. I told her! I'd caught cold! I couldn't find my traveler's checks! I was going to faint!

And here in Amsterdam, there was *dog shit* in the street, and we were going to get it on our shoes, see! "There! I *did* it, Edna! I *got it in my shoes!*"

"Well, stop being such a pain in the ass," she said, "and *clean it!*"

"It's happening all over," I said. "I knew it. I knew it would." I began to cry. She was going to leave me. And I couldn't stand being left again.

Buses went by, dogs barked, and all Edna did was laugh. She'd dragged me out for an early-morning walk, and she'd stopped dead in all the seven-thirty traffic of people rushing to work. She was wearing one of her black wool dresses and her Chinese pink jacket. Her nails glittered. Her gray hair was done up in those two knobs with Chinese combs. She stepped back to get a better look at me crying, and gave me a scornful look.

"What's the matter, Grace? *Aren't you having a good time?*"

I got as mad at her then as I ever did at all the others. At seven-thirty in the morning on those cruddy cobblestone streets with the stupid bicycles and dogs, and the canals smelling like someone had puked in them, I *said*, "I've had it with you, Edna! I can't stand you bossing me or patronizing me and making fun of me!"

But Edna said, "Maybe you'd better go home, then."

"I won't! You can't make me do it!"

She was laughing! "There's no law on earth that says I have to spend three weeks in Europe with a raging pain in the ass."

But *there should be*, I thought. There should be laws to keep people like you, people like Fran, the beautiful ones, the funny ones, with people like me. People shouldn't be *allowed* to run out. They should take it. They should take shit, like everybody else. I thought of Garnet, poor stupid boob, too stupid even to know the awful things that had happened to her. . . .

I started to cry in a different way, so that people began to notice. "I can't stand it," I said, and this time I meant it. "There's nothing for me here. I want to die. I really do."

Edna took me into a little workmen's bar. (Because they drink there, before they even go to work!) She ordered us both a beer. She fished in her purse and pulled out some Kleenex. "What's the trouble?"

"It's all right for you to say *what's the trouble!* You look wonderful, you always have a good time. People *like* you."

"Should I deny it?"

"Edna, not everybody is as lucky as you! I'm old, I'm poor! I was married to a couple of bastards, my kids hate me, my friends are either dead or too boring to talk to, I've had to work like a dog all my life!"

Edna nodded. She had to agree!

"I've suffered! I mean it! That's what a person like Garnet fails to understand! *And* Sandy! They don't understand the heartbreak there."

Edna didn't say anything, so I said it for her.

"Don't tell me they're happy on their own terms or some crap like that. If they're happy, it's because they're too stupid to know they're *not!*"

"Was there ever anything in your life that you liked?"

Oh, I knew there was a trick in that question!

But all the time we were talking, I was looking at something else. We were sitting at a little table by the door, and up at the bar some young guys were drinking. One guy had already passed out! He had a clean shirt, and he had a good haircut, but his head was down on his arms across the bar, he'd passed out cold. The way the manager was talking to the waiter, it sounded like they were going to call the police. And it was only eight in the morning. The thing is, the guy would waver every once in a while, it looked as if he might actually fall down. Fall right off the stool, poor bastard.

"Well?"

"*Well*, I did everything I was supposed to do, didn't I?"

"Grace?"

"I hated it," I said. "I hate the whole thing. I hate ironing and washing and cooking and cleaning . . . I hate vacuum cleaners and I hate changing beds. I hate the feel of soap on my fingers . . ."

"So does everyone."

"I'll tell you the truth, Edna, I wouldn't say it to everyone. One of the reasons I had so much trouble with Garnet and Sandy is I *really hate kids.* That's the biggest scam they've got going, that women are supposed to love kids. It's nothing personal with me, I just can't stand them. I hate when they're little and they're crying all the time and you have to change them and they get sick and then you worry—"

"I'm with you."

"I hate when they get older and they're such pigs. They always sit with their knees apart, and they never wash. They make up those terrible snacks and leave shit all over the kitchen. . . ."

"Some women go out and work."

"I hate typing worse than anything. I'm good at it, Edna, I'm good at my job. I even taught myself to do bookkeeping. But I hate that stuff."

"Do you ever think of getting married again?"

"If you think I'd *ever* . . ."

"You don't like men either, right?"

"They *leave* you, Edna!"

"What about before they leave?"

"Oh, I don't know. I don't even know. They're so *stupid.* They're bossy. They want sex all the time, and if they don't, they're fooling around. They keep all the money. Or if they give it to you, they think they're God on a rock! They sit around in chairs. They take naps on Saturdays. They read you things out of magazines—"

"I know. So don't you feel better about being alone?"

"I'm in bed every night by six o'clock. . . ."

"Other people live alone and manage to stay up until ten."

"I hate to see the *nights,* don't you see? I hate to even know they're there."

The guy at the bar had begun to slide.

"It's all right for you," I said. "Can't you see that? You're skinny as a rail, you've got your general secondary, whatever you pick off the rack in any store is going to fit you. . . ."

"You could eat a little less, you know. Thinness isn't an act of God."

"I don't eat a thing!"

I said it so loud the workers in that place looked around at me. All except the guy at the bar, who kept on going over toward tilt. "Just one piece of toast in the morning! You've seen that!"

Edna began to grin.

"If you're going to tell me not to drink, *forget it!* I love to drink and play cards!"

"Well, then?"

I began to cry again. And I took it from the top.

"It's easy for you, Edna. You're young—"

"Ten years younger than you?"

"You're skinny as a rail—"

"Three days a week I don't *eat.*"

"You've got a job you like."

"Yes."

"The kids even like you. . . ."

"Yes."

"Because you suck up to them all the time," I said. "Big deal!"

Eight o'clock in the morning in a creepy bar in Amsterdam. Can I say my life flashed before my eyes?

If you're mean and they hate you, at least there's a reason! I saw my mother as my brother whanged her across the face. I saw Fran, coming in late, and I'm in bed curled up like a rock. I saw you, Pearl, holding Garnet up to see the dancers. I saw Dick turn blue and fall over on his nose. I saw Garnet crying. I saw Sandy watching. What I saw made death look like the common cold.

So I did just what I could, and no more. Looking at Edna's face, so sharp and intelligent, with no loving or hating and no ax to grind, I snarled, mean as I could make it, "If *you think* I—"

But the guy at the bar fell over with a terrible crash right on the floor. The other guys jumped back. Oh, God, *it was Dick* all over again, *drunk as a skunk at nine in the morning!* The bartender looked way over the bar at him, the customers looked down—*What are they going to do now!* But then the drunk opened his eyes. "*Guti Morgi*," he said, or whatever it is they say. He was young, younger than Sandy, no more than seventeen. *Where's his mother?* Why doesn't she take care of him better? He had big blue eyes and real fresh skin.

One of the customers looked down at him. "Boom Boom!" he said. And laughed some dumb Dutch laugh. "Boom Boom!"

A couple of workers leaned over and hauled the guy up on the stool again.

"*Aren't they going to do anything? Call the police, call an ambulance?*"

Edna shrugged.

The young guy looked down at his beer, took a sip of what was left, looked around, and smiled.

"Boom Boom!" the man next to him said.

But I'd seen a nightmare. "Aren't they going to do anything?"

"They've done it," Edna said. "Listen, Grace. Just come with me to one last museum, and I promise you, on the Rhine cruise, there'll be a lot of drinking and playing cards."

But she dragged me to see a zillion pictures, and the tourist lunch in the cafeteria was lousy, and there was dog shit everywhere. *If this is what they mean by traveling, well, Christ, they can have it!*

I thought again what a poor, sad, dumb boob Fran was, all his talk, his God-on-a-rock *talk*, his tweed jackets, his Joseph *Hergesheimer*, his James Branch *Cabell*, his watercolors of *Chartres* (well, I haven't seen that one, but by the end of this pukey trip I will have seen a lot), and here was I in the art-deco cafeteria of the American Hotel in *Amsterdam*, and there was he, still in Gaviotas, shopping at Lucky's.

(Which is when I began to feel sorry for Fran. It hurt me, and I hate that.)

On the motor coach from the Jap hotel to the boat we were taking up the Rhine, one of those God-on-a-rock couples with leather everything and English accents almost had to get off. It wasn't that they'd lost their voucher, they didn't even know they had to *have* a voucher! We had to take up a collection for them. I didn't complain. (I *had* my voucher.)

All of your ideas about travel, Fran! They were just a crock of *shit*. This boat was dinky. It smelled funny. The people were mostly old and fat. Older than me. Fatter than me. The water in whatever fancy river this is is filthy. It's freezing here. I still haven't seen a windmill. My feet hurt. (But I wasn't going to faint.)

"I haven't seen such a bunch of freaks in a long time," I said to Edna. By this time all the passengers for the cruise were in the hall outside the purser's office. Everybody was standing there clutching their passports, pushing and shouting, waiting to be sorted out.

"Some of these freaks speak English, remember."

Edna is a good old gal. She enjoys herself anywhere.

It was like an old folks' home. Giant three-hundred-pound German monster women with Ace bandages on their legs. An Italian guy Fran's age with dyed hair, and his shirt open all the way down. He wanted to be waited on first. A whole family who spoke English, but *she*, the wife, looked like a hooker from Coalinga. Some languages I'd never heard before. *(Fran?* I got here, poor sucker, you didn't.) People were already beginning to start conversations with each other. Edna had her back to me talking to a good-looking American woman about her age. I hate it when Edna turns her back to me; who does she think she is? A big German broad pushed right into me and smiled. I had to smile or she'd send me to the camps!

They took away our luggage to the cabins and herded us all into a big room for a "buffet dinner." I can't eat cucumbers. I can't eat onion. I would never eat venison. Whole families were rushing out to the bar and rushing back with big bottles of wine (I don't drink wine, it makes me sleepy) or beer (I can't drink beer, it upsets my stomach).

"Want me to get something to drink for us, Grace?"

But I was looking down at this enormous plate of junk I can't eat.

"Do they have any Hill and Hill blend?"

She brought back a bottle of white wine and two glasses of white liquor.

"I don't *drink* wine, it makes me sleepy!"

"Well, you're going to sleep anyway, later."

"I don't drink vodka anymore, Edna, you know that!"

"It isn't vodka. Try it."

I sipped it. It tasted like caraway seeds. "This tastes awful," I said. But I drank it just to be polite.

We sat down at a table for two. I was starving, so I ate some cucumber. I had just a little venison. They had little pastry cups with cranberry sauce, they had prime rib and horseradish. Considering what we *had* been eating, it was pretty good.

By this time the lights were on in the dining room, people ran back and forth, little kids got in the way. People taking their *kids* on this kind of trip!

Oh, Fran, we could have done something like that, if only . . .

But I was here, now.

The captain would like to tell you something about the Rhine.

But people were making such a racket I couldn't hear much. We were going to go through three? four? countries. It would take us five days. We'd tie up at night, there would be bus tours.

"If they *think* that they're going to get me on a *bus* with these freaks!"

A voice croaked out over a set of several loudspeakers. I picked out the one closest to our table and tried to listen.

The captain would like you to join him in a welcoming glass of champagne.

And all those old freaks, all these middle-aged housewives, the few men, and even the kids scrambled for glasses.

The Rhine has been a center of culture and commerce for thousands of years.

A woman at the next table, who spoke German, crossed her legs. It's a wonder the ship didn't sink.

"I'm telling you, Edna, this place is full of freaks!"

Edna was getting oiled. "Freakee speekee Englee," she said.

At its source, in Switzerland, the cataracts of the Rhine can be heard as far away as three miles.

So what? Big deal!

The Rhine will wind through the reclaimed delta of the Netherlands on the first and second days.

On the third day, we will see the wonders of the middle Rhine, the full flower of medieval German culture.

He was saying this stuff in three languages, so his passengers could get bored in three different ways. People had drunk up their free glass of champagne and were going back to the bar to bring out some more booze. It looked a little like Las Vegas to me, a crowd like you might see at the bottom of Circus Circus, but what got me were the women! The broads! The bags! Great long tables of them—what kinds of lives had they been living? They didn't look like they'd had it so good, and that's leaving *out* World War II. They grinned big snaggle-toothed grins, they were dressed to kill in cruddy housedresses and lace-up black shoes. They looked like they'd been into some of Sandy's drugs, stoned out of their minds with the joy of it all.

"I don't think I'm going to be able to stand this for the next five days!" I whispered to Edna.

But she'd already started picking up on some guy, that fruity overripe Italian, and he'd brought us a bottle of champagne of our own.

Edna and I played cards the rest of the night in the lounge with a pretty nice Australian couple.

"The last few years, George spent most of his time in the outback and I've been busy with the kids," the wife told me.

"We'd been married nine years and we thought we'd ought to get to know each other again. We came across your states, and spent time in England. After this we go across to Singapore and then Penang and then home."

"Who's taking care of the kids?" I asked her. (I didn't have to keep much mind on the cards as long as Edna was my partner.)

The wife's face got funny. "We found a nurse for them. Do you have those in America? The kind that come in for confinements?"

What the *hell* is a confinement?

But the Australian girl said, "What do you think? Was that the right thing for us to do?"

Edna looked across to me and said, "Ask Grace. She's got two grown children."

When I think of the things I could have said! But I said, "Oh, I don't know. I think sometimes if you leave them alone, you're giving them a break. I think you did the right thing."

The husband grunted—I don't think he knew any words—you know those kind of guys, Pearl, who don't know any *words?* Or if they do, they're not going to waste them on you? Well, that's what we had at the table. But he knew how to play cards and he didn't yell at his wife, even when they lost. (Which means we won.)

When we got down to the cabin, someone had been in there to pull down the beds. *And* they'd been in our suitcases and spread our nightgowns out on our bunks.

"What the hell *is* this?" I said.

Edna grinned.

"I don't like people rummaging around in my things!"

Edna was already in her nightgown and wrapped up in her giant quilt. She turned out her light.

"Say, Edna? How'd you ever come to Coalinga anyway?"

She put one skinny arm up behind her, on the wall. "I told you. I fell in love with a guy during the war and followed him to the air base at Vandenberg."

"Did he get killed?" I was getting undressed with my back to her.

"No, he got married to somebody else, is all."

"But why—?"

"By then I kind of liked it up there."

"You've got to be kidding!"

"It's not so bad. You can play tennis and golf, and dance on the weekend. It's like everywhere else. You can take classes at the college. They've got that good Chinese restaurant. There's my quartet—I've got people to play with. You can go across the tracks and buy good tortillas. They have the fiesta every year. . . ."

The kind of life she was describing made me want to puke. Because it was a *lie*. Wasn't it?

I got in bed and laid my head back on a lump. It was hard. It was a cockroach! Ugh! But it was a piece of chocolate candy.

Edna said, "They think you should go to bed with something sweet, is all."

I couldn't eat it, but I put it on a little shelf about six inches from my nose.

"I'm not stupid, Edna," I said. "Don't patronize me! You're not the only smart person on this boat! . . . It's just," I said, after she wouldn't answer me, "it's just I've had it harder than you have. Fran leaving me. I was a nice person before that. Really. But then I had those seven years with Dick. He drove Garnet away, he turned Sandy against me . . ."

I remembered how I *strolled* for his pills when he had his heart attacks. I remember how I *tore* up the check he'd given me for my birthday. How I'd *cleaned* the vomit on the living-room floor after I'd *sat* up until two in the morning waiting for him to make his appearance after some terrible night out. . . .

Where were the tennis courts and junior colleges *then?*

Edna thought about it. "Yeah, I see it, I see what you mean. He must not have been a very nice person."

I knew there was a trick in that somewhere!

"But"—and I could *hear* her grinning in the dark—"look at the bright side. At least he had the good taste to go ahead and die. Maybe he didn't like it any more than you did, you know?"

Something I'd never even thought about.

I thought of when I last saw him, dead, his poor little mouth open like a rose, a poor little baby of a man, who took me on—because he thought he could win—

"He left me *alone*, Edna!"

"He cut you loose, is all. He set you free."

And like a dumb cue in a high-school play, the engines started, the boat gave a tremendous lurch, and we floated out sideways to, I guess, the middle of the river.

(Why did we just stay inside the house all the time and fight and drink? Dick?)

His blue face, his rosy little mouth, couldn't answer. Don't you look dignified at me, you drunken bum!

Just too *out-of-it* to live, was the only answer I come up with.

And if I'd been fighting a little baby all the time?

And if he was still alive?

I wouldn't be here?

Edna?

But she was asleep.

I tried to get the quilt wrapped up the best way around me. I looked from my bunk at the porthole, at the night sky, and sometimes, a whisk of the top of a tree. *If all my fights had been for nothing!* But I couldn't even feel sad about it now. There was the amazing sound of the engines and the gray light of the porthole. Once I thought I saw the tip of a lattice (it could have even been a windmill). I'm all alone, I thought. I'm old and alone in a foreign country! My children are afraid of me. But I couldn't keep my mind on it. And all the time I was looking at the porthole. This me, *Grace*, going upriver in a foreign country. What do you think, Mother? Daddy? Fran?

I saw something fluted out of the corner of my eye, the thin, crinkly paper they put around that little piece of chocolate candy.

You know, Pearl, I spent the next day in the observation lounge, drinking and playing cards. Except I guess I should say this, about ten o'clock we pulled into Cologne. What the fuck do I care about *Cologne?* I was playing poker with an English family from Hong Kong. The mother looked like a hooker, but she could play, and she loved to drink! Her husband looked like a tub of lard with hair on it, but he loved to play cards! He couldn't stand his sons, but they were playing too. And another American couple from Arizona. The husband thought he was God on a rock. His wife couldn't say a word, and she wouldn't *play!* She just *sat* looking out the window, at all the trees and *woods*. Come *on*, you dumb bunny! Come on and play! But she wouldn't. Maybe she couldn't. But at ten in the morning, up comes Edna, her black dress looking great on this boat.

"Come on, Grace, we're docking at Cologne."

"Nah, I'm not going, I'm going to sit here and play!"

I ended up going. We sat in a courtyard with a bigger bunch of weirdos than I'd ever seen (or ever seen up until then), and a man came around with *baskets* of beer, handing glasses out to people as fast as they could drink them. I don't drink beer, but I had a few, and then Edna said it was time to see the cathedral.

"I *hate* that shit, Edna, you know that! I can't *stand* that stuff!"

Inside, I spent some time curling my lip. Because I'd given up going to confession, any of that stuff, long ago. God's a man, isn't he? Playing dirty tricks like the rest of them.

So the incense, the big dark cave, didn't mean much to me. (Although it's okay for somebody else.)

Then Edna, who'd wandered off, came back with a funny look on her face. She grabbed my arm. "I want you to see something."

She pulled me over into an alcove where about a million

candles burned in the dark in front of an altar with a glass case on it. In the case was this little pinheaded statue of a mother and a child, and off the pinhead lady came this *tent*, with belt buckles and bracelets and pocket watches and medals and crucifixes and brooches and gold chains, and she held a scepter, which stuck out with about a dozen extra bracelets hanging on it like brass rings on a merry-go-round.

"So?"

"Do you know who she is?"

How the *fuck* was *I* supposed to know who she is!

"The Image of Grace, that's who."

I didn't even think I had to answer that, but I let Edna drag me over to have a better look. Grace looked like a pretty cool customer. God on a rock. Just sitting there, getting all the candles and bracelets.

Back on the boat, I played cards in the lounge all afternoon; I blistered the man from Hong Kong. His wife got kind of bitchy about it and said, "I hate the problem of traveling with jewelry, don't you? I mean, all the trouble with safe-deposit boxes and hotel help and going through customs? So this time I thought I'd just pick one set of things that more or less goes with everything."

"Yes, you're right," I said. "Diamonds *do* go with everything," dealing out the cards with my plain respectable hands, and took her husband for close to another fifty dollars before dinner, enough deutsche marks to keep a poor American woman going in the bar for a long time.

Oh, Pearl, honey, there isn't much more I'm going to say to you now, did you know that? But I do have to tell you about the dance.

On the second night, while the boat tied up at Koblenz, they had a dance in the observation lounge.

There were about seventeen old women for every two old men, and only about twenty middle-aged people and thirteen little kids, but they were going to have a dance. After a big meal they expected us to dance? They're going to herd us in there like a lot of senile cattle? I hate that stuff, Edna! *You* go, *you* like that sort of thing, I'll just stay *here!*

But I'd brought a long skirt, just in case, and I had a nice blouse, so I went.

(And why was I so scared? Because if there were lots of people who looked nicer and richer than me, there were lots of old crones who didn't. The big German woman with the dyed hair and the Ace bandage hadn't even changed her bandage!)

I have to tell you that the room was filled with people from every country in the civilized world. There were teachers who'd saved up for this, and ladies who'd come on this cruise to meet the man of their dreams (at age 75!?), and the Australian couple trying to get love back, and I wished them luck, but didn't have much hope for them, and old ladies with plastic shoes! And support hose if they didn't have bandages. And we'd been sitting across from an American couple in their fifties at dinner where the woman looked as if she'd swallowed a time bomb ready to go off at any second. "We're married!" she kept saying. "We're married! We've been married for . . . five years!" But a blind person could see they weren't married and weren't going to be. And at lunch and dinner Edna and I would watch her scream about backyard barbecues, and ski accidents, and shooting the rapids in Colorado, while her "husband" ate and looked out the window. If I didn't see Fran there, I was a monkey's uncle. She didn't have a chance in hell.

So I knew that this was a lounge full of . . . All I can call them is dreamers. How were they going to get up and dance?

A man came out and said that since there were all these countries represented here, the band (three old German guys, worse off than the rest of us) was going to salute us all by playing our national songs. So, okay.

The *Germans!* The band (an accordion, a sax, a broken-down drummer) belted out something with a horrendous beat, and God damn if about five couples didn't get up and dance to it, some of them terrible, some of them *not so bad.*

And what gets me, Pearl, the other ones, the old ladies lined up on the couches, just smiled like a bunch of drooling idiots and started tapping their feet and grinning and clapping.

The *French!* And a slightly higher grade of couples got up to dance. Edna, standing behind me, doing everything with dignity, was leaning up against a graying Australian bachelor (at least that was his *story)* singing "*Auprès de ma blonde, qu'il fait bon, fait bon, fait bon.*" Embarrassing!

New Zealand! They played a song I'd never heard, or anyone else on that boat either, but everyone clapped politely along and one couple got up, the *worst dancers you ever saw*, his shirt coming out of his ratty old pants, while they danced, or he walked all over her feet. But they kept it up for sixty-four bars and good old New Zealand.

Australia! "Waltzing Matilda." I let myself hum along. What do you think I am, a poor sport?

Israel? It was just one couple. They got up and waved, but sat down again, quick. How was one couple going to dance to "Hava Nagila"? About half the boat began to smile. It was loaded up with Nazis, but they clapped their brains out and sang. I knew the words because of the thousand Christmas assemblies I'd had to go to for Garnet and Sandy, where they had to stick it in the program even though there wasn't a Jew within a fifty-mile radius. Singing along:

Hava Nagila!
Hava Nagila!
Hava Nagila!
hm hm hm hm *hm!*

My flesh crawled along with the Israeli couple and then the man with the microphone said: "*Americans!*"

What did I expect, "Perdido," "Adios"? "Dancing in the Dark"? Glenn Miller and Artie Shaw *coming to me now?* What they played was: "Over hill, over dale, we will hit the dusty trail, as those caissons go rolling along! Counter march, right about, hear those wagon soldiers shout, as those caissons go rolling along!"

My face was like a beet! I looked at Edna, she was a study. All around the room, big, soft, good-hearted, stupid Americans were blushing. The rest of the populace was clapping like maniacs. The woman who sat across from us at meals and said she'd been married five years pulled and prodded the guy she was with out onto the floor, marching him through "The Halls of Montezuma."

"For God's *sake*, Edna, what *are they doing?*"

"Well," Edna yelled over at me, "come to think of it, what other American songs would they know?"

And "Waltzing Matilda" was a war song, and that French thing was a war song.

I looked at all the people. All I can tell you is, that they were having a good time.

"Edna," I shouted (and was reminded of those truly golden moments when Dick had picked a terrible bastard crazy fight, and I'd gone right back at him, screaming, weeping, hitting, whispering, marching *out* of the house and coming right back *in* again, through a different door, for six hours, eight hours, ten hours, and I'd be ready to go the whole weekend if I had to, breaking dishes and making dinner only so I could *fling* it at him, but Dick would finally say, in a tired voice, "Be reasonable, Grace. Please?").

"Edna," I said, "be reasonable. They were *killing each other* to those songs."

And she said, "Well, kid, I guess they believe in forgive and forget."

During the regular part of the dance, I danced six times. Once with the Australian bachelor—Edna put him up to it—once with the fruity Italian, once with the guy who wasn't going to marry the lady across from us, once with the man from Hong Kong, once more with the bachelor, and once with a dandruffy man I didn't know. It came to me that I was over sixty, but I still had great legs.

I didn't know the songs. They were German, mostly waltzes, and had a heavy beat. I saw all the other women watching, and most of the night I just sat and watched with them; that was all right too. For a couple of songs we linked arms and sang along. I could handle it.

The band went home around midnight. Some of us stayed up in the bar till four, dancing to the radio. I spent what I'd won on drinks for all.

That's all I have to say, sweet Pearl. I thought of you in your Empress Eugenie hat with the veil, the next day up on the observation deck; the day when we saw "all the glories of the middle Rhine," the big dark castles sweeping by, the walls and the battlements a thousand years old, people having wars with people half a mile down the river and getting all steamed up about it, and leaving such beauty behind them!

Soft gray fog, and great clean sunshine and the wild blue river, and another castle and another castle and another castle. . . .

Around the middle of the morning, the guy on the loudspeaker told us in three languages that we were going to see the legendary Lorelei rock, where boatmen used to see the Lorelei, beautiful women with golden hair who would sing this beautiful music and boatmen would love the music so much they'd pile up on the rocks and die.

I thought of Allan, caught in the muddy floodwaters of the Los Angeles River, and the tears started pouring out of my eyes. Did you see anything? Did you hear anything? Was there anything beautiful you found? (God help him, maybe I was the only beautiful thing he found.)

The loudspeaker, which usually just spoke in three languages, had begun to play a tune. And men, women, some of them, stood up, the softest looks on their faces, and began to sing, in German: "*Ich weiss nicht, was soll es bedeuten . . .*"

I wonder why I feel so sad. . . .

The dark rock slid by, and we went up the river.

Dead people, drowned people, have pearls for their eyes. Oh, Pearl, can you see what I'm trying to say?

But all that was the next day.

The night before, after the dance, we'd come downstairs—below deck! Our beds were turned down, our nightgowns laid out, the chocolate candy was waiting on our pillows.

"How much does all this cost again?" I asked Edna.

"Don't worry, you'll earn your way at the table."

I sat on the side of the bunk, took the wrapping off the candy, and bit into it. "You know," I said, "I think this is going to be fun."